A Brilliant Novel by a Master Storyteller

THE SLAVE
by
Isaac Bashevis Singer

W9-AFY-056

ISAAC BASHEVIS SINGER

The Slave

FAWCETT CREST • NEW YORK

THE SLAVE

THIS BOOK CONTAINS THE COMPLETE TEXT OF
THE ORIGINAL HARDCOVER EDITION.

Published by Fawcett Crest Books, a unit of CBS Publica-
tions, the Consumer Publishing Division of CBS Inc., by
arrangement with Farrar, Straus and Giroux, Inc.

ISBN: 0-449-24188-2

Printed in the United States of America

First Fawcett Crest printing: January 1980

10 9 8 7 6 5 4 3 2 1

The author wishes to thank
Miss Elizabeth Pollet for her
assistance in the preparation
of this book.

The Slave

PART ONE

Wanda

1

A single bird call began the day. Each day the same bird, the same call. It was as if the bird signaled the approach of dawn to its brood. Jacob opened his eyes. The four cows lay on their mats of straw and dung. In the middle of the barn were a few blackened stones and charred branches, the fireplace over which Jacob cooked the rye and buckwheat cakes he ate with milk. Jacob's bed was made of straw and hay and at night he covered himself with a coarse linen sheet which he used during the day to gather grass and herbs for the cattle. It was summer, but the nights were cold in the mountains. Jacob would rise more than once in the middle of the night and warm his hands and feet on the animals' bodies.

It was still dark in the barn, but the red of dawn shone through a crack in the door. Jacob sat up and finished his final allotment of sleep. He had dreamed he was in the study house at Josefov, lecturing the young men on the Talmud.

He stretched out his hand blindly, reaching for the pitcher of water. Three times he washed his hands, the left hand first and then the right, alternating, according to the law. He had murmured even before washing, "I thank Thee," a prayer not mentioning God's name and therefore utterable before cleaning oneself. A cow stood up and turned its horned head, looking over its shoulder as if curious to see how a man starts his day. The creature's large eyes, almost all pupil, reflected the purple of the dawn.

"Good morning, Kwiatula," Jacob said. "You had a good sleep, didn't you?"

He had become accustomed to speak to the cows, to himself even, so as not to forget Yiddish. He threw open the barn door and saw the mountains stretching into the distance. Some of the peaks, their slopes overgrown with forests, seemed close at hand, giants with green beards. Mist rising from the woods like tenuous curls made Jacob think of Samson. The ascending sun, a heavenly lamp, cast a fiery sheen over everything. Here and there, smoke drifted upward from a summit as if the mountains were burning within. A hawk, wings outstretched, glided tranquilly with a strange slowness beyond all earthly anxieties. It appeared to Jacob that the bird had been flying without interruption since creation.

The more distant mountains were bluish, and there were others, the most distant of all, that were scarcely visible—unsubstantial. It was always dusk in that most remote region. Caps of clouds sat on the heads of those unearthly titans, inhabitants at the world's end where no man walked and no cow grazed. Wanda, Jan Bzik's daughter, said that that was where Baba Yaga lived, a witch who flew about in a huge mortar, driving her vehicle with a pestle. Baba Yaga's broom was larger than the

11

tallest fir tree, and it was she who swept away the light of the world.

Jacob stood gazing at the hills, a tall, straight man, blue-eyed, with long brown hair and a brown beard. He wore linen trousers which did not reach to his ankles and a torn, patched coat. On his head was a sheepskin cap, but his feet were bare. Though he was out of doors so much, he remained as pale as a city dweller. His skin did not tan and Wanda said that he resembled the men in the holy pictures that hung in the chapel in the valley. The other peasant women agreed with Wanda. The Gazdas, as the mountaineers were called, had wanted to marry him to one of their daughters, build him a hut, and make him a member of the village, but Jacob had refused to forsake the Jewish faith, and Jan Bzik, his owner, kept him all summer and until late fall in the barn high on the mountain where the cattle could not find food and one had to feed them with grass pulled from among the rocks. The village was at a high elevation and lacked sufficient pastures.

Before he milked the cows, Jacob said his introductory prayer. Reaching the sentence, "Thou hast not made me a slave," he paused. Could these words be spoken by him? He was Jan Bzik's slave. True, according to Polish law, not even the gentry had the right to force a Jew into servitude. But who in this remote village obeyed the law of the land? And of what value was the code of the gentiles even prior to Chmielnicki's massacre? Jacob of Josefov took the privations Providence had sent him without rancor. In other regions the Cossacks had beheaded, hanged, garroted, and impaled many honest Jews. Chaste women had been raped and disemboweled. He, Jacob, had not been destined for martyrdom. He had fled from the murderers and Polish robbers had dragged him off to somewhere in the mountains and had sold him as a slave to Jan Bzik. He had lived here for four years now and did not know whether his wife and children were still alive. He was without prayer shawl and phylacteries, fringed garment or holy book. Circumcision was the only sign on his body that he was a Jew. But heaven be thanked, he knew his prayers by heart, a few chapters of the Mishnah, some pages of the Gemara, a host of Psalms, as well as passages from various parts of the Bible. He would wake in the middle of the night with lines from the Gemara that he himself had not been aware he knew running through his head. His memory played hide and seek with him. If he had had pen and paper, he would have written down what came to him, but where were such things to be found here?

He turned his face to the east, looked straight ahead, and recited the holy words. The crags glowed in the sunlight, and close by a cowherd yodeled, his voice lingering on each note, resonant with yearning as if he too were being held in captivity and longed to thrust himself into freedom. It was hard to believe that such melodies came from men who ate dogs, cats, field mice, and indulged in every sort of abomination. The peasants here had not even risen to the level of the Christians. They still followed the customs of the ancient pagans.

There had been a time when Jacob had planned to run away, but nothing had come of his schemes. He did not know the mountains; the forests were filled with predatory animals. Snow fell even in summer. The peasants kept guard over him and did not permit him to go beyond the bridge in the village. There was an agreement among them that anyone who saw him on the other side of the stream should immediately kill him. Among the peasants there were those who wanted to kill him anyway. Jacob might be a wizard or a braider of

13

elflocks. But Zagayek, the count's bailiff, had ordered that the stranger be permitted to live. Jacob not only gathered more grass than any other cowherd, but his cattle were very sleek, gave abundant milk, and bore healthy calves. As long as the village did not suffer from famine, epidemic, or fire, the Jew was to be left in peace.

It was time for the cows to be milked and so Jacob hurried through his prayers. Returning to the barn he mixed with the grass in the trough the chopped straw and turnips he had prepared the day before. On a shelf in the barn were the milking pail and some large earthen pots; a churn stood in a corner. Every day late in the afternoon Wanda came up, bringing Jacob his food and bearing two large pitchers in which to carry the milk back to the village.

Jacob milked the cows and hummed a tune from Josefov. The sun climbed beyond the mountains and the coils of fog dissolved. He had been here so long now and had become so acquainted with the plants that he could detect the odor of each flower and each variety of grass, and he breathed in deeply as the smells of vegetation were wafted into the barn through the open door. Every sunrise in the mountains was like a miracle; one clearly discerned God's hand among the flaming clouds. God had punished His people and had hidden His face from them, but He continued to superintend the world. As a sign of the covenant which He had made after the Flood, He had hung the rainbow in the sky to show that day and night, summer and winter, sowing and reaping would not cease.

II

All day Jacob climbed on the mountain. After gathering a sheetful of grass, he carried it to the barn, and then returned once more to the woods.

The other cowherds, when he had first come, had attacked and beaten him, but now he had learned how to strike back, and these days carried an oaken stick. He scampered over the rocks with the agility of a monkey, mindful of which herbs and grasses were good for the cattle and which harmful. All those things which are required of a cowherd he could do: light a fire by rubbing wood against wood, milk the cows, deliver a calf. For himself, he picked mushrooms, will strawberries, blueberries, whatever the earth produced, and each afternoon Wanda brought him a slice of coarse black bread from the village, and sometimes, also, a radish, carrot, or onion, or maybe an apple or pear from the orchard. In the beginning Jan Bzik had jokingly sought to force a piece of sausage into his mouth, but Jacob had refused stubbornly to partake of forbidden food. He did not gather herbs on the Sabbath, but gave the animals feed he had prepared during the week. The mountaineers no longer molested him.

But this was not true of the girls who slept in the barn and tended the sheep. Night and day they bothered him. Attracted by his tall figure, they sought him out and talked and laughed and behaved little better than beasts. In his presence they relieved themselves, and they were perpetually pulling up their skirts to show him insect bites on their hips and thighs. "Lay me," a girl would shamelessly demand, but Jacob acted as if he were deaf and blind. It was not only because fornication was a mortal sin. These women were unclean, and had vermin in their clothes and elflocks in their hair; often their skins were covered with rashes and boils, they ate field rodents and the rotting carcasses of fowls. Some of them could scarcely speak Polish, grunted like animals, made signs with their hands, screamed and laughed madly. The village abounded in cripples, boys and girls with goiters, distended heads and disfiguring birth marks; there were also mutes, epileptics, freaks who had been born with six fingers on their hands or six toes on their feet. In summer, the parents of these deformed children kept them on the mountains with the cattle, and they ran wild. There, men and women copulated in public; the women became pregnant, but, climbing as they did all day on the rocks, bearing heavy packs, they often miscarried. The district had no midwife and mothers in labor were forced to cut the umbilical cord themselves. If the child died, they buried it in a ditch without Christian rites or else threw it into the mountain stream. Often, the women bled to death. If someone descended to the valley to fetch Dziobak, the priest, to confess the dying and administer Extreme Unction, nothing came of it. Dziobak had a game leg and besides he was always drunk.

In comparison with these savages, Wanda, Jan Bzik's widowed daughter, seemed city-bred. She dressed in a skirt, blouse and apron, and wore a kerchief on her head; moreover, her speech could be understood. A bolt of lightning had killed her husband Stach and from then on she had been courted by all the bachelors and widowers of the village; she was constantly saying no. Wanda was twenty-five and taller than most of the other women. She had blond hair, blue eyes, a fair skin, and well-modeled features. She braided her hair and twisted it around her head like a wreath of wheat. When she smiled, her cheeks dimpled and her teeth were so strong she could crush the toughest of pits. Her nose was straight and she had a narrow chin. She was a skillful seamstress and could knit, cook, and tell stories which made one's hair stand on end. In the village she had been nicknamed "The Lady." As Jacob knew very well, according to the law he must avoid her, but if it had not been for Wanda he would have forgotten that he had a tongue in his head. Besides she assisted him in fulfilling his obligations as a Jew. Thus, when in winter, on the Sabbath, her father commanded him to light the oven, she got up before Jacob and lit the kindling herself and added the firewood. Unbeknown to her parents, she brought him barley kasha, honey, fruit from the orchard, cucumbers from the garden. Once when Jacob had sprained his ankle and his foot had swollen, Wanda had snapped the bone back into the socket and applied lotions. Another time, a snake had bitten him in the arm, and she had put the wound to her mouth and sucked out the venom. This had not been the only time Wanda had saved his life.

Yet Jacob knew that all this had been contrived by Satan; throughout the day he missed her and could not overcome his longing. The instant he awoke he would start to count the hours before she would walk to the sundial that he made from a stone to see how much the shadow had moved. If a heavy downpour or cloudburst prevented her coming, he would walk about morosely. This did not stop him from praying to God to preserve him from sinful thoughts, but again and again the thoughts returned. How could he keep his heart pure when he had no phylacteries to put on and no fringed garment to wear? Lacking as he did a calendar, he could not even observe the holy days properly. Like the Ancients he reckoned the beginning of the month by the appearance of the new moon, and at the end of his fourth year, he rectified his computations by adding an extra month. But, despite all these efforts, he was aware that he probably made some error in his calculations.

As he figured it, this long and warm day was the fourth of the month of Tammuz. He gathered great

17

quantities of grass and leaves; he prayed, studied several chapters of the Mishnah, said those few pages of the Gemara which he repeated daily. Finally he recited one of the Psalms and chanted a prayer in Yiddish that he himself had composed. He begged the Almighty to redeem him from captivity and allow him to live the life of a Jew once more. This day, he ate a slice of bread left from the day before and cooked a pot of groats over the fireplace in the barn. Having said the benediction, he felt tired, and walked outside and lay down under a tree. He had found it necessary to keep a dog to protect the cattle from wild animals. At first he had disliked the black creature with its pointed muzzle and sharp teeth, repelled by its barking and obsequious licking which had reminded him of what the Talmud said on the subject and how the holy Isaac Luria, along with other cabalists, compared canines to the satanic hosts. But at length Jacob had grown accustomed to his dog, and had even named him, calling him Balaam. No sooner had Jacob lain under the tree, than Balaam sat down near him, stretched out his paws, and kept watch.

Jacob's eyes closed, and the sun, red and summery, shone through his lids. Above him the tree was filled with birds, twittering, singing, trilling. He was neither awake nor asleep, having retreated into the weariness of his body. So be it. This was the way God had willed it.

Ceaselessly he had prayed for death; he had even contemplated self-destruction. But now that mood had passed, and he had become inured to living among strangers, distant from his home, doing hard labor. As he drowsed, he heard pine cones falling and the coo of a cuckoo in the distance. He opened his eyes. The web of branches and pine needles strained the sunlight like a sieve, and the reflected light became a rainbow-colored

18

mesh. A last drop of dew flamed, glistened, exploded into thin molten fibers. There was not a cloud to sully the perfect blue of the sky. It was difficult to believe in God's mercy when murderers buried children alive. But God's wisdom was evident everywhere.

Jacob fell asleep and Wanda walked into his dreams.

III

The sun had moved westward; the day was nearing its end. High overhead an eagle glided, large and slow, like a celestial sailboat. The sky was still clear but a milk-white fog was forming in the woods. Twisting itself into small ovals, the mist thrust out tongues, and sought to evolve into some coherent shape. Its inchoateness made Jacob think of that primeval substance which, according to the philosophers, gave birth to all things.

When he stood at the barn, Jacob could see for miles around. The mountains remained as deserted as in the days of the Creation. One above the other, the forests rose like steps, first the leaf-bearing trees, and then the pines and firs. Beyond the woods were the open ledges, and the pale snow, like gray linen unfolding, was slowly moving down from the summits ready to enshroud the world in winter. Jacob recited the prayer of Minchah and walked to the hill from which one could see the path to the village. Yes, Wanda was on her way up. He recognized her by her figure, her kerchief, her manner of walking. She looked no larger than a finger, like one of those imps or sprites about whom she told so many stories, fairies who lived in the crevasses of rocks, in the hollows of tree trunks, under the eaves of toad-stools and who came out at dusk to play, dressed in small green coats and wearing blue caps and red

19

boots. He could not remove his eyes from her, charmed by her walk, by the way she paused to rest, by her disappearance among the trees, then by the sight of her, emerging from the woods higher up the slope. Now and again, the metal pitcher in her hand gleamed like a diamond. He saw that she was carrying the basket in which she brought him food.

As she approached nearer and nearer, she grew larger and larger, and Jacob ran toward her, ostensibly to be of assistance, although the pitchers she was carrying were still empty. She caught sight of him and stopped. He was moving toward her like a bridegroom seeking his bride. When he reached her, shyness and affection, both equally intense, mingled within him. Jewish law, he knew, forbade him to look at her, yet he saw everything: her eyes which were sometimes blue, sometimes green, her full lips, her long, slim neck, her womanly bosom. Like any other peasant she worked in the fields, but her hands remained feminine. He felt awkward standing beside her. His hair was unkempt, his pants too short and as ragged as a beggar's. Being descended on his mother's side from Jews who had had constant dealings with the nobility and had rented their fields, he had been taught Polish as a child, and now in his captivity he had learned to speak the language like a gentile. At times, he even forgot the Yiddish name for some object.

"Good evening, Wanda."

"Good evening, Jacob."

"I watched you coming up the mountain."

"Did you?"

The blood rushed to her face.

"You looked no larger than a pea."

"Things look that way from a distance."

"They do," Jacob said. "The stars are as large as

20

the whole world, but they are so far off, they appear to be little dots."

Wanda became silent. He often used strange words which she did not understand. He had told her his story, and she knew that he was descended from Jews who lived in a far-off place, that he had studied books, and that he had had a wife and children whom the Cossacks had slaughtered. But what were Jews? What was written in their books? Who were the Cossacks? All of these things were beyond her comprehension. Nor did she understand his statement that the stars were as large as the earth. If they were really that large, how could so many cluster above the village? But Wanda had long since decided that Jacob was a profound thinker. Who knew, perhaps he was a wizard as was whispered by the women in the valley? But whatever he was, she loved him. Evening for her was the festive part of the day.

He took the pitchers from her and they finished the ascent together. Another man would have taken her by the arm or placed a hand upon her shoulder, but Jacob walked beside her with the timidity of a boy, exuding a sunny warmth and trailing the odors of grass and barn. Yet Wanda had already proposed marriage, or, if he was unwilling to commit himself to that, cohabitation without the priest's blessing. He had pretended not to hear her suggestion and only later had he remarked that fornication was forbidden. God looked down from heaven and rewarded and punished each man according to his deeds.

As if she were unaware of that! But in the village love was a random matter. The priest had fathered a half dozen bastards. Such a proposal as she had made to Jacob would have been refused by no other man. Were not all the villagers pursuing her, including Stephan, the bailiff's son? Not a week passed without some boy's mother or sister approaching her to arrange a match. She was forever receiving and returning gifts. Wanda found Jacob's attitude perplexing and she walked with bowed head thinking about this puzzle which she was unable to solve. She had fallen in love with the slave at first sight, and though over the years they had been much together, he had stayed remote. Many times she had come to the conclusion that from this dough would come no bread, and that she was wasting her youth on him. But the strength of the attraction he exerted upon her did not abate, and she could scarcely endure waiting for evening. She had become the subject of gossip in the village. The women laughed at her and passed sly comments. It was said that the slave had bewitched her; whatever it was, she was unable to free herself.

Thoughtfully she bent down, plucked a flower, and tearing away its petals began, "He loves me; he loves me not." The last petal assured her that the answer was "yes." But if so, how long would he go on tormenting her?

Now the sun sank rapidly, dropped behind the mountains. Accompanied by the croaking and screaming of birds, the day ended. Smoke rose from the bushes and the cowherds yodeled. The women were already preparing the evening meal, perhaps roasting some animal which had fallen into a trap.

IV

In addition to bread and vegetables, Wanda, without the knowledge of her mother and sister, had brought Jacob a rare gift, an egg laid by the white hen, and while she milked the cows, he prepared supper. He placed a few dry branches on the stones, lit a fire, and boiled the egg. He had left the barn door open although it was already dark, and the flames from the pine branches mottled Wanda's face with fiery spots and were reflected in her eyes. He sat on a log remembering the meal eaten before the fast of the ninth day of the month of Ob. An egg was consumed then as a sign of mourning: a rolling egg symbolized the changeability of man's fate. He washed his hands, let them dry, said grace, and dipped his bread into the salt. There was no table in the barn and so he used a pail turned upside down. He gained his sustenance from vegetables and fruit; meat he never tasted. As he ate, he glanced at Wanda out of the corner of his eyes, Wanda who was as devoted to him as a wife, and who every day prepared him something special. "In the mercy of the nations is sin," he said to himself, quoting a commentary on a passage from the Bible and trying to strangle the love he felt for her. Had all this been done by her for the sake of God? No, it was desire for him that had prompted her. Her love depended upon outward show, and should he become a cripple, God forbid, or lose his manhood, her love would cease. And yet such was the power of the flesh that man looked only at the surface and did not probe into such matters too deeply. He heard the sound of the milk falling into the pail and he paused in his eating to listen. Grasshoppers were singing and there was a buzzing and humming of bees, gnats, flies, multitude upon multitude of creatures each with its own voice. The stars in the heavens had kindled their fires. A sickle of a moon was aloft in the sky.

"Is the egg all right?" Wanda asked.

"Good and fresh."

"Could anything be fresher? I saw the hen lay it. The moment it fell to the straw, I thought, this is for Jacob. The shell was still warm."

"You're a good woman, Wanda."

"I can be bad as well. It depends on whom I'm with. I was bad to Stach, peace be with him."

"Why was that?"

"I don't know. He demanded, he never asked. If he wanted me in the night, he woke me from the middle of sleep. In the daytime, he would push me down in an open field."

Her words aroused both passion and digust in Jacob.

"That was not right."

"What does a peasant know of right or wrong? He just takes what he wants. I was sick once and my forehead was as hot as an oven but he came to me and I had to give myself."

"The Torah says that a man must not force his wife," Jacob said. "She must be wooed by him until she is willing."

"Where is the Torah? In Josefov?"

"The Torah is everywhere."

"How can it be everywhere?"

"The Torah tells how a man should conduct himself."

Wanda was silent.

"That's for the city. Here the men are wild bulls. Swear to me that you'll never reveal what I tell you."

"Whom would I tell?"

"My own brother threw himself on me. I was only eleven years old. He'd come back from the tavern. Mother was asleep but my screams woke her. She picked up the pail of slops and poured it over him."

Jacob paused a moment before speaking again.

"Things like that don't happen among the Jews."

"That's what you say. They killed our God."

"How can a man kill a God?"

"Don't ask me. I'm only telling you what the priest says. Really, are you a Jew?"

"Yes, a Jew."

"It's hard for me to believe. Become one of us and we'll get married. I'll be a good wife and we'll have our hut in the valley. Zagayek will give us our share of land. We'll work our time for the count, and what's left over we'll have for ourselves. There's nothing we won't have—cows, pigs, chickens, geese, ducks. You know how to read and write and when Zagayek dies you'll take his place."

It was some time before Jacob answered.

"No, I cannot. I am a Jew. For all I know, my wife is alive."

"You've said many times that everyone was killed. But even if she still lives, what's the difference? She's there and you're here."

"God is everywhere."

"And it will hurt God if you are a free man instead of a slave? You walk around barefoot, half naked. Summers you spend in the barn, winters you freeze in the granary. Sooner or later they'll kill you."

"Who will kill me?"

"Oh, they'll kill you all right."

"And so then I'll be with the other holy spirits."

"I pity you, Jacob. I pity you."

Both fell into a long silence and in the barn there was quiet except when a cow now and again stamped its hoof. The last embers in the fireplace died, and when Jacob had finished eating he walked out into the open air to say the benediction in a place unpolluted by dung. Evening had fallen but in the west the last shreds of the sunset lingered. Usually, the women who brought food to the cowherds did not loiter on the mountain since at night the way home was considered dangerous. But Wanda would often stay late despite her mother's scolding and the women's persistent gossip. She was as strong as a man and she knew the proper incantations to drive off the evil spirits.

25

She had finished milking the cows and, in the darkness of the barn, she poured milk from the pail into the pitchers. She scrubbed the churn with straw and cleaned globs of mud off the hips of the cows. All this she did swiftly and with great skill. Her tasks accomplished, she went outside, and the dog ran from Jacob to her, wagged its tail and jumped on her with its front paws. She bent down and he licked her face.

"Balaam, enough," she ordered. "He's more affectionate than you," she said to Jacob.

"An animal has no obligations."

"But they too have souls."

She delayed going home, sat down near the barn, and Jacob sat also. They always spent some time together and always on exactly the same rocks. If the moon was not out, she saw him by the light of the stars, but it was as bright this evening as at the full moon. Gazing at her in silence, Jacob was seized by love and desire, and restrained himself with difficulty. The blood in his veins seethed like water about to boil, and hot and cold fire zigzagged down his spine. "Remember this world is only a corridor," he warned himself. "The true palace lies beyond. Don't let yourself be barred from it for the sake of a moment's pleasure."

V

"What's new with your family?" Jacob inquired.

Wanda awoke from her reverie.

"What could be new? Father works, chops down trees in the woods and drags them home. He's so weak the logs almost knock him down. He wants to rebuild our hut, or God knows what. At his age! He's so tired at evening he can't swallow his food, and drops on the bed as though his legs had been cut off. He won't live much longer."

Jacob's brow furrowed.

"That's no way to talk."

"It's the truth."

"No one knows the decrees of Heaven."

"Maybe not, but when your strength gives out, you die. I can tell who's going to go—not only the old and sick, but the young and healthy too. I take one look and it comes to me. Sometimes I'm afraid to say anything because I don't want to be thought a witch. But all the same, I know. There's no change with Mother, she spins a little, cooks a little, plays at being sick. We only see Antek on Sundays, and sometimes not even then. Marisha is pregnant, will be in labor soon. Basha is lazy. Mother calls her the lazy cat. But a dance or a party revives her. Wojciech gets crazier and crazier."

"What about the grain? Is the crop good?"

"When has it ever been good?" Wanda answered. "In the valley you get rich, black earth, but here it's all stony. You could drive a cart of oxen between the stalks. We still have some rye from last year, but most of the peasants eat their knuckles. What little good earth we have belongs to the count and anyway Zagayek steals everything."

"Doesn't the count ever come here?"

"Just about never. He lives in another country and doesn't even know he owns this village. About six years ago, a bunch of them descended upon us in the middle of summer—like now, before harvest. They got the idea they wanted to go hunting and tramped back and forth in the fields with their horses and dogs. Their servants snatched calves, chickens, goats, even a peasant's rabbit. Zagayek crawled after them kissing everyone's behind. Oh, he's high and mighty enough with the people around here, but as soon as he meets someone from the city he becomes a boot licker. When they went away, there was nothing but a wasteland left. The

27

peasants starved that winter: the children turned yellow and died."

"Couldn't someone have spoken to them?"

"The nobles? They were always drunk. The peasants kissed their feet and all the thanks they got were a few strokes with a riding crop. The girls got raped; they arrived home with bloody shifts and an ache in their hearts. Nine months later they gave birth to bastards."

"We do not have such murderers among the Jews."

"No? What do the Jewish aristocrats do?"

"The Jews have no gentry."

"Who owns the land?"

"The Jews have no land. When they had a country of their own, they worked the earth themselves and possessed vineyards and olive groves. But here in Poland, they live by trade and handicraft."

"Why is that? We have it bad, but if you work hard and have a good wife, you at least own something. Stach was strong but lazy. He should have been Basha's husband, not mine. He kept putting off everything; he'd cut the hay and let it lie around until the rain soaked it. All he wanted to do was sit in the inn and talk. The truth was his time was up. On our wedding night I dreamed he was dead and his face black as a pot. I didn't tell anyone but I was sure he wouldn't last long. The day it happened, the weather wasn't bad. All of a sudden lightning struck and came straight through our window. It rolled along like a fiery apple, looking for Stach. He wasn't in the hut, but it went into the granary and found him. When I reached him his face was charred like soot."

"Don't you ever see anything good in your dreams?"

"Yes, I've told you. I foresaw that you would come to us. But I wasn't dreaming, I was wide

28

awake. Mother was frying rye cakes and father had slaughtered a chicken that was starving because it had a growth in its beak. I poured some soup on the cakes and I looked into the bowl which was filled with the great circles of fat. A mist rose and I saw you there as plain as I see you now."

"Where did you get such powers?" Jacob asked after a pause.

"I don't know, Jacob. But I've known all along that we were fated for each other. My heart knocked like a hammer when father brought you home from the fair. You weren't wearing a shirt and I gave you one of Stach's. Wacek and I were about to be betrothed, but when I saw you his image was erased from my heart. Marila has been laughing ever since. He fell into her hands like ripe fruit. I saw him at a wedding a short time ago and he was drunk. He started to cry and talk to me the way he used to. Marila was beside herself. But I don't want him, Jacob."

"Wanda, you must get such ideas out of your head."

"Why, Jacob, why?"

"I've already told you why."

"I never understand you, Jacob."

"Your faith is not my faith."

"Haven't I said that I'm willing to change my faith?"

"One can't belong to my faith unless one believes in God and his Torah. Just because one wants a man is not enough."

"I believe in what you believe."

"Where would we live? If a Christian becomes a Jew here, he's burned at the stake."

"There must be some place."

"Perhaps among the Turks."

"All right, let's escape."

"I don't know the mountains."

"I know them."

"The country of the Turks is very distant. We'd be arrested on the road."

The two once more fell into silence. Wanda's face was completely wreathed in shadows. From somewhere in the distance came a cowherd's yodel, muted and languorous as if the singer was expressing Wanda and Jacob's dilemma and bewailing the harshness of fate. A breeze had begun to blow and the rustle of branches mingled with the sound of the mountain stream as it coursed among the rocks.

"Come to me," Wanda said and her words were half command and half entreaty. "I must have you."

"No. I cannot. It is forbidden."

2

For Wanda the way down the mountain was more difficult than the way up. She was burdened now by the two pitchers filled with milk, and a heavy heart. But, terrified, she almost ran down the slopes. The path took her through towering grass, underbrush, forests; strange murmurs and rustles came from the thickets. Hostile imps and derisive spirits were abroad, she knew. They might play nasty pranks on her. A rock might be put in the path; the imps might swing from the pitchers and make them heavier; they might weave elflocks in her hair or dirty the milk with devil's dung. Demons abounded in the village and surrounding mountains. Each house had its familiar spirit dwelling behind the stove. Werewolves and trolls swarmed the roads, each monster with its own peculiar type of cunning. An owl hooted. Frogs croaked with human voices. Kobalt, the devil who spoke with his belly, was wandering somewhere in the neighborhood; Wanda heard his heavy breath-

31

ing which sounded like a death rattle. And yet fear could not dull the pain of love. Her rejection by the Jewish slave intensified her desire. She was ready to leave the village, her parents, her family, and follow Jacob naked and empty-handed. She had told herself many times that she was a fool to be angry. Who was this man? If she wished she could get one of the village boys to kill him, and no tears would be shed. But what was the use of murder when you loved the victim? The ache in her throat choked her. Her face stung as if it had been slapped. Men had always chased after her—her own brother, the urchin who tended the geese. Jacob's spirit was stronger.

"A sorcerer!" Wanda said to herself. "He's bewitched me."

But where was the charm hidden? Slipped into a knot in her dress? Tied to a fringe of her shawl? It might be hidden in a lock of her hair. She searched everywhere, found nothing. Ought she to consult old Maciocha, the village witch? But the woman was insane, babbled out all her secrets. No, Maciocha could not be trusted. Wanda became so occupied with her thoughts she didn't know how she managed the descent. But suddenly she was at the bottom of the mountain approaching her father's hut. It was little more than a hovel with crumbling beams overgrown with moss and birds' nests hanging from the thatch. The building had two windows, one covered with a cow's bladder and the other open to permit the smoke from the fire to escape. In summer Jan Bzik permitted no illumination but on winter evenings a wick burned in a shard or kindling was lit. Wanda entered, and though it was dark inside, she saw as clearly as if it had been day.

Her father lay on the bed. He was barefoot and in torn clothes. He seldom undressed. She couldn't tell whether he was asleep or just resting. Her mother and her sister Basha were busy braiding a rope of straw. The bed that Jan Bzik lay on was the only one in the hut; the whole family slept in it, Wanda included. Years before when her brother Antek had still been unmarried Jan Bzik would have intercourse with his wife before going to sleep and the children would have something to amuse them. But Antek no longer lived at home and the couple had become too old for such games. Everyone expected Jan Bzik to die shortly. Antek who was anxious to take over the house appeared every few days to ask shamelessly, "Well, is the old man still alive?"

"Yes, still alive," his mother would answer. She also wanted to be rid of this nuisance. He wasn't worth the bread he ate. He had become weak, morose, irritable. All day he belched. Like a beaver, he kept gathering wood, but the thin, crooked logs he brought home were only good for the fire.

They scarcely spoke to each other in that hut. The old woman had a grudge against Wanda for not remarrying. Basha's husband Wojciech had gone home to live with his own parents; he had become despondent after the marriage. Basha had already borne three children, one by her husband, and two bastards; all of them had died. Jan Bzik and his wife had also buried two sons, boys who had been as strong as oaks. The family had become embogged in bitterness and sadness; silent antagonism simmered and bubbled in that household like kasha on a stove.

Wanda didn't say a word to any of them. She poured the milk from the pitchers into some jars. Half of what the cows gave belonged to Zagayek the bailiff; he owned a dairy in the village where cheese was made. The Bziks would use their half the following day for cooking and drinking with bread. The family lived well compared to those around them. In a shed behind the house were two sacks, one of rye and one of barley, and also a handmill in which to grind the grain. Bzik's fields, unlike most, had been partially cleared of stones over the years and the rocks used to build a fence. But food isn't everything. Jan Bzik continued to mourn his dead sons. He couldn't tolerate Antek or his daughter-in-law Marisha. Basha he disliked because of her indiscretions. Wanda was the only one he loved and she had been a widow for years and had brought him no joy. Antek, Basha, and the old woman had become allies. They kept their secrets from Wanda as though she were a stranger. But Wanda managed the household. Her father even consulted her on how to sow and reap. She had a man's brain. If she said something, you could rely on it.

Stach's death had brought her humiliation. She had been forced to return to her parents and again sleep with them and Basha in one bed. Now she would often spend the night in the hayloft or granary, although these places were crawling with rats and mice. She decided to sleep in the granary that night. The hut stank. Her family conducted themselves like animals. It hadn't occurred to any of them that the stream that flowed before their house could be used for bathing. It was the same one that passed near Jacob's barn.

Wanda picked up her pillow; it was stuffed with straw and hay. She walked toward the door.

"Sleeping in the granary?" her mother asked.

"Yes, in the granary."

"You'll be back tomorrow with your nose bitten off."

"Better to have your nose bitten than your soul."

Often Wanda herself was amazed by the words that issued from her lips. At times they had the pithiness and wit of a bishop's talk. Basha and her mother gaped. Jan Bzik stirred and murmured

34

something. He liked to boast that Wanda resembled him and had inherited his brain. But what was intelligence worth if you didn't have luck?

II

The peasants went to bed early. Why sit around in the dark? Anyway they had to get up again at four. But there were always a few who hung around the tavern until it was late. The tavern was presumably the property of the count; it was in fact owned by Zagayek. He supplied its liquor from his still. That evening Antek was among the customers. One of Zagayek's bastard daughters waited on tables. The peasants nibbled pork sausage and drank. All sorts of strange and curious occurrences were discussed. The previous harvest a malevolent spirit named the Polonidca had appeared in the fields, carrying a sickle and dressed in white. The Polonidca had wandered around asking difficult riddles and demanding answers of all she met. For example: What four brothers chase but never catch each other? Answer: The four wheels of a wagon. What is dressed in white but black to the sight and wherever it goes speaks right? Answer: A letter. What eats like a horse, drinks like a horse, but sees with its tail as well as with its eyes? Answer: A blind horse. If the peasant didn't know the right answer the Polonidca tried to cut off his head with her sickle. She would pursue the man as far as the chapel. He would become ill and lie sick for many days.

The Dizwosina was another savage spirit. This terrifying succubus had stringy hair and came from Bohemia on the other side of the mountains. Recently she had entered the hut of old Maciek and had tickled his heels until he had died from laughter. She had taken three of the village boys as her lovers and had forced them to lie in the fields and do her will. One boy had become so emaciated he had died of the phthisis. It was also the custom of the Dizwosina to lie in wait for girls and win their confidence by braiding their hair, putting garlands around their necks, and dancing with them in a circle. But then after amusing herself with the maidens, she would spatter and cover them with filth.

Skrzots also had been seen this year in the granaries. This was a bird that dragged its wings and tail on the ground. As was well known, it came from an egg which had been hatched in a human armpit. But who in the village would do such mischief? It clearly couldn't be the men; only women would have the time and patience for things like that. In the winter the Skrzot got cold in the granary and would knock at the door of a hut and seek to be let in. Then the Skrzot brought good luck. But in all other respects it was harmful and consumed vast amounts of grain. If its excrement fell on the human eye, blindness followed. The opinion of those in the tavern was that a search party should be organized to find out what women were carrying eggs under their arms. But by far the strangest thing that had happened recently concerned a young virgin. The monster had fastened its teeth to her breasts and had drunk until dawn. In the morning the girl had been found in a swoon, the teethmarks on her skin clearly visible.

And yet concerned though they were with vampires and succubuses, they spoke even more about Jacob who lived on the mountain and who tended Jan Bzik's cattle. It was a sin, they said, to maintain an infidel in a Christian village. Who knew where this man came from or what his intentions were? He said that he was a Jew, but if that was so he had murdered Jesus Christ. Why, then, should he be given asylum? Antek said that as soon as his father "croaked," he would take care of Jacob. But the listeners replied that they couldn't wait that long.

"You've seen how your sister crawls to him every day," one peasant remarked to Antek. "It'll end up with her giving birth to a monster."

Antek deliberated before he replied.

"She claims he doesn't touch her."

"Eh, woman's talk!"

"Her belly's flat."

"Flat today, swollen tomorrow," another peasant interjected. "Did you hear about the beggar that came to Lippica? This one was a fine talker and the women followed him around. Three months after he left, five monsters were born. They had nails, teeth, and spurs. Four were strangled but one woman out of pity tried secretly to nurse hers. It bit off her nipple."

"What did she do then?"

"She screamed and her brother picked up a flail and killed it."

"Bah, such things happen," an old peasant said, licking the pork fat off his mustache.

The tavern was half in ruins. Its roof was broken; mushrooms grew on its walls. Two tables and four benches were in the room which was lit by a wick burning in a shard; the single flame smoked and sputtered. The peasants cast heavy shadows on the wall. There was no floor. One of the men got up to relieve himself and stood at a heap of garbage in the corner. Zagayek's daughter laughed with her toothless gums.

"Too lazy to go outside, little father?"

Heavy steps could be heard, and a groaning and snorting. Dziobak, the priest, entered. He was a short, broad-shouldered man; he looked as if he had been sawed in half and glued and nailed together again. His eyes were green as gooseberries, his eyebrows dense as brushes. He had a thick nose with pimples and a receding chin.

Dziobak's robe was covered with stains. He was bent and hunched up, supported himself by two heavy canes. Priests are clean shaven, but coarse, stiff hairs like the bristles of a pig sprouted on his chin. For years the charge had been made that he neglected his duties. Rain leaked into the chapel. Half of the Virgin's head had been smashed. On Sundays when it was time to say Mass Dziobak often lay in a drunken stupor. But his one defender was Zagayek, who ignored all the denunciations. As for the majority of the peasants, they continued to worship the ancient idols that had been the gods of Poland before the truth had been revealed.

"Well, good householders, I see you're all busy with the bottle," Dziobak's hollow voice came from his chest as if from a barrel. "Yes, one needs a drink to burn out the devil."

"Well, it's a drink," Antek said, "but it doesn't burn."

"Does she mix it with water?" Dziobak asked, pointing at the barmaid. "Are you swindling the householders?"

"There's not a drop of water there, little Father. They run from water like the devil from incense."

"Well said."

"Why don't you sit down, Father?"

"Yes, my small feet do ache. It's a hard job for them to carry the weight of me."

Grandiose language was still available to him; he had studied in a seminary in Crakow, but everything else he had learned he had forgotten. He opened his froglike mouth, exposing his one long black tooth which resembled a cleat.

"Won't you have a drink, Father?" the barmaid asked.

"A drink," Dziobak repeated after her.

She brought him a wooden mug filled with

vodka. Dziobak eyed it suspiciously and with visible distaste. He grimaced as if he had a pain in his stomach.

"Well, good people, to your health." He quickly gulped down the liquid. His face became more distorted; disappointment gleamed in his green eyes. It was as if he had been served vinegar.

"We're talking about the Jew Jan Bzik keeps on the mountain, Father."

Dziobak became incensed.

"What's there to talk about? Climb up and dispose of him in God's name. I warned you, did I not, little brothers? I said he would bring only misfortune."

"Zagayek has forbidden it."

"I count Zagayek as my friend and defender. We can be sure that he does not want the village to fall into the hands of Lucifer."

Dziobak peeked at the wooden mug out of the corner of his eyes.

"Just another drop."

III

Jacob awoke in the middle of the night. His body was hot and tense; his heart was pounding. He had been dreaming of Wanda. Passion overwhelmed him and an idea leaped into his brain. He must run down to the valley and find her. He knew she sometimes slept in the granary. "I'm damned already," he told himself. But even as he said it he was aware it was Satan speaking within him.

He must calm himself. He walked to the stream. The brook had its source in glacial snows and its waters were ice cold even in summer. But it was necessary for Jacob to perform his ablutions. What else remained for him but the doing of such acts? He took off his pants and waded into the stream. The moon had already set, but the night was thick

39

with stars. Rumor had it that a water devil made its home in these waters and sang so beautifully in the evening that boys and girls were lured to their destruction. But Jacob knew that a Jew had no right to be afraid of witchcraft or astrology. And if he were dragged down into the current, he would be better off.

"Let it be His will that my death redeem all my sins," he murmured, choosing those words which in ancient times had been spoken by those put to death by the Sanhedrin. The stream was shallow and filled with rocks, but at one spot the water reached to his chest. Jacob walked carefully. He slipped, almost fell. He was afraid that Balaam would begin barking, but the dog continued to sleep in his kennel. He reached the spot that was deepest and immursed himself. How strange. The coldness did not extinguish his lust. A passage from the Song of Songs came to his mind: Many waters cannot quench love, neither can the floods drown it. "What a comparison," he admonished himself. The love referred to in Scriptures was the love of God for his Chosen People. Each word was filled with mystery upon mystery. Jacob continued to immerse himself until he became calmer.

He came out of the water. Before, desire had made him tremble but now he shivered from the cold. He walked to the barn and threw his sheet over him. He murmured a prayer: "Lord, of the universe, remove me from this world, before I stumble and arouse Thy wrath. I am sick of being a wanderer among idolaters and murderers. Return me to that source from whence I came."

He had now become a man at war with himself. One half of him prayed to God to save him from temptation, and the other sought some way to surrender to the flesh. Wanda was not married, she was a widow, the recalcitrant part of him argued. True, she did not undergo ablution after her periods, but the stream was here, available to her for this ritual. Were there any other interdictions? Only the one that forbade the marrying of a gentile. But this interdiction did not apply here. These were unusual circumstances. Had not Moses married a woman from Ethiopia? Did not King Solomon take as his wife Pharaoh's daughter? Of course, these women had become Jewesses. But so could Wanda. The Talmudic law stating that a man who cohabits with a gentile could be put to death by anyone in the community was only valid if there had first been a warning and the adultery was seen by witnesses.

In Jacob's case the normal order of things had been reversed. It was God who spoke in the simplest language while evil overflowed with learned quotations. How long did one live in this world? How long was one young? Was it worth while to destroy this existence and the one that would follow for a few moments of pleasure? "It's all because I don't study the Torah," Jacob said to himself. He started to mumble verses from the Psalms, and then an idea came to him. Hereafter to occupy his time he would enumerate the two hundred and forty-eight commandments and the three hundred and sixty-five prohibitions to be found in the Torah. Although he didn't know them by heart, his years of exile had taught him what a miser the human memory is. It didn't like to give, but if one remained stubborn and did not cease asking, it would pay out even more than what was demanded. Never left in peace, it would at last return all that had been deposited within it.

To be fruitful and multiply was the first of all the commandments. ("Perhaps have a child by Wanda," the legalist within Jacob interjected.) What was the second commandment? Circumcision. And the third? Jacob could not think of another commandment in the entire book of

Genesis. So he began to reflect upon Exodus. What was the first commandment in that book? Very likely the eating of the Passover offering and of the unleavened bread. Yes, but what was the use of remembering these things when tomorrow he might forget them? He must find a way to write everything down. Suddenly he realized that he could do what Moses had done. If Moses had been able to chisel the Ten Commandments into stone, why couldn't he? Chiseling wasn't even necessary; he could scratch with an awl or a nail pried from one of the rafters. He recollected having seen a bent hook somewhere in the barn. Now Jacob found it impossible to return to sleep. A man must be clever in battling the Evil One. He must anticipate all of the Devil's stratagems. Jacob sat waiting for the light of the morning star. The barn was quiet. The cows slept. He heard the sound of the stream. The entire earth seemed to be holding its breath awaiting the new day. Now he had forgotten his lust. Once more he remembered that while he was sitting here in Jan Bzik's barn God continued to direct the world. Rivers flowed; waves billowed on the ocean. Each of the stars continued on its prescribed way. The grain in the fields would ripen soon and the harvest would begin. But who had ripened the grain? How could a stalk of wheat rise from a kernel? How could tree, leaf, branch, fruit emerge from a pit? How could man appear from a drop of semen in a woman's womb? These were all miracles, wonders of wonders. Yes, there were many questions one might ask of God. But who was man to comprehend the acts of divinity?

Jacob was now too impatient to wait for sunrise. "I thank Thee," he said, rising, and then he washed his hands. As he did so a purple beam appeared in the crack beneath the door. He walked outside. The sun had just risen from behind the mountains. The bird which always announced the coming of day chirped shrilly. This was one creature that did not oversleep.

It had become light enough to reach for the hook. Its place was on the shelf where the milk pots were stored. But it had disappeared. Well, that was Satan's work, Jacob thought. He did not wish Jacob to engrave the six hundred and thirteen laws. Jacob took down the earthen pots, one by one, and put them back on the shelf. He rummaged on the ground, searching among the straw. He remained hopeful. The important thing was not to give up. Good things never came easily.

At last he found it. It was slipped into a crack on the shelf. He didn't understand how he could have missed it. Yes, everything, it seemed, was ordained. Years before someone had left the hook there so that Jacob could engrave God's edicts.

He left the barn to find a suitable stone. He did not have to search far. Behind the barn a large rock protruded from the earth. There it stood as ready as the ram which Father Abraham had sacrificed as a burnt offering instead of Isaac. The stone had been waiting ever since Creation.

What he wrote would be visible to no one; it would be hidden behind the barn. Balaam began to wag his tail and jump as if his canine soul comprehended what his master was preparing to do.

IV

Harvest time was approaching and Jan Bzik brought Jacob down from the mountain. How painful it was for the slave to leave his solitude! He had already scratched forty-three commandments and sixty-nine interdictions into the rock. What wonders issued from his mind. He tortured mem-

43

ory and things he had long forgotten appeared. His was a never ending struggle with Purah, the lord of oblivion. In this battle force and persuasion were both necessary; patience was also required, but concentration was most important of all. Jacob sat midway between the barn and rock, concealing himself with weeds and the branches of a midget pine. He mined within himself as men dig for treasure in the earth. It was slow work; he scratched sentences, fragments of sentences, single words into the stone. The Torah had not disappeared. It lay hidden in the nooks and crannies of his brain.

But now he was forced to interrupt his task.

It had been a dry summer, and though there was never much of a harvest in the village, this year's crop was particularly meager. The stalks of grain grew further apart than usual and their kernels were small and brittle. As always, the peasants prayed to both the image of the Virgin and the old lime trees which commanded the rain spirits.

These were not the only rites. Pine branches, lurers of rain, were set among the furrows. The village's wooden rooster, a relic of ancient times, was wrapped in green wheat stalks and decked with saplings. Dancing around the lime trees with the decorated image, the villagers doused it with water. In addition to such public ceremonies, each peasant had his own unique rituals which had been handed down from father to son. Relatives of men who had hanged themselves visited the suicides' graves and begged the unsanctified bones not to cause drought. But rain was not the only problem. As everyone knew, a wicked Baba hid in the stalks and an evil Dziad in the tips. As soon as one furrow was reaped the Baba and Dziad fled and concealed themselves in another. Even when the whole crop had been bound in sheaves,

44

no one could be sure that the danger was over as tiny Babas and minuscule Dziads sought final refuge in the unhusked kernels, and had to be thrashed out with flails. Until the last small Baba had been crushed, the crop was not safe.

This year all the customs had been scrupulously followed, but somehow had been of no avail. There was a grumbling among the peasants when they learned that Jan Bzik had brought Jacob down from the mountain. The poorness of the harvest was perhaps his work. A complaint was made to the Bailiff Zagayek, but his answer was, "Let him do his job first. It's never too late to kill him."

So from early morning until sunset Jacob stood in the fields, and Wanda did not leave him. It was she who taught him how to reap, showed him how the scythe should be sharpened, brought him the food he was permitted to eat: bread, onions, fruit. The law did not allow him to drink milk now since he had not been present at the milkings. But fortunately the chickens were laying well and Wanda secretly gave him an egg each day, which he drank raw. He could also take sour milk and butter since the law stated that the milk of unclean animals does not turn. His sin was heinous enough merely eating the bread of the gentile; his soul could not tolerate further sullying.

The work was difficult, and his fellow harvesters never stopped ridiculing him. Here was a man who wouldn't drink soup or milk and never touched pork. This fellow fasted while he worked.

"You'll wither away," he was warned. "The next thing you know you'll be stretched out flat."

"God gives me strength," Jacob answered.

"What God? Yours must live in the city."

"God is everywhere, in both city and country."

"You don't cut straight. You'll ruin the straw."

The women and girls giggled and whispered.

45

"Do you see, Wanda, how your man sweats?"

"He's the strongest in the village."

Hearing that remark, Jacob cautioned her.

"The man who can control his passions is the most powerful."

"What's that fool saying?"

The women winked at each other and laughed, exchanged lewd gestures. One girl ran over to Jacob and pulled up her skirts. This made the peasants whinny with laughter.

"That's a fine show for you, Jew."

As he reaped, Jacob kept up a constant recitation, repeating to himself Psalms and passages of the Mishnah and Gemara. He had been there when the oxen plowed the fields and the seed was sowed. Now he was harvesting the grain. Weeds grew among the stalks and corn flowers on the sides of the furrows. As the scythes moved, field mice ran from their blades, but other creatures remained in the harvested fields: grasshoppers, lady bugs, beetles, flyers and crawlers, every variety of insect, and each with its own particular structure. Surely some Hand had created all this. Some Eye was watching over it. From the mountains came grasshoppers and birds that spoke with human voices, and the peasants killed them with their shovels. Their efforts were to no avail, since the more they killed, the more gathered. Jacob was reminded of the plague of locusts that God had visited upon the Egyptians. He himself killed nothing. It was one thing to slaughter an animal according to the law and in such a way as to redeem its soul, another to step on and crush tiny creatures that sought no more than man did—merely to eat and multiply. At dusk when the fields were alive with toads, Jacob walked carefully so as not to tread on their exposed bodies.

Now and again when the ribald songs of the harvesters resounded in the fields, Jacob would take up a chant of his own, the Sabbath service, or the liturgies of Rosh Hashana and Yom Kippur, or sing the Akdamoth, a Pentecost song. Wanda joined in, for she had picked up the tunes from Jacob, singing Jewish chants and recitatives with a voice that had been accustomed to ballads of a different kind. Jacob's soul throbbed with music. He kept up a constant debate with the Almighty. "How long will the unholy multitudes rule the world and the scandal and darkness of Egypt hold dominion? Reveal Thy Light, Father in Heaven. Let there be an end to pain and idolatry and the shedding of blood. Scourge us no longer with plagues and famines. Do not allow the weak to go down to defeat and the wicked to triumph.... Yes, Free Will was necessary, and Your face had to be hidden, but there has been enough of concealment. We are already up to our necks in water." So absorbed did he become in his chant that he did not notice that all the others had become silent. His voice sang alone and everyone was listening. The peasants clapped hands, laughed, and mimicked him. Jacob stood with bent head, ashamed.

"Pray, Jew, pray. Not even your God can make this a good harvest."

"Do you think he's cursing us?"

"What language is that you're speaking, Jew?"

"The Holy Language."

"What Holy Language?"

"The language of the Bible."

"The Bible? What's the Bible?"

"God's Law."

"What's God's Law?"

"That one neither kill nor steal nor covet a man's wife."

"Dziobak says things like that in the chapel."

47

"It all comes from the Bible."

The peasants became silent. One of the them handed Jacob a turnip.

"Eat, stranger. You won't get strong from fasting."

V

The crop had been poor, but nevertheless the peasants celebrated. Girls appeared in the fields with wreaths on their heads and the older women assembled also. The time had come for Zagayek to superintend the selection of the maiden who would reap the last Baba. The choice was made by drawing lots and the girl chosen cut the last sheaf of grain, thereby becoming a Baba herself. Once selected, she was wrapped in stalks tied round her body by flax, and paraded from hut to hut in a wooden-wheeled cart drawn by four boys. The whole village accompanied the procession, laughing and singing and clapping hands. It was said that in ancient times when the people had still been idol worshipers the Baba was thrown into the stream and drowned, but now the village was Christian.

The night following this ceremony, the peasants danced and drank. The Baba performed with the boy who was chosen to be rooster. The rooster crowed, chased chickens, did all kinds of antics. He had a pair of wings on his shoulders, a cockscomb on his head and on his heels wooden spurs. Last year's rooster was also there, and the two fought, pushing out their chests, charging each other, tearing each other's feathers. It was so funny the girls couldn't stop laughing. This year's rooster always won, and then danced with the Baba who was now disguised as a witch, her face smeared with soot, and with the broom in her hand on

48

which she rode to the Black Mass. The Baba seated herself in a barrel hoop and lifted her skirts, preparing to make a journey. The peasants forgot their troubles. The children refused to go to bed, sipped vodka, laughed and giggled.

Since it was no longer permissible to drown the real Baba, the boys made an effigy from straw. So skillfully did they model face, breasts, hips and feet, that the scarecrow, with two coals in the head for eyes, seemed alive. Just as the sun rose, the Baba was led to the stream. The women scolded the scapegoat, demanding that she take with her the evil eye and all their misfortunes and illnesses. The men and children spat on her, and then she was thrown into the stream. Everyone watched the straw Baba move downstream, bobbing up and down in the current. As the peasants knew, the river flowed into the Vistula and the Vistula emptied into the sea where bad spirits were awaiting the Baba. Though she wasn't alive, the over-compassionate girls wept for her. Was there such a great difference between flesh and straw? The ceremony over, vodka was passed around, and Jacob was given a drink. Wanda whispered into his ear, "I wish I were the Baba. I would swim with you to the end of the world."

The next day, the threshing began. From sunrise to sunset there was the sound of flails rising and falling. Occasionally a muffled cry or sob rose from the stalks. One of the small Babas was dying. The evenings were still warm enough for the threshers to stay out of doors, and so after supper they gathered branches and lit a fire. Chestnuts were roasted, riddles asked, stories told of werewolves, hobgoblins, demons. The most spine-tingling tale concerned the black field where only black grain sprouted and where a black reaper reaped with a long black scythe. The girls screamed and clutched each other, huddled closer

49

to the boys. The autumn days were brilliant, but the nights were dark. Stars fell; frogs croaked, spoke with human voices from the bogs. Bats appeared and the girls scurried, covering their heads and screaming. If one of these nocturnal creatures entangled itself in a girl's hair, it meant that she would not live out the year.

Someone asked Jacob to sing and he performed a lullaby he had learned from his mother. The song pleased the peasants. He was asked for a story. He told them several tales from the Gemara and Midrash. The one they liked best was about a man who had heard of a harlot living in a distant country whose fee was four hundred gulden. When the man went to the harlot, he found she had prepared six silver beds with silver ladders and one golden bed with a golden ladder. The harlot had sat before him naked, but the fringes of his ritual garment had suddenly risen and struck him angrily in the face. At the end of the story the man converted the harlot to the Jewish faith and the beds she had prepared for him were finally used on their wedding night. The story was not easy to translate into Polish, but Jacob managed to make the peasants understand. They became fascinated by the fringes. What kind of fringes were they? Jacob explained. The glow from the fire lit up Wanda's face. She pulled his arm to her lips, kissed and then bit it. He sought to free himself but she hung to him tenaciously. Her breasts rubbed against his shoulder and the heat she gave off was like an oven's.

The story had been told for her, he knew. In the form of a parable he had promised that if she did not force him to cohabit with her now, later he would take her as a wife. But could he make such a promise? His wife might be alive. How could Wanda become a Jew? In Poland a Christian who became a Jewish convert was put to death;

moreover, Jewish law forebade the conversion of gentiles for reasons other than faith.

"Well, every day I sink deeper into the abyss," Jacob thought.

Then on the last day of the threshing, a circus arrived in town. It was the first time Jacob had seen anyone from another district. The troupe included two men beside the owner, and they had a monkey, and a parrot who not only talked but told fortunes by selecting cards with his beak. The village was in an uproar. The performance was given in an open field near Zagayek's house and all of the men showed up with their wives and children. Jacob was permitted to go also. The bear whirled around on his hind legs, the monkey smoked a pipe and did somersaults. One of the men was an acrobat and did stunts like walking on his hands and lying bare-backed on a board of nails. The other was a musician and played a fiddle, a trumpet, and a drum with bells. The peasants screamed with joy and Wanda jumped up and down like a little girl. But Jacob disapproved of such entertainment, which he considered only one step away from witchcraft. More than a desire for amusement had brought him there. Circus men wandered from town to town, and perhaps this troupe had stopped at Josefov. They might have news of Jacob's family. So when the performance was done and the monkey and bear had been chained to a tree, Jacob followed the performers into their tent. The proprietor looked at Jacob in astonishment when he heard his question: had the circus stopped at Josefov.

"What business is it of yours where I've been?"

"I come from Josefov. I am a Jew and a teacher. I am a survivor of the massacre."

"How do you happen to be here?"

Jacob told the proprietor and the man snapped his whip.

"If the Jews knew where you were would they ransom you?"

"Yes, to free a captive is considered a holy act."

"Would they pay me if I told them you were alive?"

"Yes, they would."

"Give me your name. And I must have a way to convince them that I am telling the truth."

Jacob confided to the circus owner the names of his wife and children as well as that of his father-in-law who had been one of the community elders. Although the man could not write, he made a knot in a piece of string and told Jacob that he had not as yet been to Josefov, but he might well stop there. If any Jews were left in the town he would tell them that Jacob was alive and where he could be found.

3

After the harvest, Jacob returned to the barn on
the mountain. He knew that he would not be there
long. Soon the cold weather would set in and the
cattle would have no food. Already the days had
become shorter and when he gathered grass in the
morning, he found the fields covered with frost.
Haze hung over the autumn hills and it was
increasingly difficult to distinguish between fog
rising from the earth and the smoke of camp fires.
The birds screamed and croaked more shrilly these
days, and the winds blowing down from the
summits carried the taste of snow. Though Jacob
gathered as much fodder as he could, it was never
enough for the cows. The hungry beasts bellowed,
stamped on the earth, even pounded with their
hoofs while they were being milked. Once more
Jacob proceeded with his task of engraving the six
hundred and thirteen laws of the Torah onto a
stone, but he had little spare time during the day
and at night it was too dark to work.

On the seventh day of the month of Elul—according to Jacob's calculations—dusk came quickly. The sun fell behind a massive cloud which covered the entire west. But was it really that date? For all he knew his reckonings might be erroneous and when the ram's horn was blown all over the world and the Rosh Hashana litanies sung, he would be out as usual gathering fodder. He sat in the barn and thought about his life. For as long as he could remember he had been considered lucky. His father had been a wealthy contractor who bought up the gentry's timber, supervised the felling of the trees and floated the logs down the Bug River to the Vistula and from thence to Danzig. Whenever his father had gone off on such trips, he had returned bearing gifts for Jacob and his sisters. Elka Sisel, Jacob's mother, was a rabbi's daughter and came from Prussia where she had been brought up in comfortable circumstances. Susschen, as she was called, spoke German and wrote Hebrew and conducted herself differently from the other women. She had rugs on the floor of her house and brass latches on the door. Coffee, a rarity even among the rich, was served daily in her home. An expert cook, seamstress, knitter, she taught her daughters how to do needlepoint and instructed them in Bible reading. The girls married young. Jacob himself was only twelve when he became engaged to Zelda Leah, who was two years younger, and the daughter of the town's elder. He had always been a good student. At eight he had read a complete page of the Gemara unassisted; at his engagement party he delivered a speech. He wrote in a fine, bold hand, had a good singing voice, and was a gifted draughtsman and wood carver. On a canvas on the east wall of the synagogue he painted the twelve constellations in red, green, blue and purple circling Jehovah's name, and in the corners put

54

four animals: a deer, a lion, a leopard, and an eagle. At Pentecost he decorated the windows of the town's most important citizens and for the feast of Succoth adorned the tabernacle with lanterns and streamers.

Tall and healthy, when he made a fist, six boys could not force it open. His father had taught him to swim side and breast stroke. Zelda Leah, on the other hand, was thin and small—prematurely old, his sisters maintained. But of what possible interest was this ten-year-old child to Jacob? He was more interested in his father-in-law's library of rare books. Jacob received four hundred gulden as dowry, room and board at his in-laws for life.

The wedding was noisy and boisterous. Josefov was only a small town but after his marriage Jacob immersed himself so deeply in study that he forgot the outside world. True, his wife, he discovered, had odd habits. If her mother scolded her, she petulantly kicked off her shoes and stockings and overturned the soup bowl. She was a married woman and had not as yet menstruated. When her period finally came, she bled like a slaughtered calf. Every time Jacob approached her, she howled in pain. She was a perpetual sufferer from heartburn, headaches, and back aches. She screwed up her face, wept, complained. But Jacob was given to understand that only daughters were always like that. Her mother was constantly tugging her from him, but Zelda Leah bore him three children, Jacob scarcely knew how. Her recriminations and sarcasms sounded like the babblings of fools or school children; she belonged to that class of spoiled daughters whose whims can never be satisfied. Her mother, she said, was envious of her good looks. Her father had forgotten her; Jacob didn't love her. It never seemed to occur to her that she should try being lovable. Her eyes grew prematurely old from too much crying and her nose turned red. She didn't even take care of the children. That too became her mother's responsibility.

When the rabbi died, Jacob's father-in-law wanted him to take over the office, but Zaddock, the late rabbi's son, had a considerable following. True, Jacob's backer was the town's elder, a rich and influential man, but the people of Josefov had decided that this one time they were not going to let him have his way. Despite himself, Jacob found that he was involved in a quarrel. He didn't want to become rabbi, was actually in favor of Zaddock, and because of this his father-in-law became his enemy. If he refused to become rabbi, let him at least lecture to the boys in the study house. Jacob would have liked to stay in the library, studying the Gemara and its commentaries, meditating on philosophy and cabala, subjects he preferred even to the Talmud. From childhood on he had been searching for the meaning of existence and trying to comprehend the ways of God. He was acquainted with the thought of Plato, Aristotle, and the Epicureans through the quotations he had found in *A Guide for the Perplexed*, the *Chuzary*, *The Beliefs and Ideas*, and similar works. He knew the cabalistic systems of Rabbi Moshe of Cordova and the holy Isaac Luria. He was well aware that Judaism was based upon faith and not knowledge and yet he sought to understand wherever it was possible. Why had God created the world? Why had He found it necessary to have pain, sin, evil? Even though each of the great sages had given his answer, the questions remained unsolved. An all-powerful Creator did not need to be sustained by the agony of small children and the sacrifice of His people to bands of assassins. The atrocities of the Cossacks had been talked about for years before the attack on Josefov. Hearts had long been frozen with fear, then one day death had struck.

Jacob had just turned twenty-five when the Cossacks had advanced on Josefov. He was now past twenty-nine, so he lived a seventh of his life in this remote mountain village, deprived of family and community, separated from books, like one of those souls who wander naked in Tophet. And here it was the end of summer; the short days, the cold nights had come. He could reach out his hand and actually touch the darkness of Egypt, the void from which God's face was absent. Dejection is only one small step from denial. Satan became arrogant and spoke to Jacob insolently: "There is no God. There is no world beyond this one." He bid Jacob become a pagan among the pagans; he commanded him to marry Wanda or at the very least to lie with her.

II

The cowherds also had their autumn celebration. They had sought by threats and promises to make Jacob join them ever since he had first appeared upon the mountain with Jan Bzik's herd. But, one way or another, he had always put them off. He was forbidden to eat their food or listen to their licentious songs and brutal jokes. For the most part, they were a crippled, half-mad crew with scabs and elflocks on their heads and rashes on their bodies. Shame was unknown to them, as if they had been conceived before the eating of the forbidden fruit. Jacob often reflected that as yet this rabble had not developed the capacity to choose freely. They seemed to him survivors of those worlds, which, according to the Midrash, God had created and destroyed before fashioning this one. Jacob, when he saw them approaching, had acquired the habit of turning his head, or looking through them as if they didn't exist. If they foraged for grass on the lower slopes, he moved up toward the summit. He avoided them like filth. They were crawling all about him on the mountain, yet he went days and weeks without meeting any. Nor was it only disgust that kept him apart from this vermin; they were dangerous and, like wolves, would attack for no reason. Sickness, suffering, the sight of blood amused them.

That year they had made up their minds to seize him by force, and one evening after Wanda had left they surrounded the barn, deploying themselves like soldiers stealthily preparing to storm a fortress. One moment there was a stillness in which only the song of the grasshoppers was heard, and the next, the silence had been broken by howling and shrieking as both men and girls charged from all sides. The attackers were equipped with sticks, stones, and ropes. Jacob thought they had come to kill him, and like his Biblical namesake prepared to fight, or, if possible, to ransom himself through entreaties and a "gift" (the shirt off his back). He picked up a heavy club and swung it, knowing that his adversaries were so debilitated by illness he might be able to drive them off. Soon an emissary stepped forward, a cowherd who was more fluent than the others, and who assured Jacob no harm was intended. They had merely come to invite him to drink and dance with them. The man dribbled, stammered, mispronounced words. His companions were already drunk and laughed and screamed wildly. They held their stomachs and rolled about on the ground. He would not be let off this time, Jacob knew.

"All right," he finally said, "I'll go with you, but I'll eat nothing."

"Jew, Jew. Come. Come. Seize him. Seize him."

A dozen hands grasped Jacob and started to tug him. He descended the hill on which the barn was located, half running, half sliding. An awful stench rose from that mob; the odors of sweat and urine mingled with the stink of something for which there is no name, as if these bodies were putrefying while still alive. Jacob was forced to hold his nose and the girls laughed until they wept. The men hee-hawed and whinnied, supported themselves on each other's shoulders, and barked like dogs. Some collapsed on the path, but their companions did not pause to assist them, but stepped over the recumbent bodies. Jacob was perplexed. How could the sons of Adam created in God's image fall to such depths? These men and women also had fathers and mothers and hearts and brains. They too possessed eyes that could see God's wonders.

Jacob was led to a clearing where the grass was already trampled and soiled with vomit. A keg of vodka three-quarters empty stood near an almost extinguished fire. Drunken musicians were performing on drums, pipes, on a ram's horn very like that blown on Rosh Hashana, on a lute strung with the guts of some animal. But those who were being entertained were too intoxicated to do more than wallow on the ground; grunting like pigs, licking the earth, babbling to rocks. Many lay stretched out like carcasses. There was a full moon in the sky, and one girl flung her arms around a tree trunk and cried bitterly. A cowherd walked over, threw branches on the fire, and nearly fell into the flames. Almost immediately a woolly-looking shepherd attempted to put out the blaze by urinating on it. The girls howled, screamed, cat-called. Jacob felt himself choking. He had heard these cries many times before, but each time he was terrified by them.

"Well, now I have seen it," he said to himself. "These are those abominations which prompted God to demand the slaying of entire peoples."

As a boy, this had been one of his quarrels with

the Lord. What sin had been committed by the small children of the nations Moses had been told to annihilate? But now that Jacob observed this rabble he understood that some forms of corruption can only be cleansed by fire. Thousands of years of idolatry survived in these savages. Baal, Astoreth, and Moloch stared from their bloodshot and dilated eyes. He was offered a cup of vodka by one of the merrymakers but the liquid seared his lips and throat; his stomach burned as though he had been forced to drink molten lead like those culprits the Sanhedrin had condemned to death at the stake in ancient times. Jacob shuddered. Had he been poisoned? Was this the end?

His face became contorted and he doubled up.

The cowherd who had given him the drink let out a yell, "Bring him more. Make the Jew drink. Fill up his cup."

"Give him pork," someone else shouted.

A pock-marked fellow with a face like a turnip grater tried to push a piece of sausage into Jacob's mouth. Jacob gave the man a shove. The cowherd fell and lay as still as a log.

"Hey, he's killed him."

Jacob approached the fallen man with trembling knees. Had this also been destined? Thank God, the man was alive. He lay there, foam bubbling from his lips, the sausage still clutched between his fingers, screaming abuse. His comrades laughed, threatened, cursed.

"God murderer. Jew. Scabhead. Leper."

A few feet away a cowherd jumped on a girl but was too drunk to do anything. Yet the two wrestled and squirmed like a dog and a bitch. The surrounding company laughed, spat, dribbled from their noses, and goaded the lovers on. A monstrous square-headed girl with a goiter on her neck and tangled matted hair sat on a tree stump sobbing out a name over and over again. She was wringing her hands, which were as long as a monkey's and as broad as a man's, their nails rotted away. Her feet were covered with boils and as flat as a goose's. Some of the cowherds sought to comfort her and gave her a cup of vodka. Her crooked mouth opened, exposing a single tooth, but she only wailed louder.

"Father! Father! Father!"

So she also cried out, Jacob thought, to a father in heaven. Compassion for this creature who had fallen from the womb deformed and misshapen, a mooncalf, swept over Jacob. Who could tell what frightened her mother at the moment of conception, or what sinful soul had been incarcerated in the girl's body? Hers was not an ordinary cry but the wail of a spirit who has gazed into the abyss and seen a torment from which there is no escape. Through some miracle this animal comprehended its own bestiality and mourned its lot.

Jacob wanted to go and comfort her, but he saw in her half-shut eyes a fury undiminished by suffering. Such a woman might spring at him like a beast of prey. He sat down and chanted the third chapter of Psalms: "Lord, how are they increased that trouble me! Many are they that rise against me. Many there be which say of my soul, there is no help for him in God. Selah."

III

It stormed in the middle of the night. A flash of lightning lit up the interior of the barn, and the cows, dung heaps, earthen pots became visible for an instant. Thunder rumbled. After washing his hands, Jacob recited "The One Who Does the Work of Creation" and "His Power and Strength Fill the World." A gust of wind blew open the barn door. The downpour beat on the roof like hail. The rain lashed Jacob as he closed and latched the door.

This was the beginning of bad weather, he feared, and not merely one of those torrential cloudbursts that occur in summer. So it was; for a few hours later, though the rain ceased, the sky remained overcast. An icy wind blew from the mountains. At dawn the storm started all over again. Though the sun had risen, the morning was as gray as twilight. There would be no foraging for grass and other vegetation on the slopes today. Jacob would have to feed his herd with the fodder he had prepared for the Sabbath. He built a small fire to make things more cheerful and sat by it praying; he rose, faced to the east, and recited the eighteen benedictions. A cow turned its head and gazed at him with a blank humility, yet the expression of the black muzzle, wet with saliva and bristling with a few sparse hairs, made Jacob think that the creature nursed some grievance. It often seemed to him that the cattle complained, "You are a man and we are only cows. What justice is there to that?" He placated them by stroking their necks, slapping their sides, and feeding them tidbits. "Father," he often prayed. "Thou knowest why Thou hast created them. They are the work of Thy hand. At the end of days, they too must have salvation."

That morning his breakfast consisted of bread and milk and an apple brought the day before. If the rain continued, Wanda would not come. He would have to sustain himself on sour milk, a dish which he could no longer stomach. He chewed each bite of the apple slowly to savor the full flavor. In his father-in-law's house he had not known that one could have such an appetite and that bread with bran could be so delicious. As he swallowed each mouthful, he seemed to feel the marrow in his bones increase. The wind had died down, the door of the barn was now open, and from time to time he glanced up at the sky. Perhaps the weather would clear: wasn't it too early for the autumn rains? No longer was there a vista of distant places—nothing was visible but the flat crest of the hill surrounding the barn. Sky, mountains, valleys, forests, had dissolved and disappeared. Fog drifted across the ground. Mist rose from the pines as though the wet trees were burning. Here in his exile Jacob at last understood what was meant when the cabala spoke of God's hidden face and the shrinking of His light. Yesterday everything had been bright; now it was gray. Distances had shrunk; the skies had collapsed like the canvas of a tent; the tangible had lost substance. If so much could vanish for the physical eye, how much more could elude the spiritual. Every man comprehended according to his merit. Infinite worlds, angels, seraphim, mansions and sacred chariots surrounded man, but he did not see them because he was small and sinful and immersed in the vanities of the body.

As always when it rained, a variety of creatures sought shelter in the barn: butterflies, grasshoppers, gnats, beetles. One insect had two pairs of wings. A white butterfly with black markings resembling script alighted on a stone near the fire and appeared to be warming or drying itself. Jacob placed a crumb of bread near it, but it remained motionless. He touched it, but it didn't stir, and he realized it was dead. Sorrow overcame him. Here was one that would never flutter again. He would have liked to eulogize this handsome creature which had lived a day, or even less, and had never tasted sin. Its wings were smoother than silk and covered with an ethereal dust. It rested on the stone like a shrouded corpse.

Of necessity, Jacob had to war with flies and vermin which bit both him and the cows. He had no alternative but to kill. As he walked about, he could not avoid treading on worms and toads, and when he gathered grass he often encountered venomous snakes which would hiss and strike at him and which he crushed with a club or stone. But each time something like that happened he judged himself a murderer. He silently blamed the Creator for forcing one creature to annihilate another. Of all the questions he asked about the universe, he found this the most difficult.

There was nothing for him to do that day and so he stretched out on the straw and covered himself with his sheet. No, Wanda would not come. He was ashamed that he longed so much for this gentile woman, but the harder he tried to rid himself of desire, the stronger it became. His yearning stayed with him praying and studying, sleeping and waking. He knew the bitter truth: compared to his passion for Wanda, his mourning for his wife and children and his love for God were weak. If the desires of the flesh came from Satan, then he was in the Devil's net. "Well, I have lost both worlds," he muttered, and through half-shut eyes he maintained his watch. The petals of a flower stirred among the wet bushes. Field mice, weasels, moles, skunks, and hedgehogs were hiding in the thickets. All of these small creatures waited with impatience for the sun to shine. The birds, like clusters of fruit, weighed down the trees and the instant the rain let up, whistling, chirruping, croaking began.

From somewhere far off came a muted yodel. A cowherd was singing in the foul dampness, and his distant voice pleaded and demanded, lamented the injustice visited on all living things: Jews, gentiles, animals, even the flies and gnats crawling on the hips of the cattle.

IV

Though the rain ceased before evening, it was clear that this was only a short respite. Thunderheads lay low in the west, red and sulphurous, charged with lightning, and the air was heavy with mist that might at any moment turn to rain. Crows dived and cawed. There was no hope that Wanda would come in such weather, and yet when Jacob ascended his lookout hill, he saw her climbing toward him, carrying her two pitchers and the food basket. Tears came to his eyes. Someone remembered him and cared. He prayed that the storm would hold off until she reached him, and apparently his plea was answered; a moment after she entered the barn the deluge came, pouring down from the heavens as if from barrels. Neither Jacob nor Wanda spoke much to each other that afternoon. She sat down and immediately began to milk the cows. She was strangely shy and embarrassed and so was Jacob. Now and again a flash of lightning illuminated the twilight of the barn and he saw her bathed in such a heavenly glow that it seemed to him the woman he had known before had only been a sign or a husk. Had she not been created in God's image? Did not her form reflect that emanation through which the Eternal reflected His beauty? Had not Esau come from the seed of Abraham and Isaac? Jacob knew only too well where the meditations were leading, but he could not push them from him. He ate, said the benediction, recited the evening prayer, but still they did not leave him. The weather did not clear; Wanda would be unable to return home. At this late hour, moreover, the road back had already become dangerous.

"I'll sleep here in the barn," Wanda said, "unless you drive me out."

"I drive you out? You are the mistress."

They sat conversing quietly with the ease that intimacy brings. Wanda spoke of Zagayek and his paralytic wife, of their son Stephan who continued to pursue Wanda, of Zagayek's daughter Zosia whom everyone knew consorted with her father. But the bailiff had a dozen mistresses besides his daughter and so many bastards he could not remember their names. He did not conduct himself like a retainer but like a lord or king. He exacted from the peasant brides "the right of the first night," a law that was no longer in force. The peasants he treated as slaves, although they had their own fields and were only required to work for the count two days a week. He whipped them with wet rods, illegally forced them to do his business, levied private taxes upon vodka, performed operations on the sick against their will, tearing out teeth with pliers, amputating fingers with a cleaver, opening up breasts with a kitchen knife. Often he acted as a midwife and demanded a handsome payment for his services.

"There's nothing he doesn't want," Wanda said. "He would swallow the village whole if he could."

Wanda's bed was not difficult to prepare. Jacob spread out some straw and she lay down on it, covering herself with her shawl. He slept in one corner of the barn and she in another. In the silence the cows could be heard chewing their cud. She went outside to relieve herself and returned drenched from the rain. "So modesty exists even among these people," Jacob reflected. They both lay there without saying a word. "I must be sure not to snore," Jacob warned himself. He feared that he would be unable to sleep, but weariness overcame him. His jaw sagged and darkness flooded his mind. Every night he dropped onto his bed like a log. Thank God there was something stronger than his lust.

V

He awoke trembling, opened his eyes, and discovered Wanda lying next to him on the straw. The air in the barn was cool but he felt the burning heat of her body. She caught hold of him, pressed herself against him, and touched his cheek with her lips. Though he was conscious, he submitted in silence, amazed not only at what was happening but at the fierceness of his own desire. When he sought to push her from him, she clung to him with uncanny strength. He attempted to speak to her, but she stopped his lips with her mouth. He remembered the story of Ruth and Boaz and knew that his lust was more powerful than he. "I am forfeiting the world to come," he said to himself. He heard Wanda's hoarse voice imploring him; she was panting like an animal.

He lay numb, unable now to deny either her or himself, as if he had lost his freedom of will. Suddenly a passage from the Gemara entered his mind: should a man be overcome by the Evil One, let him dress himself in dark clothing, and cover himself in black, and indulge his heart's desire. This precept appeared to have been lurking in his memory for the specific purpose of breaking down his last defense. His legs became heavy and taut, and he was dragged down by a weight he could not withstand. "Wanda," he said, and his voice was trembling, "you must first go and bathe in the stream."

"I have already washed and I have combed my hair."

"No, you must immerse yourself in the water."

"Now?"

"God's law requires it."

She lay there in silence, perplexed by this strange demand, and then finally said, "I will do this also."

She rose, and still holding tight to him, opened the barn door. The rain had stopped but the night was mired in darkness and wet. There was not a trace of the sky and the only evidence of the stream was the sound of water churning and bubbling as it rushed downward. Wanda clutched Jacob's hand as they groped blindly and with the abandon of those who no longer fear for their bodies. They stumbled over stones and shrubs, were splashed by the moisture dripping from trees. They were seeking the one spot in that shallow, rock-cluttered torrent where the stream was deep enough for a man to immerse himself. When they reached it, she refused to enter the water without him, and he, forgetting to slip out of his linen trousers, followed her in. The shock of the cold water touching him took away his breath; he almost lost his footing, so swollen was the stream because of the rains. They clung to each other as if undergoing martyrdom. Thus, at the time of the massacres Jews had plunged into fire and water. At last, his feet on a firm bottom, Jacob said to Wanda, "Immerse yourself."

She let go his hand and submerged in the water. He reached about, unable to find her. She reappeared, and his eyes, now accustomed to the darkness, made out the dim contours of her face.

"Hurry," he said.

"I have done this for you."

He took her hand and together they ran back to the barn. The cold, he realized, had not extinguished the fire in his veins. Both of them burned with the heat of newly lit kindling. He dried Wanda's naked body with his sheet, breathing heavily, his teeth chattering. Wanda's eyes shone through the darkness. He heard her say to him again, "I have done this for you."

"No, not for me," he answered, "for God," and the blasphemy of his words frightened him.

Nothing could restrain him now. He lifted her in his arms and carried her to the straw.

4

The sun rose and red could be seen through the chinks in the door. A purple beam of light fell across Wanda's face. They had been asleep, but awakened by lust they again sought each other. He had never known such passion as hers. She spoke words he had never heard before, called him in her peasant dialect her buck, her lion, her wolf, her bull, and even stranger epithets. He possessed her but it did not quench his desire. She blazed with an ecstasy—was it from heaven or hell? "More, more," she cried in a loud voice, "master, husband." He found himself possessed of powers that did not seem to be his—was it miracle or witchcraft? For the first time in his life he recognized the mysteries of the body. How was such desire possible? "For Love is as strong as Death," the Song of Songs said, and at last he understood. As the sun rose, he sought to tear himself from her. She clung to his neck and again thirstily kissed him. "My husband," she said, "I want to die for you."

"Why die? You are still young."

"Take me away from here to your Jews. I want to be your wife and bear you a son."

"You must believe in God to become a daughter of Israel."

"I believe in Him. I believe."

She was screaming so loudly that he covered her mouth with his hand so the cowherds outside would not hear. He was no longer ashamed before God, but he feared the ridicule of men. Even the cows turned their heads and stared. He pulled himself from her and was baffled to discover morning brought no repentance. The opposite rather! He was astonished now that he had endured his desire. The pitcher had overturned and he could not wash his hands. He didn't even say "I thank Thee," fearing to utter holy words after what had happened. His clothes were damp, but he put them on anyway, and Wanda also tidied herself. He walked out into the cool, clear Elul morning, leaving her with the cows. Dew covered the grass and each droplet gleamed. Birds were singing, and in the distance a cow lowed, the sound echoing like the blast from a ram's horn. "Yes, I have forfeited the world beyond," Jacob muttered, and immediately Satan whispered into his ear, "Shouldn't you also give up being a Jew?" Jacob glanced at the rock on which he had already scratched a third of the commandments and interdictions and it seemed to him like a battered ruin, all that was left to him from a war that had been lost. "Well, but I am still a Jew," he said, quoting the Talmud in an attempt to rally his spirits. He washed his hands in the stream and said, "I thank Thee," and then he began the introductory prayer. When he came to the words, "Lead us not into temptation," he paused. Not even the sainted Joseph had been as tempted as he. The Midrash said that when Joseph had been about to sin, his father's image had been revealed to him. So Heaven had interceded in his behalf.

As he mumbled his prayers, he searched in himself for some extenuation of what he had done. According to the strict letter of the law, this woman was neither unclean nor married. Even the Ancients had had concubines. She could still be a pious Jewish matron. "Something done selfishly may end up as a godly act." But, nevertheless, as he prayed he contrasted, despite himself, Wanda and Zelda, peace be with her. His wife had also been a woman, but frigid and cold, forever distracted. She had been a constant stream of complaints: headaches, toothaches, cramps in the stomach, and always fearful of breaking the law. How could he have known that such passion and love as Wanda's existed? He again heard Wanda's voice, the words she had whispered to him, her groans, the swift intake of her breath, and he again felt the touch of her tongue and the sharpness of her teeth. She had left marks on his body. She was willing to flee with him across the mountains in the middle of the night. She spoke to him exactly as Ruth had spoken: "Where thou goest, I go. Thy people are my people. Thy God is my God." Her body exuded the warmth of the sun, the breezes of summer, the fragrance of wood, field, flower, leaf, just as milk gave off the odor of the grass the cattle fed on. He yawned while he prayed. He recited the Shema and stretched his arms. He had scarcely closed his eyes the night before and lacked the strength to go hunting for grass. Bending his head low, Jacob was aware of his own weariness. During the few brief moments of sleep, he had dreamed, and although he did not remember his dream clearly, its aftertaste lingered. It seemed to him that he had been descending steps

71

into a ritual bath or cave and had wandered across hills, ditches, and graves. He had met someone whose beard was composed of the roots of a plant. Who could it have been? His father? Had the man spoken to him? Wanda thrust her head out of the barn and gave him a wifely smile.

"Why are you standing there?"

He pointed to his lips to signify that she must not interrupt his prayer.

Her eyes shone with affection; she winked and nodded. Jacob closed his eyelids. Did he repent? He did not feel so much contrition as annoyance that he had been placed in a situation which made his sin possible. He stared into himself as though he were looking down the shaft of a deep well. What he saw there frightened him. Like a snake, passion lay curled at the bottom.

II

Rosh Hashana, Yom Kippur, and Succoth, according to Jacob's calendar, were past. The day which he thought to be Simchath Torah, Jan Bzik appeared on the mountain accompanied by Antek, Wanda, and Basha. The smell of snow was in the air; the time had come to drive the cattle down the valley. Both bringing them up and taking them down were difficult tasks. Cows are not mountain goats and do not climb slopes nimbly. The beasts had to be held by short, thick ropes, and restrained at every step. A cow might dig its hoofs into the ground and then one man would be forced to drag the creature while another whipped it. Others might stampede and break backs or legs bolting from the herd. But on this occasion all went well. An hour or so after the cattle had entered Jan Bzik's barn, snow fell. The mountains were no longer accessible, and were enveloped by columns of mist. The village, turned white, looked unfamiliar. Food was not plentiful in the homes of the peasants, but there was no lack of wood; smoke rose from the chimneys. The frames of the windows had been weather-proofed with lime and sealed with straw. The peasant girls had also made out of straw long-nosed monsters with horns on their heads whose task was to tease and annoy Winter.

This year, as every year, Jacob was asked to move into the hut with the family, but he preferred to take up his old abode in the granary. He made himself a straw bed and Wanda sewed him a pillow stuffed with hay; he had a horse blanket for a cover. The granary had no windows but light seeped through the cracks in the wall. Now Jacob longed for the mountains. It was better up there than down here. How strange and remote his peak seemed to him, a giant with a white beard, coiffured in clouds and with curls of mist. Jacob's heart cried out. The Jews were celebrating Simchath Torah, were reciting "Unto Thee it was shown," and circling the lectern. The Bridegroom of the Torah, who would finish the reading of the Pentateuch, was being called up from the congregation, to be followed by the Bridegroom of Genesis who would start once more the Mosaic Books, beginning with the Creation. Even boys were being summoned to the lectern, while those too young to participate were parading with flags decorated with candles and apples. Girls also were coming to the study house to kiss the holy scrolls and to wish for long life and happiness. There was dancing and drinking; people were going from house to house, partaking of wine and mead, strudel, tarts, cabbage with raisins and cream of tartar. This year, if Jacob was correct, Simchath Torah had fallen on a Friday, and the women were preparing the Sabbath pudding, dressed in their velvet capes and satin dresses.

But now all of this seemed dreamlike to him. He had been torn from his home not four but forty years ago! Indeed, were there Jews remaining in Josefov? Had Chmielnicki left a saving remnant? And if so, could the survivors rejoice in the Torah as they once had, now that all of them were mourners? Jacob stood in front of the granary and watched the snow falling. Some of the flakes dropped straight to earth and others swirled and eddied as if seeking to return to the heavenly storehouses. The rotting thatch of the roofs was covered with white, and the clutter of broken wheels, logs, poles, and piles of shavings was decorated with fleece and the dust of diamonds. The roosters were crowing with wintery voices.

Jacob reentered the granary and sat down. Some lines from the Simchath Torah liturgy which he had not thought of for four years came to his mind:

Gather you angels
And converse with each other.
Who was he? What was his name,
The man who ascended the heights
And brought down the strength of confidence?

Moses ascended the heights
And brought down the strength of confidence.

Jacob started to sing these words to the traditional Simchath Torah melody. Even the cantor had usually been a trifle tipsy by the time he reached this song. Every year it had been the same, the rabbi finding it necessary to admonish those of priestly descent not to bless the congregation while under the influence of wine. Jacob's father-in-law had himself brewed beer and vodka using grain raised in the fields he leased from the town's overlord. At this time of year, a keg with a

74

straw in it had always stood near the water barrel of his house, and nearby had hung a side of smoked mutton. Whoever visited the house sipped vodka from the straw and took a nibble of the smoked meat.

Jacob sat there in the dark, alone with his thoughts. Slowly the door was pushed open, and Wanda entered, carrying two pieces of oak bark, and some rags and string.

"I've made you a pair of shoes," she said.

He was ashamed of how dirty his feet were, but she lifted them to her lap, and while taking their measure, caressed them with her warm fingers. She took a long time making certain the shoes fit. When she was satisfied, she insisted that Jacob get up and walk about to see if they were comfortable, just as Michael the shoemaker had him do in Josefov.

"They fit, don't they?"

"Yes, they do."

"Why are you so sad, then, Jacob? Now that you are near me, I can take care of you. I don't have to climb the mountain to see you."

"Yes."

"Doesn't that please you? I was looking forward so much to this day."

III

The day began as though it were already ending. The sun flickered like a candle about to go out. Zagayek and his men were in the woods hunting bear, and the bailiff's son Stephan strode about the village in high boots, dressed in a rawhide jacket embroidered with red, a marten cap with ear flaps on his head, and a riding whip in his right hand. Stephen was called Zagayek the Second by the peasants. His career with girls had started early and by now he had his own crop of bastards. He was a short, broad-shouldered man, with a square head, a nose as flat as a bulldog's, and a chin which dimpled in the middle. He had the reputation of being a fine horseman and kept himself busy training his father's dogs and setting traps for birds and animals.

Stephan took over in the village whenever his father went hunting. On such days he went from hut to hut, throwing open doors and sticking in his head and sniffing. The peasants always had something which by law belonged to the landlord. That morning he entered the tavern and ordered vodka. His half-sister, one of Zagayek's bastards, waited on him, but their relationship did not prevent him from hiking her skirts. Then, after having his drink, Stephan proceeded to Jan Bzik's. Bzik had once been a man of importance in the village, one of those whom Zagayek had taken under his protection, but now the old man was worn out and sick. The day he had brought the cattle down from the mountain he had had a seizure and he now lay on top of the oven as his strength ebbed. He talked, spat, muttered to himself. Bzik was a small, lean man; his hair, long and matted, surrounded a single bald spot. He had deep sunken cheeks, a face as red as raw meat, and bulging, bloodshot eyes underlined by two puffy bags, a few scraggly hairs drooping from his chin. That winter he had been so sick they had measured him for a coffin. But then his condition had improved. He lay, his face turned toward the room, one eye glued shut, the other only half open. Ill though he was, this did not prevent him from running the household and overseeing each detail. "It's no good," he would grumble often. "Butter fingers!"

"If you don't like the way we're doing things, climb down from the oven and do them yourself," his wife would answer. She was a small, dark, half-bald woman, with a wart-covered face, and the slanty eyes of a Tartar. The couple did not live in peace; she kept insisting that her husband was finished and that it was time to cart him off to the graveyard.

Basha resembled her mother. Stocky and dark, she had inherited the high cheekbones and almond eyes of the older woman. She was known for her indolence. At the moment she sat at the edge of the bed studying her toes and every now and again searching for lice between her breasts. Wanda was at the oven, removing a loaf of bread with a shovel. As she bustled about the kitchen, she repeated to herself the lesson Jacob had taught her: The Almighty had created the world. Abraham had been the first to recognize God. Jacob was the father of the Jews. She had never before received any instruction and Jacob's words had fallen on her brain like a shower on a parched field. She had even memorized the names of the Twelve Tribes and knew how Joseph's brothers had sold him into Egypt. When Stephan entered, he stood at the open door listening to her mutterings.

"What's that you're saying?" he asked. "Some sort of an incantation?"

"Close the door, Pan," she directed over her shoulder. "You're letting in the cold."

"You're hot enough to keep from freezing."

Stephan walked into the room.

"Where's the Jew?"

"In the granary."

"Won't he come into the house?"

"He doesn't want to."

"They say he lays you."

Basha opened her wide, gap-toothed mouth in laughter; she licked her lips with delight, hearing her proud sister insulted. The old woman left off spinning, and Bzik wriggled his feet.

"Dirty mouths will say anything."

77

"I understand you're carrying his bastard."

"Pan, that's a lie," the old woman interrupted. "She just got over her period."

"How do you know? Did you investigate?"

"There was blood on the snow in front of the house," the old woman testified.

Stephan struck his boot tops with his whip.

"The householders want to get rid of him," he said after a slight hesitation.

"Who does he hurt?"

"He's a sorcerer, and that's the least of it. How is it your cows give more milk than anyone else's?"

"Jacob feeds them better."

"All sorts of things are said about him. He'll be done away with. Father will haul him into court."

"For what reason?"

"Don't grasp at straws, Wanda. He'll be taken care of, and you'll give birth to a demon."

Wanda could no longer restrain herself. Not everything the wicked desire comes true, she told Stephan. There was a God in heaven who avenged those who suffered in justice. Stephan pursed his lips as if about to whistle.

"Where did you hear that? From the Jew?"

"Dziobak says so also."

"It was the Jew, the Jew, who told you," Stephan said. "If his God is such a great defender, how come he's a slave? Well, answer that!"

Wanda could think of nothing to say. There was a lump in her throat and her eyes were burning; she could scarcely keep back the tears. She wanted to run quickly to Jacob and ask him this difficult question. With fingers that had become inured to heat, she picked up a fresh loaf of bread and sprinkled it with water. Anger had made her face, flushed already from the warmth of the oven, even redder. Stephan stood surveying her legs and buttocks like a connoisseur. He winked at the old woman and Basha. The latter responded flirtatiously, smiled obsequiously at him with her gap teeth. At length he walked out whistling, slamming the door behind him. Wanda stood at the window and watched him stride off in the direction of the mountain. He was a man filled with iniquity like Esau or Pharaoh. Ever since she could remember he had spoken of little else but killing and torturing. It was Stephan who assisted his father in the slaughtering and scalding of the pigs. It was he who did the actual whipping when Zagayek ordered a peasant punished. Even the trail left by Stephan's boots in the snow seemed evil to Wanda. "Father in Heaven," she began to pray, "how long will You remain silent? Send down plagues as you did against Pharaoh. Drown him in the sea."

"He wants you, Wanda. He wants you," she heard her mother saying.

"Well, he'll just keep on wanting."

"Wanda, he's Zagayek's son. He may set fire to the hut. What would we do then? Sleep in the fields?"

"God will not permit it."

Basha started to guffaw.

"What are you laughing about, Basha?"

Basha didn't answer. Wanda knew that her mother and sister were on Stephan's side. They wanted to see her humiliated. There was a crooked wrinkle on the old woman's forehead and her toothless mouth was fixed in a smile which seemed to say, "Why quarrel over such nonsense? Stephan's powerful. There's no alternative."

The old man lying on the stove mumbled something.

"Did you say something, Father?"

"What did he want?"

The old woman laughed nastily.

"What does a tomcat usually want?"

"Father's forgotten about that kind of thing," Basha said scornfully.

"You did right, Wanda. Don't let him put a bastard into your belly." Bzik spoke haltingly and with the dirge-like tone of the mortally sick uttering a last testament. "The moment you're with child, that skunk will forget you. He has enough bastards already." The old man's sing-song voice was mournful, other-worldly. Wanda remembered the Ten Commandments Jacob had taught her; one must honor one's father and mother.

"Do you want something, Father?"

Jan Bzik did not answer.

"Are you hungry or thirsty?"

He had to pass water, he said in a voice which was half cry, half yawn.

"Well, crawl outside," his wife ordered. "This isn't a stable."

"I'm cold."

"Here, Father." Wanda gave him a pan.

The old man sought to raise himself from the oven but the low ceiling interfered. He attempted to pass water and Basha giggled when he couldn't. His wife shook her head contemptuously. His member had shrunk to the size of a child's. A single drop of water fell into the pan.

"He's worthless," the old woman said.

"Mother, he's your husband and our father," Wanda replied sharply. "We must honor him."

Basha began to guffaw again. Wanda felt a cry rising in her throat. Jacob said that God was just, that He rewarded the good and punished the wicked, but Stephan, idler, whoremaster, assassin, flourished like the oak, while her father, whose whole life had been dedicated to work and who had done injustice to no one, crumbled into ruins. What sort of justice was this? She gazed toward the window. The answer could come only from Jacob in the granary.

IV

Jacob in the old days would have considered himself ridiculed if anyone had ever suggested to him that a time would come when he would discuss such matters as the freedom of the will, the meaning of existence, and the problem of evil with a peasant woman. But one never knows where events are leading. Wanda asked questions and Jacob answered them to the best of his ability. He lay close to her in the granary, the same blanket covering them both, a sinner who ignored the restrictions of the Talmud, seeking to explain in a strange tongue those things he had studied in the holy books. He told her that God is eternal, that His Powers and Nature have existed without beginning, but that, nevertheless, all that was possible for Him had not as yet been accomplished before Creation. For example, how could He have been Father until His children were born? How could He have shown pity until there was someone to pity? How could He have been redeemer and helper until there were creatures to redeem? God had the power to create not only this world but a host of others. However, Creation would have been impossible if He, Himself, had completely filled the void. So that the world might appear, it had been necessary for Him to dim his effulgence. Had He not done this, whatever He created would have been consumed and blinded by His brilliance. Darkness and the void had been required, and these were synonymous with pain and evil.

What was the purpose of Creation? Free Will! Man must choose for himself between good and evil. This was the reason God had sent forth man's soul from the Throne of Glory. A father may carry his child, but he wishes the infant to learn to walk by itself. God was our Father, we His children, and He loved us. He blessed us with His mercy, and if now and again He let us slip and fall, it was to accustom us to walking alone. He continued to watch over us, and when we were in peril of falling into ditches and pits, He raised us aloft in His holy arms.

Outside, frost glowed everywhere, but it wasn't too cold in the granary. Wanda snuggled close to Jacob, her body tight against his, her mouth leaning toward his. He spoke and she continued to question. At first it seemed to him that he was both a fool and a betrayer of Israel. How could a peasant's brain comprehend such profundities? But the more Wanda questioned, the more obvious it became to him that she grasped his meaning. She even posed problems he could not solve. If the animals did not possess Free Will, why was it necessary for them to suffer? And if the Jews alone were God's children, why were gentiles created? She clasped him so tightly he could hear her heart beating; her hands dug into his ribs. She lusted for knowledge almost as fiercely as she did for the flesh.

"Where is the soul?" she inquired. "In the eye?"

"Yes, in the eyes, but in the brain also. The soul gives life to the entire body."

"Where does the soul go when a man dies?"

"Back to heaven."

"Does a calf have a soul?"

"No, it has a spirit."

"What happens to the spirit when the calf is slaughtered?"

"It sometimes enters the body of the eater."

"Does a pig have a spirit too?"

"Yes. No. I guess so. It has to have something."

"Why can't a Jew eat pork?"

"God's Law forbids it. It is His Will."

"When I become a Jew, will I also be God's daughter?"

"Yes, if you let Him enter your heart."

"I will, Jacob."

"You must become one of us not because of love for me but because you believe in God."

"I believe, Jacob. Honestly I do. But you must teach me. Without you I am blind."

A plan was forming in Wanda's mind; they would run away together; she knew the mountains. True, a Christian could not become a Jew, but she would disguise herself as a Jewess. She would shave her head and not mix meat with milk; Jacob would teach her to speak Yiddish. She insisted that he begin immediately. She said a word in Polish and he repeated it in Yiddish. *Chleb* meant bread; *wol* was an ox; *stol*, a table, and *lawka*, a bench. Some words were the same in both languages. Wanda asked him if the two tongues were really identical.

"The Jews spoke the sacred tongue when they lived in the Land of Israel," Jacob replied. "The tongue they speak today is a mixture of many languages."

"Why aren't the Jews still in their own country?"

"Because they transgressed."

"What did they do?"

"They bowed down to idols and stole from the poor."

"Don't they do that any more?"

"They don't worship idols."

"What about the poor?"

Jacob considered this question carefully before answering it.

"The poor are not treated justly."

"Who is ever just to the poor? The peasants work

83

hard all year round and yet go naked. Zagayek wouldn't think of soiling his hands, but he takes everything the best grain, the finest cattle."

"Every man will have to make an accounting."

"When, Jacob? Where?"

"Not in this world."

"Jacob, I must go. It's almost sunrise."

She clung to his neck, pressed deeply into his mouth, kissing him one final time. Her face became hot once again, but finally she tore herself from him. As she threw open the granary door, she murmured something and smiled shyly. There was no moon but the reflection of the snow fell across her face. Jacob recalled the story of Lilith, she who seeks out men at night and corrupts them. He and Wanda had now lived together for weeks, and yet each time he thought of his transgression he shivered anew. How had it happened? He had resisted temptation for years, then suddenly had fallen. He had changed since he had cohabited with Wanda. At times he didn't recognize himself; it seemed to him his soul had deserted him and he was sustained like an animal by something else. He prayed but without concentration. He still recited Psalms and portions of the Mishnah but his heart did not hear what his lips uttered. Whatever was within him had frozen. He no longer hummed and sang the old melodies, and was ashamed to think about his wife and children and all the other martyrs whom the Cossacks had slaughtered. What connection did he have with such saints? They were holy and he, unclean. They had sacrificed themselves for the Sacred Name while he had made a covenant with Satan. Jacob could no longer control his thoughts. Every kind of absurdity and non sequitur crammed his brain. He imagined himself eating cake, roast chicken, marzipan; drinking wine, mead, beer; hunting among the rocks and finding diamonds, gold

84

coins, becoming a rich man, and riding around in coaches. His lust for Wanda reached such intensity that the moment she left the granary he began to miss her.

As with the soul, so with the body! He grew lazy and wanted only to lie on the straw. He suffered more from the cold that year than any other. When he chopped wood, the ax stuck and he couldn't pull it free. When he shoveled the snow from the yard, he tired quickly and had to rest. How strange it was! Even the cows he had reared sensed his predicament and turned nasty. Several times they tried to kick and gore him when he was milking them. The dog barked at him as if he were a stranger.

His dreams changed also. His father and mother no longer appeared in them. The moment he fell asleep he was with Wanda. Together they roamed through forests, crawled through caves, fell into pits, ravines, abysses, sank into swamps filled with putrefaction and filth. Rats and beasts with shaggy tails, large udders, and pouches chased him; they shrieked with strange voices, dribbled, spat, and vomited upon him. He awoke from these nightmares in a cold sweat but still burning with passion. A voice within him called out constantly for Wanda. He even found it difficult to stay away from her on those days when the Mosaic law declared her unclean.

V

The moon shone in a cloudless sky. That night, it was nearly as bright as day. Jacob, standing at the door of the granary, looked up at mile upon mile of mountains. Crags rising from the forests resembled shrouded corpses, beasts standing erect on their hind legs, monsters from another world. The silence in the village was so intense Jacob's ears rang as though a multitude of grasshoppers were singing under the snow. Although it had stopped snowing, occasional flakes drifted slowly to earth. A crow started from sleep and cawed once. In the granary and surrounding sheds, field mice and weasels scratched in their winter burrows as if expecting the sudden advent of spring. Even Jacob awaited a miracle. Perhaps summer would come more quickly than usual this year. There was nothing beyond God's power. The Almighty, if he wished, could remove the sun's cover as he had in the time of Abraham. But for whom would the Lord perform such a miracle? For Jacob the profligate, Jacob the sinner? He looked about him at the trees in the yard, snow hanging from their branches like white pears, petals of ice dropping from the twigs. He listened intently. Why didn't she come? The hut was dark, it seemed like a mushroom protruding from the drifts. Yet Jacob thought that he heard footsteps and voices. The door of the hut opened and Wanda appeared, but not as usual barefooted and enveloped in a shawl. She had on shoes and a sheepskin coat and she carried a cane. "Father is dead," she said, walking over to Jacob.

His mind froze.

"When? How?"

"He went to sleep like always, groaned, and that was the end of it. He died as silently as a chicken."

"Where are you going?"

"To fetch Antek."

They stood there in silence, and then Wanda said, "Hard times have begun for us. Antek's no friend of yours. He wants to kill you."

"What can I do?"

"Be careful."

She turned away from him; Jacob stood and watched her move into the distance, diminishing in size until she appeared no larger than an icicle. There had been no tears, but he knew she was

86

grieving. She had loved her father—at times she had even used that word "father" addressing Jacob—now she had lost him. Whatever soul a peasant possessed had deserted the old man's body. But where was it now? Still in the hut? Or had it already begun its ascent? Had its departure been like smoke through the chimney? The custom of the village required Jacob to visit the family and say a few words of comfort. But he was doubtful whether he ought to go. Without Wanda the hut was a nest of snakes. He was not even certain Jewish law permitted him to make this condolence call, but at length he decided to. He opened the door of the hut. The old woman and Basha stood in the middle of the room; a wick was burning in a shard. On the bed lay the body, its appearance altered by death, the face yellow as clay, the ears chalk white, only a hole where once the mouth had been. How difficult to imagine that only a few minutes before, this corpse had been alive. Yet in the wrinkled eyelids and sockets a hint of the live Jan Bzik remained, a smile, the look of a man who has encountered something both comic and propitious. The old woman sobbed hoarsely.

"He's gone, finished."

"May God comfort you."

"There wasn't a thing wrong with him at dinner. He ate a whole bowl of barley dumplings." Her remarks were only half directed to Jacob.

He stood there while the neighbors gathered. The women arrived in shawls and battered shoes, the men in sheepskins and boots made of rags. One woman wrung her hands, forced tears from her eyes, crossed herself. The widow kept repeating the identical sentence. "He had barley dumplings for supper and ate every morsel." With these words she was accusing death and giving evidence of what an exemplary wife she had been. All the faces were immersed in shadow, filled with the mystery

87

of the night. Soon the air became fetid. Someone went to fetch Dziobak; the coffin maker arrived to take Jan Bzik's measure. Jacob slipped out of the hut. He was an alien among these people, but not as much a stranger now since Jan Bzik could almost be regarded as his father-in-law. The thought of this frightened him. "Well, aren't we all descended from Terah and Laban?" he said to himself. He was cold and his teeth were chattering. Jan Bzik had been good and just, had never ridiculed him, nor called him by a nickname. Jacob had become accustomed to him. There had been a secret understanding between the two men as if Bzik had somehow sensed that some day his cherished Wanda would belong to Jacob. "Well, it's a mystery," Jacob said to himself, "the profoundest mystery. All men are made in God's image. Perhaps Jan Bzik will sit with the other God-fearing gentiles in paradise."

Again he yearned for Wanda. What was keeping her? Well, from now on there would be an end of peace. The dog barked; more and more peasants were entering the hut. Zagayek arrived, a small rotund man dressed in a coat of fox pelts, felt boots, and a fur cap similar to those Jews wore on the Sabbath. Zagayek's mustaches flared underneath his thick nose like the whiskers of a tomcat. Dawn broke and the stars faded. The sky paled and turned rose. The sun blossomed behind the mountains and reddish specks of light glistened on the snow. The shrill voices of winter birds were heard, chattering. Jacob entered the barn and found that Kwiatula, the youngest of the cows who only a short time before had been a heifer, was about to give birth. She stood with bloated stomach, saliva dripping from her black muzzle. Her moist eyes looked straight at Jacob as though imploring his help.

He started to prepare the feed. It was also

necessary to milk the animals. He mixed chopped straw, bran, and turnips together. "Well, we are all slaves," Jacob murmured to the cattle, "God's slaves." Suddenly the door opened and Wanda came in. Her cheeks were moist and red. Wanda, taking hold of Jacob, cried out as had his mother, peace be with her, before she rolled the large candle preparing for Yom Kippur Eve. "Now I have no one but you," she said.

5

The scarcity of food in the village was rarely discussed, and Christmas was celebrated with great pomp despite the dearth. Though many of the peasants had already slaughtered their hogs and suckling pigs, there was sufficient meat for the holiday meal, nor was there a lack of vodka. Children went from hut to hut singing carols. The older boys collected gifts, leading around one of their company dressed as a wolf. Since the roof of the chapel leaked, the creche showing the birth in the manger had been set up in Zagayek's granary; there, too, was put on the pageant showing the arrival of the kings and wise men come to adore God's newborn son. Staffs, flaxen beards, the gilded star, everything required for the play was on hand, having been used year after year. But the sheep were real and the sound of their bleating cheered up the dejected spirits of the peasants.

The winter had been a hard one. Sickness and pestilence! The number of small and large graves had increased in the cemetery, and gales had toppled most of the new wooden crosses. But now the time to be merry was here, Zagayek distributed toys to the children and he gave white flour to the women so that the wafers could be baked. Wanda now knew from Jacob that the Jews believed in a God who had neither son nor division into persons. Yet she had to participate in the holiday and go with the others Christmas Eve to Midnight Mass. She even took part in the pageant, stood near Stephan with a halo around her head looking like one of the saints. Stephan wore a mask, a white beard, and a miter. His breath stank of liquor, and he surreptitiously pinched Wanda and whispered obscene words in her ears.

Time after time Wanda had begged Jacob to enter the hut and take part with the others in the feasting. Even Jacob's enemy Antek sought to make peace during the holidays. Inside the hut stood a Christmas tree hung with ribbons and wreaths. The old woman had made pretzels, baked pork, stuffed cabbage, and a variety of other dishes. An extra man was needed to even out the number of guests, but Jacob remained stubborn. None of the food was kosher; all of this was idolatry, and it was well known that it was better to die than participate in such ceremonies. He stayed in the granary and ate dry bread as usual. It hurt Wanda to see him separate himself from the others and hide. The girls ridiculed him and her as well since he was her lover. Her mother openly spoke of the need to rid themselves of that accursed Jew who had brought bad luck and disgrace to the family. Now Wanda was more careful about seeking him out at night, knowing that the boys were planning to play all sorts of tricks on him. They considered dragging him out of the barn and forcing him to eat pork. Someone suggested that he be thrown into the stream as a sacrifice to the river spirit or be castrated. Wanda had brought him a knife so he might defend himself. She began to drink vodka to dispel the bitterness in her heart.

On the third day after Christmas, the village celebrated the sacred day of Turon that honored the ancient god of horses and courage, wind and power. Dziobak demanded the abolition of this pagan holiday, pointing out that with Jesus' birth all the idols had been deprived of their power, and in addition that no one in the large cities ever remembered such days. But the village paid no attention to him and there was dancing at Zagayek's house and in the huts. The musicians fiddled, banged cymbals, beat drums, played "The Little Shoemaker," "The Shepherd," "The Dove," "Good Night," and the "Dirge of a Dying Man," the last of which brought tears to the eyes of the women. The boys and girls danced a mazurka, a polka, a cracowiak, a goralsky. Everyone forgot his troubles. Sleighs crowded with young people raced across the snow, the bells on the reins and harnesses of the horses jingling. Here and there a sled yoked to a dog passed. Wanda had promised Jacob not to participate in these pagan revels, but with each passing hour she grew more restive. She had to dance and drink with the peasants. As long as she stayed in the village, it was impossible not to be one of them. The very fact that she planned to run away with him and accept his faith made the avoidance of suspicion more necessary. She hurried into the granary, her face flushed, and her eyes shining. Hurriedly she threw Jacob a few kisses, put her face on his chest, and started to sob. "Don't be angry with me," she said. "I've already become a stranger in my own house."

II

This was the first of the month of Nissan

according to Jacob's calendar, two weeks before Passover. Not once in his captivity had he eaten bread during that holiday, subsisting those eight days on milk, cheese, and vegetables. The cold had set in again and a heavy snow had fallen. Antek had gone to buy another cow in a nearby village, and had taken Wanda along to get her opinion. She had been forced to agree to the trip, fearing to quarrel with her brother as long as Jacob was there. Jacob spent the morning milking the cows and chopping wood for the fire, which was the work he liked best. His ax rose and fell and the chips flew. Little by little the pile grew until there was a sizable quantity. He went into the granary to rest, lay down, closed his eyes and dreamed of Wanda, but this dream did not have the village as its setting. Suddenly he felt himself being poked and he opened his eyes. The granary door was ajar and Basha stood near him. "Get up," she said. "You're wanted at Zagayek's."

"How do you know?"

"He's sent one of his men."

Jacob rose, realizing only too well what had happened. Zagayek had learned of his plan to escape and this was the end. Only recently Stephen had prophesied to Wanda that the Jew would be disposed of. "Well, my time has come," Jacob thought. All through the years he had been expecting this outcome. His knees trembled, and crossing the threshold, he bent over, picked up a handful of snow, and rubbed the palms of his hands with it so that he might pray. "Let it be Thy Will that my death redeem all my sins," he mumbled. For one instant he thought of making a break for it, but then saw how useless it would be. He was barefoot and without sheepskin. "No, I won't run," he decided. "I have sinned and earned my punishment." Zagayek's man was waiting outside; he was unarmed. "Let's go," he said to

Jacob. "The gentlemen are waiting."

"What gentlemen?"

"How the devil do I know?"

"So they are going to try me," Jacob said to himself. The barking of the dog brought the old woman out of the hut; she stood there, broad and squat, yellow-faced, neither joy nor pity in her slanty eyes. Basha stood next to her mother, another one of those who, cow-like, accept docilely. The dog became silent and his tail drooped. Jacob was relieved that Wanda was not there; by the time she returned it might be all over. He thought of reciting, "Hear, O Israel," but decided he should do that when the noose was fixed about his neck. His stomach felt heavy; he was cold. He hiccupped, belched, started to recite the third chapter of Psalms, but paused when he came to the verse, "For Thou, O Lord, art a shield to me, my glory, and the lifter of my head." It was too late for such hopes. When he nodded at the old woman and Basha, they remained as unresponsive as stuffed images. The one thing that astonished Jacob was that not only was his attendant unarmed but he made no attempt to manacle him. "Well, there is an end to everything," Jacob thought, walking with bowed head and measured steps. For years he had been curious about what lay on the other side of flesh and blood. He was only anxious to get the death agony over with, and was prepared to sanctify God's name if he were asked to deny or blaspheme Him.

Women came from their hovels to stare blankly. Barking dogs ran after him; others peacefully wagged their tails. A duck waddled across his path. "Well, you'll outlive me," Jacob comforted the creature. He bid the world and the village goodbye. "Do not let anxiety make her ill," he prayed, thinking of Wanda. She had not been destined to reach the truth and he sorrowed for her.

He raised his eyes and saw that the sky was once more blue and vernal. The only cloud resembled a single horned beast with a long neck. The mountains looked down on him from the distance, those hills to which he had planned to flee from slavery. "It has been ordained that I be with them," he said, thinking of his father and mother and his wife and children.

The man led him to Zagayek's house and there in front of the building stood a covered wagon hitched to a team of horses. Jacob didn't think that either the wagon or the team were from the neighborhood. The horses were covered with blankets and their harnesses were decorated with brass; a lantern hung from the rear axle of the vehicle. Jacob walked up a meticulously scrubbed staircase to the second floor. He had almost forgotten staircases existed, but here, it seemed, was a piece of the city in the center of this hamlet. As he walked down the hall, he smelled cabbage cooking; the midday meal was being prepared. He passed doors which had the kind of brass latches his parents' house had had. Straw mats lay before them. A door was thrown open and what he saw was strange and dream-like. Three men sat at a table, Jews with beards, sidelocks, and skull caps. The coat of one was unbuttoned and a fringed garment peeped through. Jacob recognized another but in his confusion forgot where he had met him. Jacob stood with his mouth open, and the Jews gaped back. At last one of them addressed him in Yiddish, "Are you Jacob from Zamosc?"

Everything went dark before Jacob's eyes.

"Yes, I am," he answered, speaking with a Polish accent.

"Reb Abraham of Josefov's son-in-law?"

"Yes."

"Don't you recognize me?"

Jacob stared. The face was familiar but he

couldn't place it. "So this is not the day of my death," he thought. He still was unable to grasp what was happening, but he was ashamed that he was barefoot and dressed in peasant clothes. Inside of him all was still and frozen and he became tongue-tied and shy as a boy. "Perhaps I am already on the other side," he thought. He wanted to say something, but couldn't utter a word. For the moment Yiddish eluded him. Another door opened and in walked Zagayek, short and stocky, red-nosed, his pointed mustaches resembling two mouse tails. He had on a braided green coat and low boots. The riding crop he carried had a rabbit's foot for a handle. Though it was early in the day, he had already drunk enough to make him walk unsteadily. His eyes were bloodshot and watery. "Well, is this your Jew?" he shouted.

The man who had just addressed Jacob spoke hesitantly. "Yes, this is he."

"All right, then, take him and go. Where's your money?"

One of the Jews, a small, pampered-looking man with a broad fanlike beard and dark eyes set widely apart, silently pulled a purse from his coat and commenced to count out gold pieces. Zagayek tested each of the coins by placing them between his thumb and index finger and trying to bend them. Only now did Jacob realize what had happened. These Jews had come for him; he was being ransomed. The man with the familiar face was from Josefov, one of the town elders. Suddenly Jacob felt terribly awkward as though the nearly five years he had lived in the mountains had taken effect this very instant and changed him into an uncouth peasant. He didn't know where to hide his calloused hands and dirty feet. He was ashamed of his torn jacket, and his unruly hair, resting upon his shoulders. A desire to bow peasant-like to the

Jews and grasp their hands and kiss them seized
him. The man who had counted out the gold pieces
lifted his eyes.

"Blessed be Thou who revivest the dead."

III

The speed with which things now happened to
Jacob was eerie. Zagayek extended his hand and
wished him a pleasant trip. A moment later, the
Jews escorted him outside and told him to get into
the covered wagon. A number of peasants had
gathered at Zagayek's house, but none of Jan
Bzik's family was in the group. Before Jacob could
say anything, the gentile driver—Jacob had not
noticed him before—snapped his whip and the
wagon careened downhill. Jacob thought of
Wanda, but he didn't mention her. What was there
to say? Could he ask that his peasant mistress be
taken along? She was not in the village and so he
couldn't even say goodbye to her. With the same
suddenness that he had been enslaved he had now
been ransomed. In the wagon the men spoke to him
all at once and confused him so he scarcely knew
what they were saying. Their speech sounded
almost like a foreign tongue. A quilt was thrown
over his shoulders and a skull cap placed on his
head. He sat among them feeling naked. Slowly he
grew accustomed to their words, gesticulations,
odor, and asked how they had known his where-
abouts. "A circus proprietor informed us," they
said.

He became silent again.

"What happened to my family?" he asked.

"Your sister Miriam is alive."

"No one else?"

They didn't reply.

"Should I rend my clothes?" he inquired,

intending the question not merely for them but for himself also. "I have forgotten the law."

"Yes, for your father and mother. But not for your children. More than thirty days have passed."

"Yes, that is now a distant event," Jacob said, employing the technical term.

Although he had known all along that his loved ones were dead, he sat there grieving. Miriam was the only one of the family who had survived. He feared to ask for details, kept looking straight ahead; the men spoke, for the most part, to each other. They discussed the clothes he must have: a shirt, a fringed garment, trousers, shoes. One of them remarked that his hair must be cut, and another untied a leather sack and rummaged in it. The third offered him cake, vodka, jam. Jacob refused to eat: he must remain in mourning for at least one day. Now he recollected the name of the man from Josefov: Reb Moishe Zakolkower, one of the town's seven most prominent citizens. The last time Jacob had seen him, he had been a young man sprouting his first growth of beard.

"It's exactly like Joseph and his brethren," one of the men remarked.

"Now we have lived to see this, we must say a benediction," another interjected, and he started to intone, "Oh, Thou who hast sustained me and made me live to reach this time."

"And I must say 'Thou hast done mercy,'" Jacob mumbled as if to prove that he too was a Jew and that no error had been made in ransoming him. But even as he said this, he was conscious of having erred. The correct thing was to praise God without further ado, but his voice sounded so coarse to him, he was embarrassed to speak before such fine people. His companions were small in stature but his head touched the roof of the wagon. He felt penned in, and so unfamiliar was the smell of the vehicle, it was difficult for him to keep from sneezing. These men should be thanked, but he didn't know the correct words for the occasion. Each time he tried to say something, Yiddish and Polish mingled in his head. Like an ignoramus about to talk to learned men he knew in advance that he would make a fool of himself. But he did ask finally, "Who is left in Josefov?"

The men appeared to have been waiting for this question and all started talking at once. The Cossacks had nearly leveled the town, had killed, slaughtered, burned, hanged, but there had been some survivors, widows and old men mostly, and a few children who had hidden in attics and cellars or taken refuge in peasant hamlets. The men mentioned some names Jacob knew, but others, since Josefov had acquired new inhabitants, that he had never heard before. The wagon continued to roll downhill, sunlight seeping through the covering, and the conversation remained elegiac. Every sentence ended with the word "killed." Now and then Jacob heard "died in the plague." Yes, the Angel of Death had been busy. The massacres and burnings had been followed by sickness, and people had died like flies. Jacob found it difficult to comprehend so much calamity. But as always, there was a saving remnant. The speakers appeared weighed down by an enormous burden and Jacob bowed his head. It was as if he had slept seventy years, like the legendary Choney, and awakened in another age. Josefov was no longer Josefov. Everything was gone: The synagogue, the study house, the ritual bath, the poor house. The murderers had even torn up the tombstones. Not a single chapter of the Holy Scroll, not a page from the books in the study house remained intact. The town was inhabited by fools, cripples, and madmen. "Why did this happen to us?" one of the men asked. "Josefov was a home of Torah."

"It was God's will," a second answered.

"But why? What sins did the small children commit? They were buried alive."

"The hill behind the synagogue shook for three days. They tore out Hanan Berish's tongue, cut off Beila Itche's breasts."

"What harm did we do them?"

No one answered these questions and they raised their eyes and stared at Jacob as if expecting him to reply. But he sat in silence. The explanation he had given Wanda that free will could not exist without evil nor mercy without sorrow now sounded too pat, indeed almost blasphemous. Did the Creator require the assistance of Cossacks to reveal His nature? Was this a sufficient cause to bury infants alive? He remembered his own children, little Isaac, Breina, the baby; he imagined them thrown into a ditch of lime and buried alive. He heard their stifled screams. Even if these souls rose to the most splendid mansion and were given the finest rewards, would that cancel out the agony and horror? Jacob wondered how it had been possible for him to forget them for an instant. Through forgetfulness, he had also been guilty of murder.

"Yes, I am a murderer," he said to himself. "I am no better than they."

6

Passover was at an end. Pentecost came and went. At first each day was so crammed with incident it seemed like a year to Jacob. Not an hour passed, scarcely a minute, without his coming upon something new or something he had half forgotten. Was it so trivial a matter to return to Jewish books, clothes, holidays, after years of slavery among the pagans? Alone in the mountain barn or in the Bziks' granary, he had felt that no trace of this world remained. Chmielnicki and his Cossacks had wiped out everything. At other times he had been half convinced that there never had been a Josefov and that all his memories were illusions. Suddenly he found himself dressed again as a Jew, praying in synagogues, putting on phylacteries, wearing a fringed garment, and eating strictly kosher food. His trip down the road from Cracow to Josefov had been one long continual holiday. Rabbis and elders had greeted and feasted him in every town. Women had brought their children to be blessed and had asked him to touch coins and speak incantations over pieces of amber. The martyrs were beyond help, and so everyone's goodness was lavished on this man who had been ransomed from captivity.

His sister Miriam and her daughter Binele awaited him in Josefov. Besides these two only a few distant relations were left to him. Josefov was so changed it was unrecognizable: grass was growing where houses had once been, buildings now stood where goats had pastured. There were graves in the middle of the synagogue yard. The rabbi, his assistant, and most of the elders came from other towns. Jacob was given a room and the authorities scratched together a yeshiva class so that he could support himself teaching. His sister Miriam had once been well-to-do, but now she was toothless and in rags. Meeting Jacob, she ran to him with a wail and never stopped sobbing and crying until she returned to Zamosc. He feared she was out of her mind. She screamed, pressed against him, bobbed up and down, all the time wringing her hands, pinching her cheeks, and enumerating all the tortures the family had undergone. She made Jacob think of those mourners and hand clappers who in the old days, according to the Talmud, had been hired for funerals. Her voice became so shrill at times that Jacob covered his ears.

"Alas, poor Dinah, they ripped open her stomach and put a dog in. You could hear it barking."

"They impaled Moishe Bunim, and he didn't stop groaning all night."

"Twenty Cossacks raped your sister Leah and then cut her to pieces."

Jacob was not under the misapprehension that one had a right to forget how the dead had been tortured. What was said in the Bible of Amalek was true of all Israel's enemies. Yet, he did beg

Miriam not to heap so many horrors on him at once. There was a limit to what the human mind could accept. It was beyond the power of any man to contemplate all these atrocities and mourn them adequately. A new Tischab'ov and a new seventeenth day of Tammuz had to be proclaimed. The year was not long enough to pray for and lament each of these saints singly. Jacob would have liked to run off and hide in some ruined building where he could remain in silence. But there was no such place in Josefov, which was all hustle and bustle. Houses were being built, buildings roofed; on every side men were mixing lime and carrying bricks. There were new stores in the market place and once again the peasants flocked to town on market day to deal with the Jews. Jacob, returning, was immediately involved in religious activities. It was the time when the matzoths were baked and he helped prepare them for the town's most pious citizens, drawing the water and assisting in the rolling. On the first night of Passover he entertained some widows at his seder, and it seemed strange to him now to speak of the miracles that had transpired in Egypt when in his day a new Pharaoh had brought to pass what the old Pharaoh had been unable to accomplish. There was not a prayer, law, passage in the Talmud that did not seem altered to him. The questions that he asked about Providence became increasingly sharp and searching and he found he had lost the power to stop asking them.

But, as he realized with astonishment, what was so new for him was stale for everyone else. The yeshiva boys laughed and played practical jokes on each other. Alert young men wove chains of casuistry. Merchants were busy making money, and the women gossiped in the same old way. As for the Almighty, He maintained his usual silence. Jacob saw that he must follow God's example, seal

103

his lips, and forget the fool within, with his fruitless questions.

So the days flew by: Passover, Pentecost! Jacob's body had returned home but his spirit remained restless. No, if anything, his condition was worse, for now he had nothing to hope for. To prevent himself from thinking, he kept busy all day: teaching, studying, praying, reciting Psalms. Other towns had contributed a number of worn out, dog-eared books to Josefov and Jacob mended the pages and filled in the missing letters and words. The new study house needed a beadle, and he took that job also. His day began at dawn and did not end until he was ready to collapse from exhaustion. If his thought could dwell only on complaints against Heaven or on memories of lechery in a barn on a mountain, then it was unclean. Let those whose minds were pure indulge in meditation.

Those pious women who took care of Jacob sought to repay him for his years of exile, but an undeclared war developed between them and their charge. They prepared him a bed of down and he stretched out on the hard floor and lay there all night. They cooked him soups and broths, and he wanted dry bread and water from the well. When visitors came to speak to him about his years of absence, he answered curtly. How else could he behave? The windows of the study house overlooked the hill where his wife and children lay buried. He could see cows grazing there in the newly grown pasture. His parents, relations, friends, had been tortured. As a boy he had pitied the watchman in the cemetery at Zamosc whose life had been passed near the cleansing house, but now the whole of Poland had become one vast cemetery. The people around him accommodated themselves to this, but he found it impossible to come to terms with. The best he could do was to

104

stop thinking and desiring. He was determined to question no longer. How could one conceivably justify the torments of another?

One day seated alone in the study house, Jacob said to God, "I have no doubt that you are the Almighty and that whatever you do is for the best, but it is impossible for me to obey the commandment, Thou Shalt Love Thy God. No, I cannot, Father, not in this life."

II

How revolting to lust for some peasant woman and not adore the Creator. Out of contrition, one should bury oneself alive. But what then could be done with the gross body and its desires? How silence the criminal within? Jacob lay on the floor moving neither hand nor foot. The window was open and the night billowed in. He traced the path of the constellation in the ascendant and saw the stars drift from roof to roof, noting how these lights, whiter than the sun, twinkled and shimmered. The same God, who had given the Cossacks strength to chop off heads and rip open stomachs, directed this heavenly multitude. The midnight moon floated in mother-of-pearl and its face, said by the children to be Joshua's, stared straight at Jacob.

Josefov by day was a confusion of sounds: chopping, sawing; carts arriving from the villages with grain, vegetables, fire wood, lumber; horses neighing, cows bellowing; children chanting the alphabet, the Pentateuch, the commentaries of Rashi, the Gemara. The same peasants who had helped Chmielnicki's butchers strip the Jewish homes now turned logs into lumber, split shingles, laid floors, built ovens, painted buildings. A Jew had opened a tavern where the peasants came to swill beer and vodka. The gentry, having blotted out the memory of the massacres, again leased

105

their fields, woods, and mills to Jewish contractors. One had to do business with murderers and shake their hands in order to close a deal. It was rumored that Jews, too, had fattened on the catastrophe, dealing in stolen goods and digging up caches hidden by refugees. Deserted wives were another subject of gossip. These women wandered through town searching for their husbands or for witnesses to testify they were dead. Many Jews had not been strong enough to resist conversion and the Polish government had decreed that those unwillingly baptized might reassume their own faith.

But the greatest sensation of all was caused by the Cossack wives, Jewish women forced into marriage, who now fled the steppes and returned. One of them, Tirza Temma, who had arrived in Josefov shortly before Jacob, had forgotten how to speak Yiddish. Her first husband was still alive, having escaped to the forest where he had lived on roots at the time of the massacre. He had not recognized Tirza Temma and had denied it was she. She had exhibited her evidence in the bath house, a honey-colored speck on one of her breasts and a second birthmark on her back. But her petition that her husband be forced to divorce his second wife had been denied. Tirza Temma, informed by the court that it was she who would be divorced, had berated the community in Cossack, and still persistently sought to break into her old home and take over the household. Another woman had been possessed by a dybbuk. One girl barked like a dog. A bride whose groom had been murdered on their wedding day suffered from melancholia and spent her nights in the cemetery dressed in her bridal gown and veil. Only now, years after the calamity, did Jacob realize how deep were the wounds. Moreover, new wars and insurrections were feared. The Cossacks on the steppes were again preparing an invasion of Poland, and Muscovites, Prussians, and Swedes stood poised with sharpened swords. The Polish nobility did nothing but drink, fornicate, whip peasants, and quarrel among themselves over the distribution of honors, privileges, and titles.

Only at night was there silence—the song of grasshoppers and the croak of frogs. Warm breezes wafted the smell of flowers, weeds, ripening grain from the fields, and Jacob recognized each faint aroma. He heard birds and animals stirring among the thickets. Lately he had taken a solemn oath, to root Wanda from his heart and never think of her again. She was a daughter of Esau who had lured him into adultery, a woman whose desire to accept his faith came from impure motives. In addition she was there, he here. What good was this brooding? Nothing but sins and imps born of evil thoughts arose from it. He marshaled the images of the cripples he had seen on the road and here in Josefov, men without noses, ears, tongues—each time he lusted for her, he thought of them. He should be more concerned with the misery of these unfortunates than with dreams of luxury in the lap of their torturer's sister. He determined to punish himself: every time he thought of Wanda he would fast until sunset. He drew up lists of torments: pebbles in his shoes, a stone beneath his pillow, bolting his food without chewing it, going without sleep. The debt he owed for allowing Satan to ensnare him had to be paid off once and for all. But Belial was as persistent as a rat. Who was the rat? Jacob, himself? Some force beyond him? But there was, as he well knew, a Spirit of Good and a Spirit of Evil. In his case the latter was more firmly seated in his brain and had much more to say. The instant Jacob dozed off, Evil took over, sketched lascivious pictures, brought Wanda's voice to the sleeper's ears, revealed her naked body to him, defiled and polluted Jacob. Sometimes he heard her voice even when he was awake. "Jacob, Jacob," she called. The sound came from without, not within him: he saw her working in the fields, grinding the grain, bearing food to the cowherd who this year slept in the barn with the cattle. She had taken up residence within him and he could not drive her forth. She nestled close to him beneath the prayer shawl when he prayed. She studied with him as he sat poring over the Torah. "Why did you show me how to be a Jew if you meant to leave me among the idolaters?" she complained. "Why did you pull me to you only to thrust me away?" He looked into her eyes, heard her sob, walked with her among the cattle in the fields. Once more they bathed together in the mountain stream and he bore her in his arms to the straw. Balaam barked; the mountain birds sang. He heard her panting, "More, more." She whispered, bit his ear, and kissed it.

The matchmakers were busy trying to marry off Jacob, and one of the men who had ransomed him was among those who had found a prospect. Jacob at first said "no" to all these suggestions. He had no intention of remarrying, would remain celibate. But the contention was that he should not travel so dangerous a road. Why endure temptation daily? Moreover, he should obey the precept: "Be fruitful and multiply." A widow from Hrubyeshoyv was among the possibilities and she was to come to Josefov shortly to meet him. She had a drygoods store in the Hrubyeshoyv market and a house that the Cossacks had neglected to burn. The widow was a few years older than he and had a grown daughter, but this was no great handicap. The Jew does not tempt Evil by denying the body but harnesses it in the service of God. Jacob knew that he could never love this woman from Hrubyeshoyv, but possibly he might be able to find forgetfulness with her.

He was exhausted by the struggle within him, sleepless at night, weary during the day. He found he lacked the patience to teach and had lost his taste for Torah and prayer. He sat in the study house longing for the open air, dreaming of gathering grass again, scaling crags, chopping wood. The Jews had ransomed him but he remained a slave. Passion held him like a dog on a leash. The hounds of Egypt bayed but he could not drive them off.

One day when he was seated in the study house explaining the procedures involving the horns of rams sacrificed as burnt offerings, a small boy entered and said, "My father would like to see you, Reb Jacob." Jacob shivered as he always did now when he saw a child.

"Who is your father?"

"Moishe Zakolkower."

"Do you know what he wants with me?"

"The widow from Hrubyeshoyv is here."

The class burst out laughing and Jacob, becoming confused, blushed. "Recite the Gemara while I am gone," he directed. But even before he left the building, he heard his pupils pounding on the table and arguing querulously. Active boys, accustomed to playing wolf and goat, hide and go seek, tag, they were forever joking among themselves and laughing boisterously. One of the principal objects of their humor was gloomy Jacob seated before them lost in somber thoughts, and, now that he was being led away to meet a woman, they had something more to ridicule. Jacob walked beside the boy, having decided not to go home to change to his Saturday gabardines. The child, who had not even been alive at the time of the massacres, prattled about a bird that had flown through his bedroom window. They came to Moishe Zakolkower's newly erected house, even more comfortable than the one the Cossacks had burned, and Jacob, entering, found himself in a hall, smelled food, cutlets, and onions frying. The door of the kitchen was open and he could see Moishe's second wife (his first had been killed) standing near the oven. Another woman was kneeding dough and a girl was grinding pepper in a mortar. For a moment he caught a whiff of the past and then Moishe, the man who had counted out the gold pieces for Zagayek, opened the living room door and bade Jacob enter. In the room Jacob noted the newness of everything, walls, floors, tables, chairs, newly bound books from Lublin in the bookcases. The evil ones destroyed, the Jews created. Once more Jewish books were being printed and authors were traveling here and there to sign up subscribers. Jacob felt a stab in his heart every time he saw the past visibly resurrected. No doubt the living must go on living, but this very affirmation betrayed the dead. A song he had heard a wedding jester sing came to his mind: "What is life but a dance across graves?" Yes, his coming to meet a prospective bride was a scandal. Only a few feet from here his wife and children lay buried. Yet better a wife than this perpetual brooding about a gentile woman.

Moishe and he were deep in a discussion of yeshiva and community matters when the woman of the household entered, bringing cookies and a dish of cherries—the hospitality of the wealthy. Blushing, she apologized for not being properly dressed, and nodded as if to say, "I know what you think, but you can't do a thing about it. This isn't a man's world." Finally the widow from Hrubyeshoyv arrived, a small dumpy woman, decked out in a silk dress and satin cape, wearing a matron's bonnet decorated with colored ribbons and pearls. Her round face had so many wrinkles that it looked as if it had been pieced together, and her eyes were black and soft, resembling those pulps found in cherry brandy. From her neck hung a gold chain with a dangling pendant, her fingers gleamed with rings. The odor of honey and cinnamon trailed into the room with her, and she looked Jacob over shrewdly.

"My, what a giant of a man! May the evil eye not fall on you."

"We are as God created us."

"True, but better big than a midget."

She spoke with a lilt and a sob, and kept wiping her nose with a batiste handkerchief. The wagon that had brought her to Josefov had lost a wheel, she said, and they had had to stop for repairs at a blacksmith's. Then she sighed and began to fan herself, meanwhile talking about her drygoods store and how hard it was to get the goods that the customers wanted. She refused the refreshments that Moishe's wife offered her, and then broke down and drained a glass of blueberry wine while she swallowed three cookies. Some crumbs fell on the folds of her cape and she picked them up and ate them. True, her business was large, thank God, but the girls she had working for her, on the other hand, couldn't be trusted. "A stranger's hand is useful only for poking a fire," she said, quoting the proverb and looking at Jacob slyly fron the corners of her eyes. "One needs a man in the house, otherwise everything goes."

She liked him, Jacob saw, and was ready to sit down and write the preliminary agreement. But he hesitated. This woman was too old and syrupy, too cunning. He didn't want to spend his life overseeing clerks and bargaining with customers. Such a person needed a husband who was wrapped up, body and soul, in money. She was going to add a new wing to the house, she said, and also enlarge the store. The more she spoke, the more disconsolate Jacob became. I have ceased being a part of this world, he said to himself, the match would be good for neither of us. "I am not a business man by nature," he said aloud.

"Who's born a business man?" she asked, picking up a cluster of cherries with her flabby fingers.

She began to examine Jacob on his years of captivity—a subject avoided since the Jews regarded time spent among the pagans as wasted and better not discussed—but such a wealthy woman did not have to conform to convention. Jacob told her of Jan Bzik, of the barn on the mountain in which he had spent his summers, of the granary where he had slept in the winter. "How did you get food when you were on the mountain?" she asked.

"It was brought from the valley."

"Who brought it? The peasant?"

"No, his daughter."

"Unmarried?"

"A widow."

"Did you collect grass on the Sabbath?"

"I never broke the Sabbath. Nor did I eat unkosher food." He was ashamed to hear himself boasting of his piety.

The woman thought over what he had said carefully, and then remarked as she reached out her hand to take another cookie, "What choice did you have? Oh, what those murderers did to us!"

III

It was noon; the boys went for their midday meals, some to their families and others to the houses where they boarded. Alone in the study house, Jacob prepared a lecture. He was pleased to be once more deep in the study of books, yet he found earning his living by teaching distasteful. Most of

112

his students were bored and the clever ones spent their time in hair-splitting or in complicating the obvious. His years away from Torah had changed his views. Now conscious of much he had not realized, he saw that one law in the Torah generated a dozen in the Mishnah, and five dozen in the Gemara; in the later commentaries laws were as numerous as the sands of the desert. Each generation added its own strictures, and during his years of exile the Shulcran Oruch had been further interpreted and additional forbiddances added. A wry thought occurred to him: if this continued, nothing would be kosher. What would the Jews live on then? Hot coals? And why had these interdictions and commandments not preserved the Jews from Cossack atrocities? What more did God require of his martyred people?

Moreover, as Jacob looked about him, he saw that the community observed the laws and customs involving the Almighty, but broke the code regulating man's treatment of man with impunity. His return before Passover had brought him to town when a quarrel was in progress. Flour for matzoths was scarce and the rabbi, finding no proscription in the Mosaic Law, in the Talmud, or even in Maimonides, had authorized the eating of peas and beans during the holidays. This ruling had incensed certain members of the congregation, some because they wanted to show how pious they were, others because they were angry at the rabbi; and they had broken the windows in the rabbi's house and driven nails into his bench at the east wall. One of the zealots had approached Jacob and sounded him out about becoming rabbi. Yes, men and women who would rather have died than break the smallest of these ritualistic laws, slandered and gossiped openly, and treated the poor with contempt. Scholars lorded it over the ignorant; the elders divided privileges and preferments among themselves and their relatives and exploited the people generally. Money lenders gouged their clients—using loopholes in the law against usury; merchandise was kept off the market until it became scarce. Some went so far as to give false weight and measure. But when Jacob entered the study house he met them all: the angry, the haughty, the obsequious, the crooked. They prayed and schemed, erected tall towers and legalisms while they broke God's commandments. The catastrophe had impoverished the community, but the town still had more than its share of hatred and envy. Moishe Zakolkower told Jacob that there were those who were anxious to prevent his match with the widow of Hrubyeshoyv. An anonymous letter had been received denouncing Jacob.

Yet Jacob's thoughts worried him, since he knew his concern with such things was of evil origin. Satan tried to prove that corruption being general, sin could be taken lightly. The Spirit of Good replied: "Why concern yourself with what others do? Look to yourself." But Jacob had no peace. Everywhere he heard people asserting things that their eyes denied. Piety was the cloak for envy and avarice. The Jews had learned nothing from their ordeal; rather suffering had pushed them lower.

Chanting as he studied, he found it difficult now to keep the lilt of the cowherds' songs out of his voice. Moments came when he longed for the barn. His love for the Jews had been wholehearted when he was distant from them. He had forgotten the shifty eyes and barbed tongues of the petty—their tricks, stratagems and quarrels. True, he had suffered from the primitiveness and savagery of the cowherds, but what could be expected from such a rabble?

The marriage contract was almost completed,

the date of the wedding set for the Friday after Tischab'ov. The widow, though well along in her thirties, could still bear children and was anxious to have a son. Already flatterers considered Jacob a rich man and showered him with compliments. Yet he lay awake worrying, still uncertain about the marriage. The widow needed a business man, a good mixer; he was withdrawn, a recluse. The years of slavery had estranged him from life; he looked healthy, but was shattered within. He kept rummaging in the cabala and leafing through books of philosophy. Sometimes he was overwhelmed by the desire to flee, but he didn't know where. He doubted everything, with, as the saying goes, the kind of doubt which "the heart does not share with the lips." He had not tasted meat in all the years of slavery and the idea of feeding on God's creatures now repelled him. Meat and fish were both eaten customarily on the Sabbath, but the food stuck in his throat. Jews treated animals as Cossacks treated Jews. The words "head," "neck," "liver," "gizzards," made him shudder. Meat in his mouth gave him the fantasy he was devouring his own children. On several occasions he had gone outside and vomited after the Sabbath dinner.

He was alone in the study house, not studying, but merely leafing through volume after volume. Possibly Maimonides had the answer. Or the *Chuzary*. Might it be contained in *The Duty of the Heart* or *The Vineyard?* He read a few words, turned the page, opened another book in the middle, turned pages again. Putting his hands to his face, he closed his eyes. He longed for both Wanda and the grave. The instant his desire for her left him, he wished to die. "Father in Heaven," his lips said as if possessed of a will of their own, "take me."

Footsteps approached; a charity worker entered,

bringing him a bowl of soup. Jacob studied her. Lame though she was, with a wart on her nose and hair on her chin, this woman was a saint. Kindness, gentleness, candor dwelt in her eyes. She had lost her husband and children but exhibited no bitterness, envied no one, nursed no grievances, uttered no slander. She washed Jacob's linen, cooked for him, waited on him like a maid, and would not allow him even to thank her. Her answer to his praise was, "For what other reason were we created?"

She placed the bowl on the table and brought bread, salt, a knife, as well as a pitcher of water for him to wash his hands; and then stood humbly at the door waiting for him to finish. What was the source of her kindness? Jacob wondered. Only the wise behaved as she. Even if she were the sole representative of virtue in Josefov, she would still be a witness to God's mercy, and this was the woman he should marry. Would she consider marriage, he asked, if a proper husband were found for her? Her eyes clouded. "God willing, in the next world with my Baruch David."

IV

Wanda came to Jacob one night as he lay sleeping. He saw her in the flesh, her body surrounded by light, her cheeks tear-stained, and knew she was pregnant. The smell of fields and haystacks entered with her. "Why did you leave me?" she asked wanly. "What will happen to your child? It will be brought up among pagans." Startled, Jacob awoke; the image lingered an instant at the boundary of sleep and waking. When it at last dissolved, the darkness retained an afterglow as if a lamp had just been extinguished. Hearing Wanda's voice re-echo in his ears, Jacob trembled. He could almost feel the warmth of her body.

Straining his ears, he waited for her to reveal herself again. He dozed off. She reappeared, wearing a calico apron, carrying a kerchief with a fringed border, and approaching him, threw her arms about him and kissed him. Because of the child she bore, he had to bend to her and he tasted her lips and the salt of her tears. "It's yours," she said, "your flesh and blood."

Once more he awoke, and did not close his eyes again that night. He had seen her, she was carrying his child. Jacob began to recite Psalms. The eastern sky became scarlet; he rose and washed his hands. All was clear to him now. The law obliged him to rescue Wanda and his child from the idolaters. He had money, for as sole heir of his father-in-law he had received fifty gulden for the property in the market place where the old house had stood. He threw his belongings into a burlap sack and walked to the study house. Reb Moishe, always one of the first ten to enter God's house, had his Gemara already open, and was busily studying. His dark eyes grew large seeing Jacob approach with a sack slung over his shoulder.

"What are you up to?"

"I'm off to Lublin."

"But the date of the wedding's been set."

"I can't go through with it."

"What'll happen to your class?"

"You'll find another teacher."

"Why? And so suddenly?"

Wanting neither to lie nor tell the truth, Jacob said nothing. He counted out twenty gulden from a small bag. "Here's part of the money the town spent ransoming me." Astonished, Reb Moishe tugged at his beard. "Repaying the community," he mumbled. "We can expect the Messiah any day."

"It should be of some assistance."

"What do I tell the widow of Hrubyeshoyv?"

117

"Say we weren't meant for each other."

"Are you coming back?"

"I don't know."

"What's your plan—to become a recluse?"

Without waiting for the arrival of a quorum, Jacob turned his head and began the morning prayer. He had learned the day before that a wagon would leave for Lublin in the morning, and quickly finishing his devotions, he set out to find Leibush the carter. If he passed someone carrying a filled container, he had decided that would be an omen that there would be room on the wagon, and that Heaven approved of the trip. Lo and behold, there was Calman the water carrier lugging two pails of water. "Well, we can always squeeze in one more," Leibush said.

The morning was warm; the village quiet. It was late in the month of Sivan. Shutters opened. Sleepy-eyed women poked out their bonneted heads. Men converged on the study house carrying bags containing their prayer shawls and phylacteries. Cows were being led to pasture. A great golden sun was aloft in the east, but dew continued to fall on the grass and the young trees planted after the destruction. Birds sang and pecked at the oats fallen from the horses' feedbags. On such a morning it was difficult to believe this a world in which children were slain and buried alive, and that the earth still drank of blood as in the days of Cain. "You sit with me on the box," Leibush said to Jacob. The other passengers were mostly women off to buy goods in the Lublin stores.

One woman had forgotten something. Another had to run home to nurse her baby. A man arrived with a package to be delivered to the Lublin inn. So the wagon did not start immediately as scheduled. Two men, storekeepers, who were seated among the women whiled away the time swapping spicy stories and innuendoes with the giggling matrons.

Jacob heard his name mentioned and then the name of the widow of Hrubyeshoyv. Unintentionally, he had humiliated her. No matter what one does one stumbles into sin, he thought. He had been reading books of ethics, filled with the best advice on how to avoid the pitfalls of evil, but Satan always outwitted one. He participated in all business transactions and marriages; no human enterprise proceeded without him: touch something and you hurt someone. Have a little success, and, no matter how decent you were, you provoked envy. But why was he on his way to Lublin? He told himself he didn't know. He wanted advice from the city's wisest rabbis and would do as they recommended. Yet all the time he was aware he was traveling to Wanda, like one of the Israelite rabble that had wanted to turn and march back to Egypt and slavery for a kettle of meat. But did he dare let his child grow up among the pagans? He had not thought that the gentile woman would become pregnant. Generally he had withdrawn and spilled his seed like Onan.

Well, it makes no difference whether I go or stay, Jacob remarked to himself. I'm lost either way. The wagon had begun to move without his noticing it, and was now passing fields where the peasants were weeding and transplanting. How beautiful the countryside was and how contrary to his despair. Doubt, dissension, discord dwelt within him, but the fields exuded harmony, tranquillity, fruitfulness. The sky was blue, the weather warm with the mercy of summer, the air fragrant as honey, each flower exhaling its own perfume. A hidden hand had shaped and modeled each stalk, blade of grass, leaf, worm, fly. Each hovering butterfly's wings exhibited a unique design; every bird sang with its own call. Breathing deeply, Jacob realized how much he had missed the country. Grainfields, trees, every single

119

growing thing refreshed his eyes. If only I could
live in perpetual summer and do harm to no one, he
murmured, as the wagon entered a pine wood
which seemed less a forest than some heavenly
mansion. The trees were as tall and straight as
pillars and the sky leaned on their green tops.
Brooches, rings, gold coins were embossed on the
bark of their trunks. The earth, carpeted with moss
and other vegetation, gave off an intoxicating
odor. A shallow stream coursed through the
woodland, and perched on rocks in the water were
birds Jacob had never seen in the mountains. All
of these creatures knew what was expected of
them. None sought to rebel against its Creator.
Man alone acted viciously. Jacob heard the women
behind him slandering the whole of Josefov.
Raising his eyes, he gazed through the screen of
branches and needles where jewels glittered. The
light which filtered through shone with all the
colors of the rainbow. Cuckoos sang, woodpeckers
drummed. Gnats circled quickly, dark, eddying
specks. Jacob closed his eyes as though begrudg-
ing himself the sight of so much splendor. A
roseate light seeped through his lids. Gold mingled
with blue, green with purple, and, out of this
whirlpool of color, Wanda's image formed.

V

Great crowds filled the community house in
Lublin. The Council of the Four Countries was not
in session, but the Council of Poland was. Deserted
wives petitioning for the right to remarry, "Cossack brides" returned from the steppes and
Russian Orthodoxy, widows whose brothers-in-
law had refused to perform the Levirate ceremony
or had insisted on being payed exorbitantly to do
so, moved through the rooms. Mingled with them
were husbands whose wives had run off or gone

mad and who needed the consent of a hundred rabbis to remarry, fathers looking for prospective sons-in-law, authors asking religious authorities for endorsements, contractors seeking partners to invest in the lumber business, and individuals who merely wanted witnesses for wills. Both social and commercial activity went on in the Lublin community house. Merchants passed around samples; jewelers and goldsmiths displayed their wares; authors hawked their books and met with printers and paper jobbers; usurers discussed loans with builders and contractors; managers of estates brought objects their gentile patrons wanted to pawn or sell—a carved ivory hand ornamented with rubies, a lady's gold comb and hairpins, a silver pistol with a mother-of-pearl handle studded with diamonds.

Despite the upheaval, Poland's commerce remained in the hands of the Jews. They even dealt in church decorations, although this trade was forbidden them by law. Jewish traders traveled to Prussia, Bohemia, Austria, and Italy, importing into the country silk, velvet, wine, coffee, spices, jewelry, weapons, and exporting salt, oil, flax, butter, eggs, rye, wheat, barley, honey, hides. Neither the aristocracy nor the peasantry had any real knowledge of business. The Polish guilds continued to protect themselves through every form of privilege, but nevertheless their products were more expensive than those of the Jews and often inferior in workmanship. Nearly every manor harbored Jewish craftsmen, and, although the king had forbidden Jews to be apothecaries, the people had confidence in no others. Jewish doctors were sent for, sometimes from abroad. The priests, particularly the Jesuits, harangued against infidel medicine from their pulpits, published pamphlets on the subject, petitioned the Sejm and the governors to disqualify Jews from medical practice, but no sooner did one of the clergy fall ill, than he called in a Jew to attend him.

Jacob had come to Lublin to get advice from the local rabbi or from the members of the Council, but he loitered in the city doing nothing. The Sabbath came and went. The more he reflected on the question perplexing him, the clearer it became that no one could advise him. He was familiar with the law. Would he find a man anywhere who could determine the authenticity of a vision or who could weigh in the scales which was the greater transgression, the abandonment of one's issue to the idolaters or the conversion of a woman lacking a true vocation? Once more Jacob remembered the saying, "Something done selfishly may end up as a godly act," and argued accordingly. Cakes, candies, and almonds were given to a child starting cheder to encourage him to love the Torah. Didn't one speak of a convert as new-born? Who could know all the motives of those who had become Jews in the past? No saint was entirely selfless. Jacob decided to take the sin upon himself and instruct Wanda in the tenets of his faith. Now that the Polish government permitted converted Jews to return to their religion, Wanda could pass as one of them. No one would bother to investigate. She would shave her head, put on a matron's bonnet, and he would teach her every single law.

In Lublin, Jacob was known as the man from Josefov who spent so many years as a slave. Speaking thus, they set him apart. The scholars addressed him as if he were a simpleton who had forgotten all he learned. When they mentioned a Hebrew word or quoted the Talmud, they translated it into Yiddish for his benefit. In his presence they whispered among themselves and smiled patronizingly as city people do when they converse with bumpkins. The elders were interested in how

122

he had conducted himself in slavery: had he kept the Sabbath and the dietary laws? How odd that he had not attempted to escape but had waited to be ransomed. Jacob became convinced they knew something dreadful they dared not say to his face. Could they have been told about Wanda? Zagayek might have passed a comment to the group who had come to ransom him. If so, this secret was traveling from mouth to mouth.

From the first he had noted the difference between himself and the others, and the longer he stayed in Lublin, the sharper the contrast seemed. He was tall, blond, blue-eyed; they, for the most part, were short, dark-eyed, black-bearded. They liked esoteric scholarly jokes, used snuff, smoked tobacco, knew the names of all the rich contractors, were acquainted with who had married whom, and what Jew was the favorite of which nobleman. All this was foreign to Jacob. I have turned into a peasant, he said, rebuking himself. But he recalled that it had not been so different before the calamity. The rabbis, elders, and rich men in the old days had also been of one party and he of another. They had eyed him suspiciously as if they suspected he had gentile blood. But how could this have been? Descended from an eminent family, his grandfathers, and their fathers also, had all been Polish rabbis.

Stranger than this, however, was the attitude of the Jews who, having just survived their greatest calamity, behaved as if they no longer remembered. They groaned and sighed, but without feeling. The rabbis and elders were again quarreling over money and power. The problem of the deserted wives and "the Cossack brides" was for them an opportunity to display their casuistic brilliance in long, time-consuming discussions little connected with the spirit of the law. The unhappy petitioners waited weeks and months for verdicts that could have been handed down in a few days. The Council of the Four Countries had taken upon itself the task of collecting the Crown taxes in addition to those which went for its own support, and everywhere complaints were heard that the burden of the tax was inequitably distributed and the rate excessive. Occasionally an accuser pointed a finger at these eminent men, threatening to complain to the administration, to stand up in the synagogue and denounce them before the reading of the Torah, or to wait for them outside and give them a good beating. The man was immediately made a member of the elite, offered a few crumbs, and sent out to sing the praises of the very individuals he had been defaming. Jacob even heard of emissaries who misappropriated money they collected or took too high a percentage for themselves. The catastrophes over, the stomachs of many of the rabbis and elders had increased in size; their necks wrinkled with fat. All this flesh was dressed in velvet, silk, and sables. They were so heavy they wheezed; their eyes shone greedily. They spoke an only half-comprehensible language of innuendoes, winks, and whispered asides. Outside the community house, angry men proclaimed these rulers robbers and thieves and warned prophetically of the plagues and afflictions their sins would produce.

Yes, it was clear to Jacob that these, the grabbers, were worthless, but there were also the givers, and more of these than the others. Thank God, not all Jews were community elders. Men still prayed, studied, and recited Psalms in God's house. Many of them still bore the wounds they had received from the Cossacks. Jacob saw cripple after cripple, men deprived of ears, fingers, noses, teeth, eyes, and all sang: "We will sanctify"; "Bless ye." They listened to the sermons, sat down to pore

124

over the Mishnah. Anniversary candles were lit and men continued to mourn.

Wandering through the narrow alleys, Jacob saw how great the poverty was. Many lived in what were only dark burrows; tradesmen worked in shops that looked like kennels. A stench rose from the gutters; ragged women, often on the point of giving birth, foraged for wood shavings and dung to be used for heat. Half naked children with scabby heads and rashes walked around barefoot. Many of the urchins had rickety legs, sores on their eyes, puffed bellies, distended heads. There was some kind of epidemic in progress and hearses with corpses in them passed constantly, each followed by lamenting women. A beadle rattled his alms box and cried out, "Charity will preserve you from death." The insane were everywhere, wild in the streets, another remembrance of the Cossacks.

It shamed Jacob that he thought so much of Wanda. People were starving before his eyes. A groschen here could save a life. He was continually changing silver to smaller coins and distributing his money. But what he gave was little when confronted with this vast need. Bands of beggars pursued him, clutched at his coat, blessing and cursing him. They hissed, spat at him, threw lice in his direction, and he was barely able to escape. Where was God? How could he look down on such want and keep silent? Unless, Heaven forbid, there was no God.

7

Jacob traveled from Lublin to Cracow by wagon. Changing to peasant dress, he proceeded on foot from Cracow to the mountains. The sack slung over his shoulder contained bread, cheese, a prayer book and shawl, phylacteries, a volume of the Mishnah, and presents for Wanda: a matron's bonnet, a dress, a pair of shoes. He had made his plans in advance; he would avoid the high road and take meadow and forest trails. The sun had gone down before he left Cracow, and all night he walked, aware of the dangers around him. Wild beasts and robbers lived in the hills; he remembered Wanda's stories of vampire owls disguised as cats and of witches' mares galloping through darkness on their evil errands.

The roads were dangerous at night, as Jacob knew. The King's Daughter, filthiest of witches, confused travelers and shoved them into bogs. The demonic Lillies made their homes in caves and the hollows of tree trunks. Ygereth, Machlath, and

126

Shibta enticed men off the highways until they defiled themselves with nocturnal emissions. Shabriry and Briry polluted the waters of springs and rivers. Zachulphi, Jejknufi, Michiaru, survivors of the generation that had built the Tower of Babel, confounded men's speech and drove them mad or into the mountains of darkness. But Jacob's longing for Wanda made him willing to take any risk. Even though the journey must result in sin, he sang Psalms and begged God to keep him safe. His investigations of the cabala since his return had uncovered the doctrine that all lust was of divine origin, even Zimri's lust for Kozbi, the daughter of Zur. Coupling was the universal act underlying everything; Torah, prayer, the Commandments, God's holy names themselves were mysterious unions of the male and female principles. Jacob thrashed this way and that, constantly seeking exoneration: a soul would be saved from idolatry; his seed would not be mingled with that of Esau. Such virtuous acts must tip the scale in his favor.

The summer night passed, but Jacob could not have told how. The sun rose and he discovered himself in a forest with a stream close by. Washing his hands, he recited the Shema, and said the morning prayer in his shawl and phylacteries. He breakfasted on bread, dried cheese, and water, and then, having said grace, rested his head on the sack and fell asleep. The analogy between him and his Biblical namesake had already occurred to him. Jacob had left Beersheba and journeyed to Haran for love of Rachel and had toiled seven years to win her. Had she not been the daughter of a pagan? Awaking with such thoughts in his mind, he resumed his own journey, heading upstream past mushrooms and blackberry brambles in bud, noting which plants were edible. Uncertain of the road, he kept his eye out for the blazes the Gazdas notched into trees. Cows bellowed close at hand; he could see camp fires. As long as the path climbed, it was taking him to Wanda.

Late in the afternoon, when the sun was moving westward, a strange figure appeared as if risen from the earth. White-haired, bearded, the man wore a brown robe and felt boots. A rosary and crucifix hung from his neck. He stopped before Jacob, leaning on a crooked staff. "Where are you bound for, my son?" he asked.

Jacob told him the name of the village.

"There is the way," the old man said, and he showed him the path.

Before leaving, he blessed Jacob. If it had not been for the cross he wore, the old man might have been mistaken for the prophet Elijah. But, perhaps, Jacob thought, he was an emissary of Esau, sent by those powers who wished Jews and gentiles to mate. Jacob was now nearing the village, and he lengthened his stride. He felt anxious: Wanda might have remarried or fallen ill. God forbid, she might be dead. She might be in love with someone else. The sun went down; though it was midsummer, it became cold. Columns of mist rose from the mountains. In the distance, a huge bird, an eagle perhaps, hung suspended in mid air, wings motionless as though kept aloft by cabala. The moon rose and one by one, like candles being lit, stars appeared. Suddenly there was a noise, a kind of roaring. An animal or the wind? Jacob wondered. Though he was prepared to fight, he recognized that Providence would be justified in allowing some predatory creature to destroy him. How had he deserved better?

Stopping, he looked about him. He was as solitary here as the original Adam, with no sign anywhere of man and his works. The birds silent, only the song of the grasshoppers and the bubbling of a stream were heard. Glacial breezes blew from the mountains. Jacob breathed in deeply, savoring the familiar odors. Strange how he had missed not only Wanda but this. The stale air of Josefov had been unbearable, windows tightly shut, nothing but books all day. Tired though he was from his exertion, the journey had invigorated him. The body required use as well as the soul. It was good for men to haul, drag, chop, run, perspire, to hunger and thirst and become weary. Raising his eyes, he saw more stars appearing, large and brilliant here in the mountains. The workings of the heavens were visible to him, each orbiting light going its prescribed way and fulfilling its function. Notions he had had as a boy returned to him. Suppose he had wings and flew in one direction forever, would he come to the end of space? But how could space end? What extended beyond? Or was the material world infinite? But if it was, infinity stretched both to the east and west, and how could there be twice infinity? And what of time? How could even God have had no beginning? How could anything be eternal? Where had everything come from? These questions were impertinent, he knew, impermissible, pushing the inquirer toward heresy and madness.

He continued to walk. How strange and feeble was man. Surrounded on every side by eternity, in the midst of powers, angels, seraphim, cherubim, arcane worlds, and divine mysteries, all he could lust for was flesh and blood. Yet man's smallness was no less a wonder than God's greatness.

Pausing, he took some dry cheese from his sack and refreshed himself. Would he find Wanda today or have to wait until tomorrow? He feared the peasants and their dogs. He began to mumble prayers—a slave returning to bondage, a Jew again putting on Egypt's yoke.

II

Jacob entered the village at midnight, stealing through fields and pastures at the back of the huts. The moon had set, but it was light enough for him to recognize each house and granary. The mountain where he had spent five summers was visible also and he constantly lifted his eyes to it. Those years seemed dreamlike now, a vanished miracle, an interlude achieved by sorcery. Thank God, the dogs slept. His feet no longer felt heavy and his steps were faunlike; his body was buoyant from lack of food. He broke into a run, down the hill leading to Jan Bzik's hut, his single desire to find Wanda. Was she in the house? In the granary? Could she have gone to Antek's? He thought of his life and was amazed at what had happened to him. He had been taken captive; his family had been wiped out. Now, disguised as a peasant, he was hurrying to find his beloved. This was the sort of ballad his sisters had told or sung when his father was absent, not daring to when the pious man was at home, knowing that he regarded the female voice as lascivious.

Jacob stopped and held his breath. There it was, Jan Bzik's hut. He was trembling. He could make out every detail: the thatched roof, the windows, the granary, even the stump on which he had chopped wood. The kennel in the center of the yard appeared to be empty. Tiptoeing toward the granary, he smelled an odor he only now remembered. Was Wanda there? Could he be sure she would not cry out and wake everyone? He recollected the code she had used during those months when he had feared an attack by Antek or Stephan—three knocks, two loud and one soft. He rapped out the signal. There was no answer. Now for the first time he realized how dangerous this undertaking was. If he were discovered, he might be killed as a thief. And what if he did find Wanda, where could they go? This adventure was putting him in constant jeopardy. The Christians burned gentiles who became Jews. Nor would the Jews accept the convert. It was still not too late to run back, he knew. He tingled with anxiety. Where had passion led him? Quietly he pushed open the granary door, meanwhile defending himself—I am no longer responsible for my acts. He heard breathing. Wanda was there. Hands ready to stifle her scream, he approached. Now he saw her in the darkness: she lay on the straw, her breasts exposed, half-naked. The story of Ruth and Boaz floated through his brain. He was awake, yet dreaming. He put down his sack.

"Wanda."

Her breathing stopped.

"Wanda, don't scream. It's me, Jacob." He broke off, unable to say more.

She sighed. "Who is it?"

"Jacob. Don't scream."

Thank God she did not, but sat up like someone delirious from fever.

"Who are you?" she said uncomprehendingly.

"Jacob. I've come for you. Don't scream."

At that very instant she did. Her scream made Jacob shudder and he was certain those in the hut must have heard. He fell to the straw, and, struggling with her in the darkness, he clamped his hand over her mouth. She freed herself, got to her feet, and he clutched her again, glancing at the open door, expecting to see peasants running toward the granary.

"Be still," he said, his breath coming in gasps. "They'll kill me. I've come for you, Wanda. I couldn't get you out of my mind."

Scarcely knowing what he was doing, he pulled her closer. They dared not stay there, the granary was a trap. He was breathing hard and sweating; his heart was pounding. "We must leave here while it's still dark," he whispered.

No longer struggling, trembling now, she pressed herself to him, her teeth chattering as though it were winter. "Is it really you?" he heard her say:

"Yes, I. Hurry, we must go."

"Jacob. Jacob."

The scream must have gone unnoticed as no one was coming. But perhaps the peasants lay in wait outside. Now, for the first time, it occurred to him that this was not the Wanda of his vision. There was no indication that she bore his child. A dream had deceived him. Her arms about his neck, she whimpered like a sick animal, "Jacob, Jacob." He could not doubt that she had been longing for him. But every minute counted now. Over and over again he cautioned her that she must dress quickly and come with him. He grasped her by the wrists, shook her, begged her not to delay—they were in great peril. She pulled him to her again, pressing her face against his. In his anxiety he couldn't make out what she was saying. "We must leave," he warned her.

"One minute."

Turning, she ran from the granary. He saw her enter the hut and wondered if she would tell the old woman. He lifted his sack and walked out into the open air, prepared to run for the fields if there was trouble. It was difficult for him to believe that the woman he had awakened was Wanda. She looked smaller and thinner than she had been, more like a girl than a woman. Outside it was dark and still—that moment before dawn when night borders on day. Sky, earth, and mountains waited in an expectant hush. Though he remained terrified and shocked at what he had done, there was also a silence in Jacob. His mind seemed frozen. He no longer cared what the outcome of this adventure would be. His fate was decided. He had passed beyond freedom, was both himself and another. The still point within him watched as though his actions were those of a stranger.

He waited, but Wanda did not come. Had she decided not to leave with him? The sun must have risen already on the other side of the mountains. He stood enveloped in the chill darkness of dawn. Suddenly Wanda ran from the hut, now wearing shoes and with a kerchief on her head. A sack was slung over her shoulder. "Did you wake them?" he asked.

"No, they sleep like the dead."

III

Wanda chose another route to leave the village than the one he had had in mind. Like an elusive shadow she ran before him scarcely visible in the darkness. His legs shook from too much walking and too little sleep. He stumbled over rocks, slid into ditches. He wanted to call to her not to get too far ahead, but dared not raise his voice. How could she run so quickly bearing a sack? He felt drowsy; he kept dreaming. Something rose from the darkness. He drew back startled and instantly the image dissolved. An alien voice spoke inside him. Things were happening, but he didn't know what. Wanda had dressed and packed without waking her mother and sister—how? An absurd idea, patently false, came to him: could she have strangled them?

That instant a fragment of day fell on the mountains and made them shine. The east reddened and the sun lifted itself behind the peaks. Jacob caught up with Wanda and saw that they

133

were in a meadow at the edge of the forest. He noticed that she had on the fringed kerchief and the calico apron she had worn in his dream. Yes, she had altered, was shrunken and emaciated. Though her face was tinted purple by the sun, nevertheless her complexion was as pale as that of a consumptive. Her eyes had grown large and protruded from their sockets. It was even more difficult now to understand how she could have run so swiftly.

"Let's stop for a moment," he said.

"Not here—in the forest," she answered in a whisper.

But they did not stop immediately upon entering the woods. Among the trees Wanda's figure became more elusive than ever, and Jacob feared he would lose sight of her. The grade became steeper. He slipped on the pine needles. Wanda climbed like a bear, or a doe. He had returned to a changed woman. How could she have altered so quickly?

The forest grew lighter as if a lamp had been lit. Golden light fell over everything. Birds whistled and sang. Dew fell. Wanda stopped at the narrow opening of a cave. She threw her sack into the aperture and crept in head first, her feet kicking outside for a second. Jacob pushed his sack in and followed her through the opening. He recalled the commentary in the Talmud on the passage in the Bible, "And the pit was empty, there was no water in it." The Talmud added, "There was no water in it, but there were snakes and lizards." Well, whatever happens, happens, Jacob said to himself. It was as if he had entered the mouth of an abyss. He slipped and Wanda gripped him by the shoulders. The dampness choked him. He stumbled into her, and they fell over the sacks. Finally the cave became larger and he was able to sit up. When he spoke, his muffled voice sounded far off and unfamiliar to him.

"How did you know about this cave?" he asked.

"I knew. I knew."

"What's wrong with you? Are you sick?"

Wanda did not speak immediately.

"If you'd waited a little longer, you would have found me dead."

"What's wrong?"

Wanda paused again.

"Why did you go away? Where did they take you? I was told you'd never come back."

"You knew that the Jews had ransomed me?"

"All they said was that some devils had seized you."

"What do you mean? They paid Zagayek fifty gulden. They arrived in a wagon."

"When I was out of the village. But I knew I wouldn't find you when I got back. I didn't need the women to tell me."

"How did you know?"

"I know everything, everything. I was walking with Antek and the sun became black as night. The horse Wojciech was riding began to laugh at me."

"The horse?"

"Yes, and then I knew that my enemies would revenge themselves on me."

Jacob considered what she had told him.

"I was lying in the granary, when your sister came to call me."

"That! I know. As soon as I came into the village, they all laughed at my bad luck. How did the Jews know where you were?"

"I spoke to that circus proprietor and he carried the message."

"Where to? Palestine?"

"No, to Josefov."

135

"You didn't even say goodbye to me. It was as if the earth had swallowed you up, as if there had never been a Jacob. Stephan came to me but I spat in his face. He got back at me by killing the dog. Mother and Basha said I was either possessed or crazy. The peasants wanted to tie me to a tree trunk but I ran away to the mountains and I stayed there until they brought up the herd. For four weeks I didn't taste a thing but snow and cold water from the stream."

"It wasn't my fault, Wanda. The Jews came and took me. What could I have told them? The wagon was waiting. When Zagayek sent for me I thought I was going to be hanged."

"You should have waited. You shouldn't have left me like that. If I'd had a child by you I would have had some comfort. But all I was left with was the stone behind the barn and what you had scratched on it. I beat my head against it."

"But I did come."

"I knew you would. You called to me but I didn't have the strength to wait. I went to the coffin maker and had myself measured. I had the priest confess me and I chose a grave next to father's."

"But you told me you no longer believed in Dziobak."

"What? He sent for me and I came. I fell on my knees and kissed his feet. All I wanted was to lie near Father."

"You'll live, but as a daughter of Israel."

"Where will you take me? I'm sick. I can't be a wife to you now. The witch told me what to do—it was she who brought you here and no one else."

"Wanda, what are you telling me? One cannot use witchcraft."

"You didn't come of your own free will, Jacob. I made a clay image of you and I wrapped it in my hair. I bought an egg laid by a black hen and buried it at the crossroads with a piece of glass

136

from a broken mirror. I looked into it and I saw your eyes...."

"When?"

"After midnight."

"One mustn't do such things. That's sorcery. It's not allowed."

"You wouldn't have come by yourself."

Suddenly clutching him, she let out a wail that made Jacob shudder. Crying, she kissed his face, licked his hand. A howl tore itself from her throat.

"Jacob, don't leave me again, Jacob."

PART TWO

Sarah

8

Once more the Cossacks attacked Poland, once
more they slaughtered Jews in Lublin and the
surrounding areas. Polish soldiers dispatched
many of the survivors. Then the Muscovites
invaded from the east and the Swedes from the
north. It was a time of upheaval and yet the Jews
had to conduct business, supervise the tilling of
leased fields, borrow money, pay taxes, even
marry off daughters. A house built today would be
burned tomorrow. Today a girl was engaged, a few
days later raped. One day a man was rich, the next
poor. Banquets were held one day, the next
funerals for martyrs. The Jews were constantly on
the march, from Lemberg and back to Lemberg,
from Lublin and back to Lublin. A city that was
secure one day was under siege the next. A wealthy
man would wake to find he must carry a beggar's
sack. Entire communities of Jews turned Christian and though some later reassumed their own
faith, others remained in darkness. Poland teemed

with deserted wives, raped women, brides run away from their gentile husbands, men who had been ransomed or who had escaped from prison. God's wrath poured down on his people. But the moment the Jews caught their breath, they returned to Judaism. What else could they do? Accept the religion of the murderer?

A handful of Jews, survivors of burned-out and pillaged towns, gathered in Pilitz, a village on the other side of the Vistula, having gained the consent of the overlord to settle there. The Swedish war had ruined Adam Pilitzky, but not even the Swedes could steal earth, sky, and water. Again the peasants plowed and sowed. Again the earth, soaked with the blood of the innocent and the guilty, brought forth wheat and rye, buckwheat and barley, fruit and vegetables. The retreating Swedish army had set fire to Pilitzky's castle, but a rain storm had extinguished the blaze. A revolt of the peasantry had followed the withdrawal of the Swedes and one of Pilitzky's marshals had been stabbed. Arming his retainers, Pilitzky attacked the rebels, hanging some, and flogging others to death. He ordered the heads of the executed to be placed on poles and publicly exhibited as a warning to the serfs. Birds pecked at the flesh until only naked skulls remained.

Pilitzky had no time for his manor and was a poor manager; his Polish bailiffs were drunkards, drones, and thieves. True, the Jews also swindled if they got the chance, but the owner could brandish a whip over them. A Jew could be flogged like a peasant, imprisoned in a sty, even beheaded. Moreover the Jew was thrifty, saved money, and put it out for usury. One could always go bankrupt and make a settlement with him.

Though Adam Pilitzky was already fifty-four, he looked much younger. He was tall, dark, had brown hair untouched by gray, black eyes and a

141

small goatee. He had spent his youth in France and Italy and had returned with what he termed new ideas. For a time he flirted with Protestantism, but that mood passed and he soon became a zealous Catholic and an enemy of the reformation. The neighboring landowners found him strange, spoke of him as an "odd bird." He continually predicted the collapse of Poland. All of the prominent leaders were rascals, thieves, scum. He himself had taken no part in the Cossack and Swedish wars but accused his countrymen of cowardice. He swore by all that was holy that everyone in Poland could be bought, from the smallest clerk in a town hall to the king. Phrases from the diatribes of the priest Skarga were perpetually on his lips, though he drank heavily and was considered a libertine. The *jus primae noctis* (obsolete elsewhere) was in force in his estates. It was said that his daughter had drowned herself after having been possessed by him. His son had gone mad and had died of jaundice. The rumor was that his wife Theresa was his procuress and had taken the coachman as her lover. Another report was that she copulated with a stallion. Both wife and husband had recently become religious enthusiasts. When the monastery at Czestochow was besieged and Kordecki put up his heroic resistance, they had worked themselves into a religious frenzy.

Pilitzky's castle was crowded with his and his wife's relatives, who, though they belonged to the aristocracy, did the work of maids and lackeys. Once when Lady Pilitzky found a hole in the tablecloth she emptied a glass of wine over a female cousin. She required that the tablecloths, towels, shirts, underwear, silver, and porcelain be counted weekly. When Adam Pilitzky became angry, he took a rod and beat the old maids. The great fortune he and his wife had inherited between them had been dissipated. The neighborhood joke was that all that remained of Theresa Pilitzky's jewelry was a single gold hairpin. At every opportunity Adam Pilitzky warned that Poland would have no peace until all Protestants, Cossacks, and Jews were killed—particularly the Jews who had secretly bribed the traitor Radziszewski and conspired with the Swedes. Pilitzky had given his word to the priests that when Poland was rid of its enemies, no Jew would lay foot on his property. But, as usual, he did the opposite of what he said. First he permitted a Jewish contractor to settle. This Jew began to complain that he needed a quorum. Soon the Jews were granted the right to build a synagogue. Someone died and a cemetery was necessary. Finally the Jews of Pilitz imported a rabbi and a ritual slaughterer. So now Pilitz had become a community. Adam Pilitzky cursed and spat, but the Jews had done much to get him back on his feet. It was they who saw to it that the peasants plowed, harvested, mowed hay. They paid cash to Pilitzky for grain and cattle, repaired the pond in which he stocked fish, built a dairy. They even brought beehives for honey into the estate. Pilitzky no longer had to go looking for a tailor, a shoemaker, a furrier, a bell maker. Jewish craftsmen repaired his castle, patched the roof, rebuilt the ovens. Jews could do anything; rebind books, mend parquet floors, put glass in windows, frame pictures. When someone was ill, a Jewish doctor bled him or applied leeches and had a stock of medicines ready. A Jewish goldsmith made a bracelet for Lady Pilitzky and took a note instead of cash. Even the Jesuits, despite their slander and pamphlets, dealt with the Jews and used their handicraft.

At first Pilitzky had kept count of the number of Jews who settled on his property. But before long, he lost track. He didn't know their language and

143

could scarcely tell one Jew from another. He warned constantly, "Unless the Poles change radically, there'll be another Chmielnicki. Anyway, everything's collapsing."

II

One day a man and woman trudged into Pilitz, sacks on their shoulders, bundles in their hands. The Jews emerged from stores and workshops to welcome the newcomers. The man, tall, broad-shouldered, blue-eyed, had a brown beard. Wearing a kerchief, seemingly younger than her husband, the woman looked almost gentile. The man was called Jacob. Asked where he was from, he mentioned the name of a distant city. The women soon learned that the young wife was a mute, and at first were amazed that so handsome a man should have made such a marriage. But, then, was it so astonishing? Marriages were made in heaven. Jacob gave his wife's name as Sarah, and she was immediately nicknamed, "Dumb Sarah."

The Jews inquired if Jacob was a scholar because they were looking for a teacher. "I know a chapter or two of the Pentateuch," Jacob said hesitantly.

"That's all that's needed."

It was springtime, the period between Passover and Pentecost. So now Pilitz had a school. Jacob and his mute wife were given a room and promised a house of their own if Jacob proved a good teacher. Pilitzky owned many forests and lumber was cheap in the town. The new teacher was supplied with a table, a dunce's stool, and a cat-o'-nine-tails; he whittled a pointer and printed the letters of the alphabet on paper. Most of the children were in the early grades and the class assembled under a tree. Jacob sat with his charges

144

in the shade, teaching them the alphabet, how to read syllables and words, instructing each child according to his age and knowledge. Because of the great amount of construction in progress, logs and lumber were piled all around, and the children built swings out of the boards and made little houses from chips and shavings. The town had no woman teacher and some of the parents sent daughters as well as sons to the cheder to learn their prayers and master a little writing. The girls made mud pies and sang and danced in a circle. The smaller boys and girls played house. The husband went to the synagogue to pray, his wife fixed supper for him and served it on a broken plate. The bread was a sliver of bark, the soup sand, the meat a pine cone. Jacob misplaced his cat-o'-nine-tails. He never whipped the children or scolded them, but lovingly pinched their cheeks and kissed their foreheads. These children had been born after the catastrophe.

The community liked Jacob immediately and pitied him for having a mute wife. True, Dumb Sarah behaved as a Jewess should, went to the ritual bath, soaked the meat and salted it, on Friday prepared the Sabbath pudding, burned a piece of chalah dough, blessed the candles; on the Sabbath, she stood in the woman's section of the synagogue and moved her lips as though praying. But sometimes she behaved in a way unbecoming a teacher's wife, took off her shoes and walked barefooted, laughed unrestrainedly, exhibiting a mouthful of unblemished peasant-like teeth. Dumb Sarah labored with the skill of a country woman, chopped wood, tended a vegetable garden she had planted behind the house, washed clothes in the river. When her own washing was done, she helped other women who had small children. She was remarkably strong and worked for everyone— and for nothing. Once she undressed in front of the

145

women and swam in the river naked. Certain that she would drown at the spot where the waters swirled dangerously, the matrons, none of whom knew how to swim, broke into screams. But Dumb Sarah fearlessly crossed the whirlpool. Her audience was astounded. Dumb all right! Just like an animal.

This incident was soon followed by another which gave the people of Pilitz more to gossip about. The construction of Jacob's house was begun; and not only did Jacob assist in the work but Sarah also, although she was already pregnant and had stopped going to the ritual bath. Jacob went to the forest and felled trees, trimmed them with his ax and dragged them to the village. Sarah hauled logs and lumber as though she were a man. The house didn't cost the community a groschen. Nor was Jacob as unlearned as everyone had believed. One Saturday the reader lost his voice and Jacob read from the scroll; several times he was observed opening a Gemara in the study house. When he prayed he stood in a corner, swaying piously, and occasionally sighing. He said little about his past and the community concluded that he must have lost his family in the massacres. If they sought to engage him in conversation, he walked away, saying, "What happened happened. One must start over again."

The men respected him and the women liked him. When the matrons sat on their benches in front of their houses Sabbath afternoons, they agreed among themselves that Dumb Sarah had more luck than brains. No one denied that she was young, good-looking, and healthy, but what did a man want with a dumbbell? A husband liked to talk to his wife and hear her opinions. What a calamity, God forbid, if the child should take after its mother. Such things happened. One woman known as a wit remarked: "Well, some men would

146

regard a silent wife as a blessing. No tongue, no torment."

"Oh, that's just talk."

"Well, it's better than having a blind one."

"Have you noticed," a young woman asked, "that as soon as it's dark she closes the shutters?"

"What does that prove?"

"That she loves him."

"Who wouldn't?"

On the Sabbath, Dumb Sarah discarded her kerchief, put on a bonnet, pointed shoes, an embroidered apron, and a dress with flowers that she had brought from far off. Going to synagogue, she held a prayer book in one hand and a handkerchief in the other. [This was allowed since the town of Pilitz had been enclosed in a wire which removed the Sabbath ban against carrying things.] When the women tried to communicate with her by hand signs, she smiled and shook her head, apparently unable to understand. The women poked fun at her, yet agreed she had a kind heart. She visited the sick and massaged their bodies with turpentine and alcohol. She prepared stewed apples and prunes as a treat for her husband's pupils on the Sabbath afternoon. Her stomach swelled, became pointed, and the women calculated she would give birth around Succoth or early in the month of Cheshvan.

Since the mute are also deaf, the women did not watch their words in her presence. Once, while Sarah sat with her prayer book open, a woman remarked, "She reads as well as the sacrificial rooster."

"Perhaps she's been taught."

"How can you teach the dumb?"

"Maybe she became dumb with fright."

"She doesn't look frightened."

"Perhaps the murderers cut out her tongue."

The women asked to see her tongue. At first,

Sarah didn't seem to understand, then she began to laugh and her cheeks dimpled. She stuck out a pink tongue, as pointed as a dog's.

III

Wanda, not Jacob, had thought of playing the mute, realizing Yiddish would take her too long to learn; the few words she knew she spoke like a gentile. Her idea of passing herself off as a "Cossack bride" who could now only speak the language of the steppes was discarded because she didn't know that tongue either. She was not an adroit liar and would have been unmasked immediately. Jacob and she underwent many hardships and dangers before she decided on the role of a mute. They went to distant Pilitz because Jacob was too famous in Lublin and the surrounding areas as the slave who had returned. At night when Sarah, as all Jewish converts were called, closed the shutters, Jacob spoke with her and instructed her in their religion. He had already taught her the prayers and how to write Yiddish and now they studied the Pentateuch, the Books of Samuel and Kings, the Code of the Jewish Law; he told her stories from the Gemara and Midrash. Her diligence was amazing, her memory good; many of the questions she asked were the same the commentators had raised. Teaching her, he dared not lift his voice. Not only did he dread the gentiles and their laws, but also the Jews who would expel him from the village if they learned his wife was a convert. Sarah's presence in Pilitz imperiled the town. If the Polish authorities learned that a Christian girl had been seduced into Judaism, there would be reprisals. God knows what accusations would be made. The priests only wanted a pretext. And if the Jews got wind of it, the elders would immediately investigate the circumstances

148

of the conversion and would guess correctly that Sarah had left her own religion because of Jacob—women being little interested in speculative matters; and Jacob would be excommunicated.

There was so much concern with the lineage and matrimonial connections of scholars that Jacob had not divulged that he was learned. The few scholarly books he had brought he kept hidden. He built his house with thick walls and constructed an alcove, windowless and hidden from the world by a clump of trees, where he and his beloved wife could study in secret. True, they had lived together illicitly, but since then they had fulfilled the law of Moses and Israel by standing under the canopy. Sarah now fervently believed in God and the Torah and obeyed all the laws. Now and then she erred, doing things upside down according to her peasant understanding, or speaking in a manner that was inappropriate. But Jacob corrected her kindly and made her understand the reason for each law and custom. Teaching others, Jacob realized, one also instructed oneself; correcting Sarah's behavior, answering her questions, eradicating her errors, many problems about which he would not have otherwise thought were clarified for him. Often her questions demanded answers which were not to be found in this world. She asked: "If murder is a crime, why did God permit the Israelites to wage war and even kill old people and small children?" If the nations distant from the Jews, such as her own people, were ignorant of the Torah, how could they be blamed for being idol worshipers? If Father Abraham was a saint, why did he drive Hagar and her son Ishmael into the desert with a gourd of water? The question that recurred more often than any other was why did the good suffer and the evil prosper. Jacob told her repeatedly he couldn't solve all the world's riddles, but Sarah kept on insisting, "You know everything."

He had warned her many times about the unclean days, reminding her that when she was menstruating she could not sit on the same bench with him, take any object from his hand, nor even eat at the same table unless there was a screen between her plate and his. He was not allowed to sit on her bed, nor she on his; not even the headboards of their beds ought to touch at this time. But these were some of the things that Sarah either forgot or ignored, for she kept on insisting she must be near him. She was capable of running over and kissing him in the middle of her period. Jacob rebuked her and told her such acts were forbidden by the Torah, but she took these restrictions lightly, and this caused Jacob sorrow. She was very scrupulous about less important things. She immersed all the dishes in the ritual bath, and kept on inquiring about milk and meat. At times she forgot she was a mute and broke into song. Jacob trembled. Not only was there the danger of her being heard, but a pious daughter of Israel should not provoke lust with the lascivious sound of her voice. Nor had she let the bath attendant shave her head like the other women's, though Jacob had asked her to. Sarah cut her own hair with shears; occasionally ringlets pushed out from under her kerchief.

Though Jacob had built them a house, Sarah complained nightly that she wished to leave Pilitz. She could not remain silent forever, and she feared what would happen to her child. The young must be taught to speak, and given love. She kept asking whether her Yiddish had improved; Jacob assured her she was doing well but it wasn't so. She mispronounced the words, twisted the constructions, and whatever she uttered came out upside down. Often her mistakes made Jacob laugh. Even a few words dropping from her tongue and there was no mistaking she had been born a gentile. Now that she was pregnant Jacob was more frightened than ever. A woman in labor cannot control her screams. Unless she could endure the birth pangs in silence, Sarah would give herself away.

Yes, the day Jacob had left Josefov for the village where he had been a slave for five years, he had picked up a burden which became heavier with the passage of time. His years of enforced slavery had been succeeded by a slavery that would last as long as he lived. "Well, Gehenna is for people and not for dogs," he had once heard a water carrier say. Yet he had saved a soul from idolatry, even though he had stumbled into transgression. At night when Sarah and he lay in their beds which were arranged so as to form a right angle (the room wasn't long enough to have one at the foot of the other), the couple whispered to each other for hours without tiring. Jacob informed Sarah about the moral life, spicing his text with little parables. She spoke of how much she loved him. They often recalled the summers he had lived in the barn when she had brought food to him. Now those days were far off and as shadowy as a dream. Sarah found it difficult to believe that the village still existed and that Basha and Antek and possibly her mother still lived there. According to the law, Jacob said, she no longer was a member of her family. A convert was like a newborn child and had a fresh soul. Sarah was like Mother Eve who had been formed from Adam's rib; her husband was her only relative. "But," Sarah urgued, "my father is still my father," and she began to cry about Jan Bzik who had had so hard a life and now lay buried among idolaters. "You will have to bring him into Paradise," she told Jacob. "I won't go without him."

151

The peasants, now busy in the fields preparing for harvest, rarely brought produce to town. Jewish peddlers traveled to the country with packs on their backs to buy chickens, millet and corn. Sarah, needing supplies, picked up a sack and set out, though Jacob had insisted this was no errand for a pregnant woman, much less the wife of a teacher. But Sarah longed for the fields and pastures. The moment Pilitz was behind her, she kicked off her shoes and slung them over her shoulder. The townswomen smirked, seeing her go, asked each other, "Now how will the dumbbell bargain?"

Sarah's presumed deafness left the women free to slander and ridicule her in her presence. She was referred to as a dumb animal, a golem, a simpleton, a cabbage head. Jacob was pitied for having brought home such a goose. The guess was she had a rich father who had given a substantial dowry to marry her off. Still, Jacob was a fool to have led such a nanny goat under the canopy. Sarah had to keep smiling though she could scarcely retain her tears. The peasants were openly scornful. Running their fingers across their throats, they would point toward the road, pretending the Cossacks were coming. Pan Pilitzky, they said, was infesting Poland with Jewish lice, and they prophesied wars, plagues, and famines, Heaven's revenge for permitting the God murderers to settle there. Sarah found it difficult to remain silent.

When she was alone with Jacob at night she cried and repeated what the Jews said. "You must not repeat such things," Jacob scolded her. "That's calumny. It's as great a sin as eating pork."

"So they're allowed to abuse us but I can say nothing?"

"No, they're not behaving properly either."

"Well, they all do it, even Breina, and she's the wife of an elder."

"Those who do such things will be punished in Heaven. The sacred books warn that all those who gossip, ridicule, or speak evil of others, will burn in the fires of Gehenna."

"All of them?"

"There's no lack of room in Gehenna."

"The rabbi's wife laughed too."

"There are no favorites in Heaven. When Moses sinned, he was punished."

Sarah became thoughtful.

"No, speaking evil can't be one thousandth the sin of eating pork, or no one would do it."

"Come, I'll show you what it says in the Torah."

Jacob, opening the Pentateuch, translated the text and told her how each of the sins had been interpreted by the Gemara. Several times he walked to the door to assure himself no one was listening or looking through the keyhole. "Why do the Jews obey some laws and break others?" Sarah whispered.

Jacob shook his head.

"That's the way it's always been. The prophets denounced it. The temple was destroyed for that reason. It's easier not to eat pig than to curb your tongue. Come and I will read you a chapter from Isaiah."

Jacob turned to Isaiah and translated the first chapter. Sarah listened in amazement. The prophet said the same things as Jacob: God had had enough of the blood of bullocks and the fat of lambs; people were not to come into his presence with bloody hands. The elders of Israel were compared by the prophet to the lords of Sodom God had destroyed. Late though it was, the wick in the shard continued to burn and moths circled the flame. The shadow of Jacob's head wavered on the ceiling. A cricket chirped from behind the oven. Love and fear mingled in Sarah. She dreaded the angry God who dwelled in Heaven and overheard every word and thought; she feared the peasants desirous of murdering Jews again and burying children alive; she was anxious about the Jews who were provoking the Almighty by obeying only one part of the Torah. Sarah promised not to repeat the evil gossip she heard, though as it was she had not told him everything. It was said in town that one of the storekeepers gave false measure. There was a rumor that a man had stolen from his partner at the time of the massacres. Sarah had been told that the Jews were the chosen people and she wanted to ask how they could be so favored when they committed such crimes. But that Jacob was righteous was evident to her. If God loved him as much as she did, he would live forever.

In her prayers she told God that she had no one but Jacob. She could never love another. She had joined a community but felt like a stranger. Though she had fled the peasants, she had not become one of the Jews of Pilitz. Jacob was husband, father, and brother to her. The moment the candle was extinguished she called him to her bed. "You, gentile," Jacob said jokingly: "Don't you know that a daughter of Israel mustn't be immodest or she'll be divorced without a settlement?"

"What can a daughter of Israel do?"

"Bear children and serve God."

"I intend to bear you a dozen."

He would not lie with her immediately, but first told her stories of upright men and women. She asked what went on in Paradise and what would occur when the Messiah came. Would Jacob still be her husband? Would they speak Hebrew? Would he take her with him to the rebuilt temple? When the Messiah came, Jacob said, each day would be

154

as long as a year, the sun would be seven times as bright, and the Saints would feed on leviathan and the wild ox and drink the wine prepared for the days of redemption.

"How many wives will each man have?" Sarah asked.

"I'll have only you."

"I'll be old by then."

"We'll be young forever."

"What kind of a dress will I wear?"

Lying with Jacob was for her a foretaste of Paradise. She often wished that the night would last forever and she could continue to listen to his words and receive his caresses. That hour in the darkness was her reward for what she had endured during the day. When she fell asleep, her dreams took her to her native village; she entered the hut where she had lived; she stood on the mountain. Strange events involving Antek, Basha, and her mother occurred. Her father, once more alive, spoke wisely to her, and though she forgot his words as soon as she awoke, their resonance rang in her ears. Sometimes she dreamed Jacob had left her, and cried in her sleep. Jacob always awakened her.

"Oh, Jacob, you're still here. Thank God." His face would become hot and wet from her tears.

V

A coach drawn by a team of four horses, with two coachmen in front and two footmen in the rear, rode into the market place at noon. One of the coachmen blew his horn. The Jews of Pilitz became alarmed. Pilitzky rarely came to town in such pomp, and never in summer before the harvest. He was carrying a sword; he looked drunk. Leaping from the coach, he drew his sword from its scabbard and screamed, "Where is

155

Gershon? I'm going to cut off his head. I'm going to tear him to pieces and pour acid into his wounds—him and his family as well. I'm going to throw the whole batch of them to the dogs."

Some of the Jews scurried off. Others rushed to Pilitzky and threw themselves at his feet. The women began to wail. The children in Jacob's class heard the tumult and came running to have a look at the lord, at the coach, at the horses with their heads held high in their fine harnesses. One of Gershon's sycophants hastened to him and warned him that Pilitzky was drunk and looking for him. Gershon was the most powerful man in Pilitz, since he leased the fields of the manor and managed them as if they were his own. He was known in town as a shady dealer. He'd built himself a large house and had acquired three sons-in-law, all from wealthy families, who had become respectively the town's rabbi, ritual slaughterer and public contractor. The last supplied the flour at Passover and had built the synagogue. Gershon had retained the wardenship of the burial society and charged exorbitant prices for graves, although Pilitzky had donated the land for the cemetery. Gershon also collected the taxes, usurping the function of the town's seven elders as set forth by the Council of the Four Countries. Taxation in Pilitz worked on the principle that the friends and flatterers of Gershon paid little or nothing; all others tottered under the weight of his levies. Gershon was ignorant but had granted himself the title "Our Teacher" and did not allow the cantor to intone the eighteen benedictions until he, Gershon, had said them over to himself. When he got the whim to take a steam bath in the middle of the week, the bath attendant was forced to heat the water at the community's expense.

Those whom Gershon had trampled threatened

to denounce him to Pilitzky and to the Council in Lublin, but Gershon feared no man. He had friends who sat on the Council and he held Pilitzky's note for a thousand gulden. He was an intimate of other landowners, Pilitzky's enemies. Gershon, it seemed, had forgotten that the Jews were in exile. Yes, Pilitzky was looking for him and Gershon was advised to take cover in an attic or cellar until the wrath of the lord of Pilitz subsided. But Gershon was not one to have himself thought a coward, and he put on his silk overcoat, his sable hat, wrapped a sash around his waist, and walked out to meet Adam Pilitzky. Though Gershon dressed like a rabbi, he had the florid complexion of a butcher. His nose was flat, his lips thick; his belly stuck out as though he were pregnant. One of his eyes was higher and set in a larger socket than the other. He had heavy, bushy eyebrows. Not only was he aggressive but stubborn. When he rose to make a speech, every third word was a barbarism; he babbled until everyone fell asleep, and the opposition never had a chance to voice its opinion.

Now, walking slowly, Gershon approached his overlord. He did not come alone but accompanied by his entourage: the butchers, the horse dealers, and the men of the burial society whom he banqueted twice a year and who got all the sinecures in town. Before Gershon could open his mouth, Pilitzky screamed: "Where's the red bull?"

Gershon considered the question for a moment and then replied. "I sold him to the butcher, my lord."

"You dirty Jew. You sold my bull."

"Sir, while I lease the manor land, I'm in control."

"So you're in control. Seize him, boys. We'll hang him here." All the Jews shouted in terror—even Gershon's enemies joined in. Gershon tried to speak and retreated a few steps, but the coachmen and footmen caught hold of him. Pilitzky cried out, "Get the rope."

Some of the Jews fell to their knees, prostrated themselves, bowed—as on Yom Kippur when the cantor repeats the ritual service of the ancient temple in Jerusalem. Women screamed. Gershon struggled with his captors. The sash was torn from his waist. Pilitzky shouted, "A pole. Bring me a pole."

"We can hang him from the lamp post, my lord."

Jacob, hearing the clamor which was not unlike that when the Cossacks had attacked Josefov, came running. Gershon's wife was clasping one of Pilitzky's knees, refusing to let go. Pilitzky was trying to shake himself free of her and had his sword raised as if about to sever her head. The women were pushing and milling and wailing insanely. One dug her nails into her cheeks, another clutched her breasts, a third scratched at her husband to do something. Gershon was a crass man. The Jews of Pilitz disliked him but they could not stand by and see him hanged summarily. Gershon's daughters-in-law fell into each other's arms. The rabbi also prostrated himself at Pilitzky's feet; his skull cap having come off, his long side locks dragged in the dirt. It was almost as if the massacres had again begun. Gershon's followers, instead of disarming Pilitzky's servants which they might have done easily, just stood gaping with legs spread wide, amazed it seemed at their own impotence. But when had a Jew ever defied a Polish noble? Then out of the study house walked the beadle bearing the holy scroll as if it would quiet Pilitzky's wrath. There were shouts bidding the old man advance closer; others among the crowd motioned him back, protesting the sacrilege. He stood swaying indecisively on his rickety legs as though about to fall. Seeing him totter, a great cry of lamentation rose from the people. Jacob stood transfixed, knowing he must say nothing, yet equally certain he could not remain silent. Stepping forward, he ran quickly to Pilitzky and took off his hat.

"Mighty lord, a man is not killed for selling a bull."

The market place became quiet. Everyone knew that Gershon had declared war on Jacob because Jacob had taken the place of the reader. Gershon didn't like scholars, would never have tolerated Jacob's appointment if he had known that this was a man who could understand both text and footnotes. Now Jacob came to his assistance. Astonished, Pilitzky stared at the Jew in front of him.

"Who are you?"

"I am the teacher."

"What's your name?"

"Jacob."

"Oh! Are you that Jacob who cheated Esau out of his birthright?" An inhuman laugh burst from Pilitzky's throat.

Hearing the lord of Pilitz laugh, everyone joined in—the Jews, Pilitzky's men; Pilitzky doubled up with mirth. Was it merely a joke, a nobleman's prank such as the Polish landowners often played on their Jewish tenants? These games always terrified the Jews since such fun sometimes turned serious. But the men still held onto Gershon—who was the only one not laughing. His yellow eyes had lost none of their arrogance; his thick, mustached lip was drawn back into a snarl, revealing sparse, yellow teeth. Gershon looked like an animal at bay about to die in a struggle with a stronger adversary. Pilitzky howled with laughter, clapped his hands, clutched at his knees, and gasped. Those who had prostrated themselves rose and, relieved, bellowed with a mad exuberance. Even the rabbi laughed. The women collapsed into each other's arms, their knees buckling, their laughter turning to tears.

"Mommalas, Poppalas, tsitselas," Pilitzky mimicked and started braying again. The whole community joined in, every face with its own particular expression and grimace. The sight of one old matron, who had lost her bonnet and whose unevenly clipped scalp resembled a newly sheared ewe, started the women off once more, but this time their laughter was genuine.

Then all laughter ceased. Pilitzky gave a final burst and scowled again.

"Who are you? What are you doing here?" he asked Jacob. "Answer me, Jew."

"I am the teacher, my lord."

"What do you teach? How to steal the host? How to poison wells? How to use Christian blood to make matzoth?"

"God forbid, my lord. Such acts are prohibited by Jewish law."

"Prohibited, are they? We know. We know. Your cursed Talmud teaches you how to fool the Christian mob. You've been driven from every country, but King Casimir opened our gates wide to you. And how do you repay us? You've established a new Palestine here. You ridicule and curse us in Hebrew. You spit on our relics. You blaspheme our God ten times a day. Chmielnicki taught you a lesson, but you need a stronger one. You love all Poland's enemies—Swedes, Muscovites, Prussians. Who gave you permission to come here?" Pilitzky screamed at Jacob, shaking his fist. "This is my earth, not yours. My ancestors shed blood for it. I don't need you to teach Jewish vermin how to defile my country. We have enough parasites already. We're more dead than alive."

Pilitzky ceased his invective and foamed at the mouth. Once more, eyeing each other in dread, the

Jews bent, ready to fall to the ground and beg for mercy. The elders signaled among themselves. Picking up his skull cap, the rabbi placed it, still dirty, on his head. The woman whose bonnet had fallen off clapped it back on, askew, its beaded front to the side. Pilitzky's men tugged at Gershon again, as though trying to shake him out of his clothes. The beadle still swayed back and forth with the scroll. Evidently the story was not to end happily. Men and women began to detach themselves from the crowd and to slip away, some going to close their shops, others running into their houses and locking the doors. "Don't run away, Jews," Pilitzky shouted. "There's no escape. I'll strangle you wherever you are. When I finish with you, you'll mourn the day your wretched mothers squeezed you from their leprous wombs."

"Magnanimous lord, we are not running away. Mighty benefactor, we await your pleasure."

"I have asked you something," Pilitzky shouted, turning to Jacob. "Answer me."

Jacob didn't remember the question. Pilitzky reached out as if to grab the teacher by his collar. But Jacob was too tall for him.

"Forgive me, my lord," Jacob bowed his head. "I have forgotten the question."

Pilitzky, having forgotten himself, looked confused. He had noticed that this Jew, unlike the others, spoke good Polish. His anger left him and he felt something akin to shame at having made such a display before these paupers, the survivors of Chmielnicki's blood bath. He had always considered himself a compassionate man. Tears came to his eyes. Prayers to Jesus and the apostles passed through his head. From boyhood on, he had expected to die young; a fortune teller had predicted an early end. Now he looked for some excuse to terminate this saturnalia. His turbulent spirit stood midway between contrition and anger.

Should he ask forgiveness of the Jews, that wilful people God had chosen? There was a bitter taste in his mouth and his nose tickled. I wouldn't behave this way if my life weren't chaos. That cursed woman has ruined me. Suddenly he had an impulse to toss coins to the crowds. That would show them that he was no Haman. But when he reached into his pocket he remembered he didn't have a groschen, and he was overwhelmed with self-pity. That's what these Jews have done to me, he thought, bled me dry. Seeing the old beadle, swaying unsteadily with the holy scroll on his shoulder, he yelled, "Why did you bring out the scroll? How can that help you? It would be better if you followed what is written there instead of using it to mask your crimes. Carry it back to the synagogue, you old rascal."

From every side shouts came, "Carry back the scroll. Carry back the scroll." The lord of Pilitz had relented, the Jews sensed. The beadle gave a final sway and bore the scroll into the study house. But the men still held Gershon pinioned. Pilitzky's mood might change again. He surveyed the crowd, a bitter look in his eyes as if searching for another victim. Dumb Sarah walked into the square carrying an apronful of herbs. Having gone into the fields, she had not heard the noise of Pilitzky's arrival and knew nothing of what had happened. She saw the coach and horses, Pilitzky's men, Pilitzky himself, and Jacob, hat in hand, standing humbly before the lord of Pilitz. Sarah raised her arms, wailed, and the herbs fell from her apron. What she had dreaded had come to pass. Her nightmares had been true omens. Breaking through the crowd, she pushed her way to Jacob, and screaming wildly threw herself at Pilitzky's feet. Pilitzky turned pale and retreated. She followed him, crawling like a worm and clutching at his legs. "Have pity, Pan," she lamented in

Polish. "Mercy, gentle lord. He's all I've got. I carry his child in my womb. Kill me instead. My head for his. Let him go free, Pan. Let him go free."

"Who is this woman? Get up."

"Forgive him, my lord. Forgive him. He's committed no crime. He's honest, my lord. A holy man."

Jacob bent to raise her and then paused, terrified. Only then did he realize that Sarah had given herself away: she had spoken. In the confusion, no one appeared to have understood what had happened. Then men spread their hands and raised their eyebrows; women clutched their heads; Pilitzky's servants momentarily let go of Gershon. Even the horses, until then standing silently, lost in equine meditations remote from the struggles of men, turned their heads. Gershon looked baffled and outraged. Like many overbearing men, he resented having things happen he could neither control nor comprehend. A woman slapped both of her cheeks screaming, "Oh, I've seen everything."

"What is this? Who is she?" Pilitzky asked.

"My lord, she's a mute."

"What? A mute?"

"Gracious Lord, she's as dumb as a fish. Deaf and dumb."

"Yes, gracious lord, dumb, dumb, a mute." Cries came from all directions.

"Hey, rabbi, is that a fact? Is this woman a mute?" Pilitzky said, turning to the rabbi.

"Yes, my lord, she's the wife of the teacher. She's deaf and dumb. This is a miracle."

"Children, I'm going to faint"—and a woman fell to the ground.

"Help. Water! Water!"

"Oh, my God"—and another woman fainted.

Jacob, bending, pulled Sarah to her feet. Her limp body lay against his shoulder, supported by his arm; she trembled, gasping, sobbing. Pilitzky rested his hand on the hilt of his sword. "What is this, Jew? Some kind of farce?"

"No farce, my lord. She's deaf and dumb. Deaf as the wall and dumb as a fish."

"My lord, we all know she's mute," witnesses from the crowd attested.

"Are you prepared to swear to that?"

"My lord, we've invented nothing."

"Hey, you, Jew, is your wife really dumb?"

"Yes, my lord."

"Always been that way?"

"As long as we've been married."

Jacob did not consider this a lie since Sarah had assumed her role before stepping under the canopy. All around him the townswomen were screaming that it was indeed so, swearing by their husbands and their children that this was Dumb Sarah who everyone knew was unable to talk. Pilitzky's men stood gaping while their master considered this strange occurrence.

"I don't believe you, Jews, not a word of it. This is just another one of your tricks. You want to fool me and make me look ridiculous. Remember Jews, if this is a lie, you'll be flayed alive, I'll herd you into your synagogue and set it on fire. We'll roast you slowly, as sure as my name is Adam Pilitzky."

"Gracious lord, we are telling the truth."

VI

Pilitzky realized the Jews were telling the truth. Their open mouths and bewildered looks told him this was a miracle. Adam Pilitzky had been waiting for a miracle ever since the start of the wars and invasions. One was needed to save Poland. Prior Chodecki's resistance at Czestochow and Stephan Czanecki's campaign against the Swedes, which had rallied the Polish armies and revived the cause of Catholicism, had seemed to be that miracle. Now from every side came reports of new wonders. An image of the Virgin had wept real tears which the people gathered in a silver chalice. On church steeples stone crosses flamed in the dark of night. Dead armies, dressed in the uniforms of a hundred years ago, marched against the enemies of Poland and drove them from fortified positions. Ghost riders were seen galloping on phantom horses. Legendary heroes, dressed in helmets and breastplates, brandished swords and spears as they led charges. Monks and nuns, long since residents of Paradise, put on bodies again and roamed the countryside comforting the people and urging them to pray.

Here a church bell rang by itself, and there an ancient coach was seen driving down a road into a wall and disappearing as if swallowed up. Birds spoke with human voices and a dog led a battalion out of ambush. In one village it had rained blood, in another fishes and toads. In one instance wine had been lacking for the mass and God's mother had opened her lips and wine had flowed out. An almost blind crone had watched a flaming ship flying the Polish ensign sail across the sky. These signs and portents had invigorated the nation's spirit and renewed its belief in heaven.

Nevertheless, Adam Pilitzky had seen no miracles himself and resented this. The devil subverted and denied the wonders of God in a thousand ways; hidden in every heart was some doubt. Often when Pilitzky lay awake thinking of what was going on in the country, Lucifer came and whispered in his ear: "Don't they all speak of miracles? The Greek Orthodox, the Protestants, even the infidel Turks? How does it come about that God sometimes rides with the Protestants bringing them victories? Why doesn't he visit them with the plagues of Pharaoh or rain down stones as he will on Gog and Magog?" Pilitzky listened to Lucifer; at heart, he may have believed man merely an animal who returns to dust, and hence condoned his wife's licentiousness.

The revolt of his serfs and the cruelties with which he had suppressed the rebellion had further mortified Pilitzky's spirit. He knew that widows and orphans sorrowed because of him. At night he had visions of bodies hanging from the gibbets, their feet blue, their eyes glassy, their tongues extended. He suffered from cramps and headaches; his skin itched. There were days when he prayed for death or planned suicide. Not even wine and vodka could calm him now. Nor were the pleasures of the body as intense as they had been. He was always on the lookout for new sensations to stave off impotency. Because of the perverseness of that witch Theresa, now only her infidelities aroused his lust. He made her describe her affairs in detail. When she had exhausted the catalog of her debauchery, he forced her to invent adventures. Husband and wife had driven each other into an insane labyrinth of vice. He procured for her and she procured for him. She watched him corrupt peasant girls and he eavesdropped on her and her lovers. He had warned her many times that he would stab her, she teased about poisoning his food. But both were pious, lit candles, went to confession, and contributed money for the building of churches and religious monuments. Often Adam Pilitzky opened the door of their private chapel and found Theresa, her cheeks wet with tears, a crucifix pressed to her bosom, kneeling before the altar deep in contemplation. Theresa spoke of entering a nunnery; Pilitzky toyed with the idea of becoming a monk.

Pilitzky could never have described the torments he had endured during the last few years. Only God, aware of all the temptations and pitfalls besetting man, and compassionately viewing His creatures' follies and weaknesses, knew how much Pilitzky had suffered through shame and guilt. What the lord of Pilitz wanted was a sign that some supernal eye looked down and took notice, some proof that more than blind chance governed the world. Now heaven, it seemed, had decided to put an end to his doubts.

Pilitzky looked at Sarah and Jacob, the wife clinging to the husband. No, this was no fraud. He could see the Jews glancing at each other and staring at the couple incredulously. There was a lump in Pilitzky's throat; he found it difficult to keep from crying. Then, remembering that the mute had spoken of Jacob as a holy man, he said in a firm voice, "Forgive me, Jacob. I did not mean to insult you. If you are truly a holy man as the mute has attested, I respect you even though you are a Jew."

"Gracious lord, there is nothing holy about me. I am an ordinary individual, a Jew like all the others; perhaps even less than they."

"What? Saints are all modest. Hey, there, men, let that crook Gershon go. I'll settle with him some other time. You are no longer my tenant, Gershon," Pilitzky said. "Don't step on my land again or let me see your face. If I find you trespassing, I'll unleash the dogs."

"Your excellency owes me money," Gershon said. His voice did not waver; his manner showed he did not fear the bluster of overlords. "I have leased the manor lands. I have a contract and your note."

"Huh? Jew, you have nothing. You can wipe yourself with those papers."

"My lord, this is not just. A man's word is sacred. There is a court in Poland."

"Drag me into court, will you, Jew? You're crazy, Jew. You'd be already swinging and the birds

167

would be eating the flesh of your head, as the Bible says, if what just happened had not. You thief, you swindler. I've heard that you filch from the Jews, even. I intend to investigate and see you're punished. As for the court: I fear no one. I am the court and the law. I rule supreme on my manor. Poland is not France where the king tyrannizes over the nobles. Here we have more power than the king. We make and break our kings. Keep that in mind and you'll also keep your head on your shoulders."

"I have paid for the contract."

"What you paid, you got back a long time ago. I'll have no further dealings with you. Move—before I break every bone in your body."

There was a murmuring among the Jews. Gershon's friends and family whispered to him to leave the market place immediately. His wife and daughter tugged at his sleeves, begging him to come home. But Gershon shook his head; his nose wrinkled and his heavy under lip sagged. Powerless though a Jew was against a nobleman, Gershon did not intend to stand by and see himself ruined. He had friends who were richer and more eminent than Pilitzky. He knew that the lord of Pilitz had broken every law of church and state. Moreover, he was involved in law suits that threatened to ruin him. The nobility still preserved their code and demanded that notes and contracts be honored, even those made with the contemptible Jews. Gershon took a step forward.

"I am still the tenant until the expiration of my lease."

"All you are is a dead dog."

Adam Pilitzky turned violently, drew his sword, and ran at Gershon. The Jews wailed and screamed.

9

Jacob saw that he had lost control of himself. Satan fiddled and he danced. "Transgression draws transgression in its train," the Book of Aboth said, and this was surely true in his case. His lust for a forbidden woman had involved him in deception. An entire Jewish community—no, not merely one, a host of them—had been deluded into believing his wife was a mute. Now, grieving women sought out Sarah who was already in her eighth month and begged her to lay her hands on them and bless them. Nor would the elders of Pilitz hear of Jacob not accepting Pilitzky's offer. Gershon had lost the contract; Pilitzky warned that if Jacob refused to become his administrator, he would import one from another town. He even threatened to expel the Jews from Pilitz. A deputation of the elders, led by the rabbi, came to plead with Jacob. Gershon let it be tacitly understood that he was not opposed to this arrangement; Jacob should administer the estate for the time being. Gershon's appraisal was that the teacher, unable to distinguish rye from wheat, would mismanage Pilitzky's interests and this would lead the nobleman to conclude that Gershon was indispensable.

As is usual in the affairs of men, the relationships were complex, and all were based on deception. Woe to the house founded on falsehood. But what could Jacob do? If he told the truth, Sarah and he would be burned at the stake. Sacred though the truth was, the law did not permit one to sacrifice oneself for it.

Lying awake at night, Jacob addressed God: "I know that I have forfeited the world to come, but nevertheless you are still God and I remain your creation. Castigate me, Father, I will submit to your punishment willingly."

The punishment might arrive any day. Sarah would shortly go into labor, and might scream and talk. The truth would sooner or later make itself known. Jacob waited for the rod to strike and worked; there was more than enough for him to do. God had blessed the fields with plenty; the Polish and Swedish armies had not trampled the newly sown crops that year. Jacob woke early and retired late; the lord of Pilitz expected a profit. Gershon also anticipated getting a covert share. However, Jacob, unlike Gershon, received no contract and was only Pilitzky's manager, supervising the peasants and dealing with the grain merchants. He took as wages merely what he needed to subsist.

It was strange to be in the fields surrounded by vegetation again. Sarah and Jacob lived in the house Gershon had built for himself near the castle. Jacob's own house as well as the school he had begun to build remained unfinished. The town was looking for a new teacher—meanwhile someone tutored the children a few hours a day—and the current joke was that since Jacob was managing Pilitz, Gershon should take over the cheder.

Jacob had always been aware that everything in this world is transitory. What was man? Today alive, tomorrow in his grave. The Talmud spoke of the world as a wedding; the poet in the liturgy compared man to a drifting cloud, to a wilting flower, to a fading dream. Yes, everything passed. But never before had Jacob felt the transience of things so keenly. One week a field of grain stood ripening; the next the field was bare. The days were now bright and clear, but rain and snow would soon follow. Jacob had become important in Pilitz; the lord of the manor was now accessible to him. When he passed peasants, they tipped their caps and addressed him as "Pan." The Jews considered him the husband of a holy woman. Jacob knew the end of all this would be disgrace and a walk to the gallows. But meanwhile he saw to it that the grain was harvested, threshed, and stored. He superintended the autumn plowing and the sowing of the winter crop. What he had learned in those years of slavery had become useful. Now when Sarah and he retired at night, they discussed not only the Torah but also the affairs of the manor. Even though Jacob did not keep the account books, little by little he uncovered evidence of Gershon's bad practices. True, Pilitzky in turn stole from the peasantry and he who robs a thief is guilty of no crime; nevertheless Gershon had broken the Eighth Commandment, made enemies for Israel, and committed sacrilege. Well, but everyone has his temptations.

Jacob had risen in the world, but he knew his ascent was of that kind of which it is written, "Pride goeth before a fall." The peasants did not seek to trick him, as they had Gershon, but followed his instructions and even offered him

171

advice. The inhabitants of the castle, Pilitzky's dependents as well as his servants, respected Jacob. The dogs, whose ferocity had made Gershon tremble, for some mysterious reason took to Jacob immediately, wagging their tails when he approached the gate. Everyone in the castle was kind to him, and the Lady Pilitzky sent a maid to help the pregnant and mute Sarah. Pilitzky, himself, went out of his way to talk to Jacob and admired the manager's fluent Polish. Gershon had been another sort, an ignoramus unable to answer any of his patron's questions about Jews and their religion. Jacob replied quoting the holy books. Accustomed to discussing difficult questions lucidly, he invented parables the gentile mind could accept. Pilitzky brought up the same problems that had disturbed Wanda.

One day when Pilitzky sat with Jacob in the library showing him a Bible concordance in Latin which had Hebrew marginalia, Lady Pilitzky entered. Jacob rose from his chair and bowed deeply. Theresa Politzky was a small, plump woman with a round face, short neck, and a high bosom. Her blond hair, twisted in a coronet, reminded Jacob of a Rosh Hashana chalah. She had on a pleated, black silk dress, decorated with ribbons, and around her neck lay a gold cross set with jewels. She had a small nose, full lips, bright dark eyes and a smooth forehead. Jacob had been told that she behaved like a whore, but she walked with sprightly steps and seemed almost girlish, despite her stoutness. She smiled upon seeing the men and her cheeks dimpled. Pilitzky winked at her, "This is Jacob."

"Of course, I've seen you many times from my window."

Lady Pilitzky offered her hand to Jacob who hesitated an instant and then, bowing again, carried her fingers to his lips. One more sin, Jacob thought, kissing her hand, and blushing to the roots of his hair. Pilitzky laughed.

"Well, now that that's done let's have a glass of wine together."

"Forgive me, my lord, but my religion forbids it."

Pilitzky's body tensed.

"Oh, so you're forbidden. It's all right to fleece the Christians, but you mustn't drink wine with them. And who forbids it? The Talmud, naturally, which teaches you how to cheat the Christians."

"The Talmud makes no mention of Christians, only idolators."

"The Talmud considers Christians idolators. Your people gave the world the Bible, but then you denied God's only begotten son, thereby turning from the Father. Today Chmielnicki punishes you; tomorrow another *hetman* will continue your castigation. The Jews will never have peace until they recognize the truth and..."

Lady Pilitzky frowned. "Adam, these discussions have no value."

"No, I will not keep back the truth. That Jew Gershon was a crook and a jackass besides. He didn't know a thing, not even his own Bible. Jacob appears to be not only honest but well-educated. That's why I want to ask him a few questions."

"Not now, Adam. He's busy seeing to the fields."

"Where are the fields running? Sit down, Jew. I'm not going to hurt you. Sit here. Very good! Neither Lady Pilitzky nor I believe in forcing our Faith on anyone. We don't have an inquisition here as they do in Spain. Poland is a free country, too free for its own good. That's why it's collapsing. But that's not your fault. Let me ask you this. You've been waiting for the Messiah for a thousand years—what am I talking about?—for more than fifteen hundred, and he doesn't appear. The reason is clear. He has come already and revealed God's truth. But you are a stubborn people. You keep yourself apart. You regard our meat as unclean, our wine as an abomination. You are not permitted to marry our daughters. You believe you are God's chosen people. Well, what has he chosen you for? To live in dark ghettos and wear yellow patches. I've been out of the country and seen how Jews live abroad. They're all rich and all they think about is profit. Everywhere they're treated like spiders. Why don't you take a good look at yourself and throw away the Talmud? Perhaps the Christians are right after all. Have any of you visited heaven?''

"Really these religious arguments are stupid," Theresa Pilitzky protested.

"What's so stupid about them? People have to discuss things. I'm not speaking to him in anger, but as an equal. If he can convince me that the Jews are right, I'll become a Jew." Pilitzky laughed.

"I can convince no one, my lord," Jacob began to stammer. "I inherited my faith from my parents and I follow it to the best of my ability."

"The idolators had fathers and mothers too. And they were taught that a stone is God. But you Jews demanded the destruction of their temples and the annihilation of their children. The Old Testament says so. Doesn't that prove that one doesn't necessarily follow the parents' faith?"

"The Christians also regard the Bible as sacred."

"Naturally. But one must be logical. Everyone but your people and the infidel Turks have accepted Christianity. You Jews consider yourself cleverer than anyone in Europe or the world. All right, God loves you. What kind of love?—your wives are raped and your children buried alive."

Jacob swallowed hard. "Those were the acts of the Christians."

"What? The Cossacks are no more Christians than I am Zoroastrian. Only the Catholics are Christian. The Russian Orthodox are as idolatrous as their allies the Turks. Protestants are even worse. But this is all irrelevant, Jew."

"None of us knows the ways of Providence, my lord. The Catholics also suffer. They wage war against each other..." Jacob broke off in the middle of his sentence.

For a moment Adam Pilitzky meditated in silence on Jacob's words.

"Of course we suffer. As the Bible says, man was born to suffer. But we suffer for a reason. Our souls are purified through what we endure and rise to heaven. But the real torment begins for the unbeliever after death."

Theresa Pilitzky shook her head. "Really, Adam, where's this getting you? The truth cannot be proved. It can only be found here." Theresa Pilitzky pointed to her heart.

"Yes, that is true, my lady," Jacob said softly.

"Well, I suppose it is. But of what use is this stiff-necked clinging to your faith? In your misguided way, you are attentive to God, and your synagogues are always filled. Once when I was in Lublin, I walked past your prayer houses. Such ecstatic singing! A song rose as if from a thousand voices. But a few years later ten thousand Jews were slaughtered. I talked to someone who saw the Cossacks enter Lublin. The Jews crushed each other in their panic. More died from being trampled on than were killed by the invaders. While this went on, was the sky any less blue? Did the sun stop shining? Where was the God you praise and beseech, whose dear children you claim to be? How do you deal with these facts, Jew? How can you sleep at night remembering?"

"When you're tired enough, your eyes close by themselves."

"I see you avoid answering me..."

"He's right, Adam, he's right. What's there to say? Can we explain our misfortunes any better than he can his? Even searching for an answer is blasphemous. You know that very well."

Pilitzky drew his eyeballs downward and stared crosseyed at Lady Pilitzky. "I know nothing, Theresa. Sometimes I think that the Epicureans and Cynics were right. Have you ever heard of Democritus, Jew?"

"No, my lord."

"Democritus was a philosopher who said that chance ruled everything. The Church has proscribed his writings, but I read him. He believed in neither idols nor God. The world, he said, was the result of blind powers."

"Don't repeat those heresies," Theresa Pilitzky said, interrupting.

"Perhaps he was right."

"Really, Adam."

"Very well, I'll go and lie down. Your eyes close by themselves," he said, echoing Jacob. "Isn't there something you have to say to Jacob, Theresa?"

"Yes, there is."

"Goodbye, then, and don't be afraid of us. Is your wife really a mute?"

"Yes, my lord."

"That means that miracles also happen among the Jews, doesn't it?"

"Yes, my lord."

"Well, I'll go and take a nap."

II

As he left the room, Pilitzky glanced back over his shoulder. Jacob bowed. Lady Pilitzky slowly moved her fan of peacock feathers.

"Sit down. So! Where do such discussions ever

lead? One has to trust that God knows how to manage the world. When the Swedes took the manor, they flogged me in my own castle. I thought it was the end. But the Almighty wanted me to continue living."

Jacob paled. "They flogged you, my lady?"

Lady Pilitzky smiled.

"My dear Jacob, the rod is not particular about rank. Dukes, ladies, your royal highnesses even, are all the same to it. It strikes. The officers found it more amusing just because I was an aristocrat."

"Why did they do this, my lady?"

"Because I said no to the general. My husband was in hiding and I had no one to protect me. If my suitor had been young and handsome, or at least healthy" (Lady Pilitzky's tone changed) "I might have been tempted. 'All's fair in love and war,' as they say. But not with that ugly ape. One look and I said, 'Sir, death is preferable.'"

"I had thought such behavior was limited to Muscovites and Cossacks."

Lady Pilitzky smiled. "Ah, the Swedes are angels? No, Jacob, all men are alike. Frankly, I don't blame them. Women have only one use for them. A child must nurse and doesn't care if the breast belongs to a peasant or a princess. Men are like children."

Demureness and coquetry met in Lady Pilitzky's smile. She looked Jacob straight in the eye and fluttered her lids slightly. Jacob's neck became hot.

"A man has his wife."

"What? To begin with, in wartime, wives don't count. Secondly, one gets tired of a woman. My tailor makes me an expensive dress; so after I wear it three times I'm bored with it and give it to one of my husband's cousins. Men feel the same way. A woman's no longer attractive to a man when he can have her as much as he pleases—and he's off

177

after another. But why should I tell you this? You're a man—tall and with blue eyes..."

The blood rushed to Jacob's face. "The Jews do not behave so."

Lady Pilitzky petulantly shook her fan. "Jew or Tartar, a man is a man. Why, your men were allowed a host of wives. The great kings and prophets had harems."

"Now that's forbidden."

"Who forbade it?"

"Rabbi Gershom, the Light of the Diaspora. He issued the edict."

"The Christians forbid it too. But what does human nature care about edicts? I don't condemn a man for anything. If he gets a woman to say 'yes' I don't condemn her either. My view is that everything comes from God—including lust. And not everyone's a saint, and not every saint was always saintly. Anyway, how does it hurt God? Some take the position that a secret sin where there is no sacrilege injures no one. My husband spent a few years in Italy. There the ladies have both a husband and lover. The lover is called an 'amico.' When a lady goes to the theater, she is escorted by both her gentlemen. Don't forget this happens in the shadow of the Vatican. The amico is often a cardinal or some other Church dignitary. The Pope knows of it, and, if it were such a crime would he tolerate it?"

There was a pause in the conversation. Finally, Jacob said, "Nothing like that occurs among the Jews. A man may not even glance at another woman."

"Just the same they do glance. I know a man's a hypocrite if he claims to be only interested in his wife. Let me ask you something."

"Yes, my lady."

"Where are you from? How does it happen you settled here? Don't think it odd that I pry; I have

178

my reasons. It seems strange that you married a mute. Most Jews aren't as good-looking as you, or as well-bred, and you speak good Polish. You could have had the prettiest girl."

Jacob shook his head. "This is my second marriage."

"What happened to your first wife?"

"The Cossacks killed her and our children."

"In what town?"

"I am from Zamosc."

"Well, that is sad. What do they have against the women and children? And where does your present wife come from?"

"From near Zamosc."

"Why did you marry her? There must have been other women."

"Only a few. Most of the women were killed."

"You must have liked her. It can't be denied that she's good-looking."

"Yes, I did."

Lady Pilitzky rested her fan on her bosom.

"I'll be frank with you, Jacob. Your enemies among the Jews—don't think you don't have any—are spreading the story that your wife is not as mute as she pretends. When my husband first heard this, he was out of his mind with rage, and he wanted to put your Sarah to the test. But I dissuaded him. His idea was to shoot off a pistol behind her and see what happened. I told him you don't play such tricks on a pregnant woman. Adam Pilitzky listens to me. He does whatever I tell him to. In this one respect he's an unusually good husband. You understand yourself that the Jews of Pilitz will suffer if there was no miracle. The clergy in this part of the country, particularly the Jesuits, have their own interests to look out for. All that I want you to know is that you have a close friend in me. Don't be shy and secretive. We are all only flesh and blood underneath our clothes. I want to protect you, Jacob, and I am afraid that you may need protection."

Jacob raised his head slowly.

"Who is spreading these rumors?"

"People have mouths. Gershon is sly and even conspires against my husband. He will come to a bad end, but before that happens he will make trouble."

III

Fear such as he had felt when Zagayek sent for him, arose in Jacob. But now Sarah's life was in danger, also. The Jesuits had interests to protect. Pistols were to be fired near Sarah! I am in a trap, thought Jacob. I must flee. But the child must be born first. With winter approaching, where could he run? What course should he follow—tell Lady Pilitzky the truth? Deny the rumor? He sat silent and helpless, ashamed of his cowardice. Lady Pilitzky surveyed him expertly out of the corner of her eyes, a polished smile on her lips.

"Don't be afraid, Jacob. You remember the saying, 'A great wind but a small rain.' Nothing bad will happen."

"I trust not. Thank you, my lady. I can't thank you enough."

"You can thank me later. Have you seen the castle?"

"No, only this room."

"Come, I will show it to you. The invaders did a great deal of damage, but they left something. At times I agree with my husband—everything's collapsing. The peasants report having seen a huge comet in the sky with a tail stretching from one horizon to the other. It's as it was at the end of the first millennium, or during the Black Plague."

"When did they see the comet? I've seen nothing."

"Nor have I. But my husband has. It's a sign that we can expect some cataclysm: war, pestilence or flood. The Turks are sharpening their scimitars. Suddenly the Muscovites are a power. The Prussians, of course, are always ready for pillage. 'Eat, drink, and be merry. For tomorrow we die.'"

"A life lived in constant fear loses its flavor."

"What? Some have the opposite attitude. I've been through one war after another. But I know how to keep calm when others shiver. I laugh when most people cry. 'Draw the curtains,' I order my maid, and say to myself, 'Theresa, you have only one more hour to live.' Do you ever drink in bed?"

"Only when I'm sick..."

"No, when you're well. My husband's room is across the hall from mine and so I can isolate myself completely. I prop myself up with a pillow and order the maid to bring me wine. I like mead especially, although it's supposed to be a peasant's drink. They call it 'the nectar of the Slavs' in other countries. But I'm happy when I'm just this side of being drunk. When my mind's a trifle foggy, I don't worry; I lose all sense of obligation. I only do those things that please me."

"Yes, my lady."

"Follow me."

As Lady Pilitzky led Jacob through the halls and chambers, he did not know what to admire first: the furniture, the rugs, the tapestries or the paintings. Everywhere were trophies of the hunt: stags' and boars' heads staring down from the walls; stuffed pheasants, peacocks, partridges, grouse, looking as if they were alive. In the armory were displayed swords, spears, helmets, and breastplates. Lady Pilitzky pointed out the portraits of the lords of Pilitz and their families. Pictures of the kings of Poland were also on the walls: the Casimirs, the Wladislaws, the Jagelos,

King Stephan Batory, along with famous statesmen from the ancient families of Czartoryski, and Zamoyski. Whichever way he turned, Jacob's eyes fell on crosses, swords, nude statuary, paintings of battles, tournaments, and the chase. The very air of the castle smelled of violence, idolatry, and concupiscence. Lady Pilitzky threw open the door of a room in the center of which was a large canopied bed. Jacob caught sight of himself in a mirror, but his image, standing as it were in deep water, was barely recognizable. He saw himself hatless, blushing, his hair and beard disheveled, resembling, it seemed, one of the savages portrayed in the other room. "It isn't the best taste to show the bedrooms," Lady Pilitzky said, "but you Jews don't go in too much for courtly forms. My father had a manor Jew whom we were all fond of. He was very vivacious and would dress up like a bear when we had a ball. You know, he could dance exactly like a bear! But he wouldn't drink and though he took part in the fun, he stayed sober. My father always said only a Jew could do that."

"He had to do it."

"Do you know, not only could he speak in rhymes but in a mixture of Polish, Yiddish, and the patois of the peasants? The Jews considered him a scholar. He married his daughter to the son of a rabbi and the fellow lived at his expense and just sat swaying over prayer books."

"What happened?"

"You mean to the old fellow? He was killed by brigands."

Strange, but Jacob had known she was going to say that. His skin prickled. When Lady Pilitzky spoke, he had the impression she understood that what she told him had made him sad.

"Well, he had had a full life. But what difference does it make how long one lives? One thing is certain; we all die. Sometimes I find it impossible to believe that the world will go on after I'm gone, that the sun will shine, the trees blossom—but I won't be there. No, it's unimaginable. But then, one often hears old people speak of things that happened before one was born. Well, while one's here one longs for happiness, particularly at night. I lie by myself with the darkness surrounding me. Jacob, have you ever seen a werewolf?"

"No, my lady."

"Nor have I. But there are such creatures. There are nights when I want to crawl out into the dark on my hands and knees and howl."

"Why, my lady?"

"Oh, for no reason. I may decide to visit you one of these nights, Jacob, and then be on your guard because I'm dangerous."

Suddenly Lady Pilitzky took hold of Jacob's wrists and said, "I am not so old yet. Kiss me."

"My lady, I am not allowed to. My religion forbids it. I must humbly beg your pardon, your excellency."

"Don't apologize. I'm a fool and you're a Jew. You have borscht, not blood in your veins."

"My lady, I fear God."

"Well, go to him."

IV

It was a warm, summerlike evening in the month of Elul. The crops had been harvested and the fields lay bare. A tepid mist rose from the empty furrows. Jacob as he walked heard the croak of frogs; he kept his eyes fixed on the heavens where a half moon shone, attended by a brilliant blue-green star twinkling with a strange light. Jacob could almost see this small point as the vast orb it really was. Here on earth he was as good as destroyed by the dangers hemming him in on every side. But it was a comfort to realize that God and his angels and seraphim dwelt in their heavenly mansions. Jacob, not wanting to lay himself open to investigation and persecution, had to be careful about opening a book in Pilitz; he did not want to be known as a scholar and certainly not as a cabalist. But here on the manor, he could study whatever he wanted in his free moments. He had brought with him the *Book of Creation, Angel Raziel,* and the *Zohar* to use as charms against devils and to put under Sarah's pillow when she was in labor. These were the books he kept returning to now. A man like himself could not expect to understand what was written in such volumes, but the very words had a sacred look about them. Merely gazing at a page edified him. Even if you were a sinner, it was a privilege to exist surrounded by so many spheres, chariots, powers, and potentates. Jacob remembered from his readings in *The Tree of Life* that evil, synonymous with absolute emptiness, only arose because God had contracted and hidden his face. Repentance could change sins to pieties, justice to mercy. A transgression might at times even lead to good. So, he, Jacob, had sinned when he had lusted for Wanda, but now Wanda had become Sarah, the daughter of Abraham, and in giving birth to a child was about to summon a Jewish soul from the Throne of Glory. It had been right for him to rebuff Lady Pilitzky but would his virtue help him avoid the traps lying all around him?

He was walking on an embankment between fields and insects and other small creatures scurried from beneath his advancing tread. They had received their share of wisdom, but the Creator had left their bodies unprotected. Whoever had feet trod on them; they killed and fed on each other. Yet Jacob found no sadness anywhere but within himself. The summer night throbbed with joy; from all sides came music. Warm winds bore the

184

smells of grain, fruit, and pine trees to him. Itself a cabalistic book, the night was crowded with sacred names and symbols—mystery upon mystery. In the distance where sky and earth merged, lightning flashed, but no thunder followed. The stars looked like letters of the alphabet, vowel points, notes of music. Sparks flickered above the bare furrows. The world was a parchment scrawled with words and song. Every now and then Jacob heard a murmur in his ear as if some unseen being was whispering to him. He was surrounded by powers, some good, some evil, some cruel, some merciful, but each with its own nature and its own task to perform. At times he heard laughter, at other times sighs. He tripped but his foot was guided to the ground. The struggle was going on without as well as within him. He trembled thinking of Lady Pilitzky's wrath but thanked God continually that he had not involved himself with her. He longed for Sarah who might already be in labor, and wished he were home. The maid was in the house, and in an emergency the servants' midwife could be sent for, but Jacob wanted a daughter of Israel to bring the baby into the world. He would not stay on in the manor during the High Holidays. The moment he had finished his most important work he would move back to Pilitz. That is if he were still alive.

"Don't be frightened," Jacob said to himself to keep up his courage, and suddenly a few lines of commentary entered his mind. They concerned the Biblical passage in which the patriarch Jacob blesses his son Jehudah, saying, "Jehudah thee shall thy brethren praise." His teacher at cheder had given the following gloss: Jehudah had been hiding in a corner from his father afraid that he would be reminded of his transgression with Tamar. But Jacob had said reassuringly, "Don't be afraid and don't tremble. Thy brethren will

185

praise you because King David will descend from your loins."

So many years had passed since he had been a school boy, but his teacher's voice still rang in his ears. The old man had died a martyr; Jacob could see his wrinkled face and his gesticulating hands. He remembered the cheder boys also, each with his particular facial expression and mannerism. Where were Moishe'le, Kople, Chaim Berl? Probably dead; and inhabitants now of higher worlds, where thousands upon thousands of mysteries had already been revealed to them. As Jacob walked, his shadow paced with him, a double shadow, composed of a light shell and a dark kernel. He had come to a swamp and, fearful of sinking into the slime, retraced his steps and made a long detour. Nets of moonlight fell in front of him; he heard the hissing and rapid retreat of frightened snakes. Sorcery lay all around him. The castle appeared and disappeared, one moment in front of him, the next to the rear, and he realized that he was lost. He noticed a light in one of the castle windows and thought he caught a glimpse of Lady Pilitzky.

When, at length, he reached home, he found Sarah preparing supper on a tripod, and looking almost girlish despite her pregnancy. Thank God she was all right. The pine branches over which she was cooking blazed and smoked and Jacob smelled the odors of resin and fresh milk. Before he had a chance to speak, Sarah pointed to the rear. On a log outside the house sat three women and a man who had heard of Sarah's miracle and come to be blessed.

Jacob covered his face with his hands. His lies had made him a party to this abominable fraud. These people had left home, wasted their money, exhausted themselves to seek out Sarah. He walked outside and saw a broad-shouldered man with a ragged beard, heavy eyebrows, and a pimply nose. The man's tattered coat was unbuttoned revealing his hairy chest and long fringed garment. A beggar's sack stood close by on the ground. The man rose upon seeing Jacob. The three women were all small and wore kerchiefs and aprons. One of them had a bundle in her lap, the second a basket; the third nibbled on a piece of turnip. They also rose when Jacob appeared.

"Good evening, vistors. Bless you."

"Good evening, rabbi," the man answered in a deep, gruff voice.

"I am not a rabbi," Jacob said, "only a humble Jew."

"God has granted you a saint for a wife," one of the women answered, "so you must be a saint also."

V

The guests were invited to remain for the night and Sarah prepared supper for them. When the meal was over she blessed the travelers, placing her hands on the womens' heads and mouthing a silent prayer over the man. Then, knowing that this was a wasted evening, she wearily retired to her bed in the alcove. There would be no studying of the Torah that night; the guests had to be hospitably treated. Though the women had had beds made up for them in the adjoining bedroom, and the man his in the shed, none of the travelers felt like retiring and they walked out into the warm evening. Jacob followed, anticipating that this would be one of those nights when he would not close his eyes. The incident with Lady Pilitzky had made his position untenable. He expected to be arrested at any moment.

As always the talk turned to the catastrophe. In a rasping voice, the man, Zeinvel Bear, told how he had fled Chmielnicki's Cossacks.

"Yes, I ran. No, my body ran. I was scared. I meant to stay with my family, but my feet said 'no.' Look, I'm a wanderer now. Well, in the old days I just stayed put. All I did was pound cleats into shoes. So how did I, a shoemaker, know where to go? I'd heard of two hamlets, Lipcy and Maidan. In Lipcy there was this fellow who would walk through fire for me. Only a peasant, but a builder and wood carver too. The count humored him, let him dress like one of the gentry. I made his boots. Such boots aren't made any more. The king's aren't as good. But Maidan had a bad reputation. The peasants there were sorcerers and brigands, and allies of the murderers. So, there I stood at the crossroads, wanting to get to Lipcy, but not knowing whether it was right or left. Suddenly I saw a dog. Where had it come from? Out of the earth. It wagged its tail, and pointed its nose straight at me. It couldn't talk, but it was saying, 'Follow me.' It started off down one of the roads and kept turning its head. It was making sure that I was following. Where did it lead me? Right into Lipcy. When I saw the town I went to pat the dog and give it a piece of bread. But it vanished before my eyes. I knew then that it wasn't a dog at all but a messenger sent from heaven."

"Did the gentile really hide you?"

"I lived in the granary for weeks and he brought me everything I needed."

"What became of your family?"

"None of them are left."

The woman with the basket nodded her head.

"Heaven wanted you to be saved, so you were. But why was I kept alive? My husband and my little swallows were killed in front of me. Woe to a mother who must endure that. I begged them to do away with me first but they wanted to torture me. Two Cossacks held me while the others did their dirty work. They discussed the plans that they had

188

for me. One of them had a rabbit and they were going to sew it into my stomach. Suddenly there was a scream and they ran like crazy. I still don't know who screamed. It was such an awful yell I get cold shivers even now when I think of it."

"They must have thought it was some soldiers."

"What soldiers?"

The woman, still holding on to her turnip, took a bite and spat it out. "Trine, tell them about the Cossacks," she said to the woman with the bundle.

Trine didn't answer.

"What's wrong? Are you angry?"

"What's there to tell?"

"She was the wife of a Cossack for three years."

"Be quiet. Why talk? It was worse than when the temple was destroyed. I look old, but I'm not as old as all that. I'll be thirty-six on the fast day, the seventeenth of Tammuz. My husband was a scholar and known all over Poland. When the rabbis were stumped by a question, they came to him. He would pick up a book and open it: there was the answer. They wanted to make him assistant rabbi, but he would have no part of it. 'When the town buys you bread, soon you wish you were dead.' He sat and studied and I took care of our drygoods store. When a fair opened, I went there with our stock, and God did not forsake me. My only grief was that I had no children. Ten years after our marriage, my mother-in-law (may it not be held against her) said that my husband should divorce me because I was barren. We married young. I was eleven and he twelve. He was bar-mitzvahed in my father's house. My mother-in-law had the law on her side, but my husband answered, 'Trine is mine.' He liked to talk in rhyme. He would have been a good wedding jester. Well, the murderers came. We all ran to hide, but he put on his prayer shawl and walked out to meet them. They made him dig his own grave. As he

189

dug, he prayed. I sat in the cellar for days and I didn't have the strength to rise. I fainted from hunger. The others went out at night to hunt for food. I was already in the other world and I saw my mother. There was music and I didn't walk but floated like a bird. My mother flew beside me. We came to two mountains with a pass between. The pass was as red as sunset and smelled of the spices of Paradise. My mother skimmed through, but when I tried to follow someone drove me back."

"An angel?" the shoemaker asked.

"I don't know."

"What happened then?"

"I cried, 'Mother, why are you leaving me?' I couldn't make out her answer. It was just a faint echo in my ear. I opened my eyes and someone was dragging me. It was dark out. I was being pulled from the cellar by a Cossack. I begged him to kill me, but those who want to die live. He tied me to his horse. His name was Vassil."

"Is that the one you married?"

"Married-shmarried."

"Where did he take you?"

"Who knows? Some place on the steppes. We rode day and night. Maybe a week, maybe a month. I didn't even know when it was Sabbath."

"So?"

"Please let me alone."

"He kept her for three years," the woman with the basket said.

"I'll bet you had children by him, huh?" Zeinvel Bear asked.

His question remained unanswered.

No one spoke for a while, and everyone looked up at the moon. Then Zeinvel Bear asked, "What about the steppes? Is it like here?"

"It's beautiful, beautiful. They have strange birds there that talk like people. The grass is very tall and you have to watch out for snakes. The

190

horses are small but faster than our big ones. The Cossacks ride bareback and laugh at anyone who uses a saddle. The women ride too. All the men wear a single earring, and they carry riding crops. When they get angry, they hit with their whips, first from the right, then from the left. They'll beat their own mothers. When a boy comes of age, he and his father wrestle in front of the village. They call it *stanitza*. If the son throws the father, they're jubilant, even the mother. We milk cows but they milk mares. I saw a lot of Tartars where I was. The Tartars shave off their hair and leave only a pigtail. They gamble with hard-boiled eggs on holidays. We do everything inside the house, but they wash and cook outside. They make a fire in a hole, and if they don't have wood, they burn cow dung. They don't have a king. If they have to decide something, all the men get together and talk it over. Every Cossack has his own sword and saber. If a man suspects his wife's unfaithful, he just kills her and no one says anything. Everyone sings there, even the women. At dusk they sit around in a circle and an old man starts the chant and the others join in. They also know how to dance and play musical instruments.

"When I got there, I was more dead than alive. My Cossack had ridden with me all day and half of the night. We didn't eat much, mostly only mushrooms and berries and whatever else he could find in the forest. When he went to look for food, he'd tie his horse to a tree and me to the horse. One time it started to rain and thunder and I tried to get free. But when they tie you up, you stay tied. The horse got frightened too and started to stamp his hoofs and neigh. He came back carrying a wild boar. I refused to put the meat in my mouth. He'd roasted it but it was still half raw. They all eat meat that's hard as a rock and filled with blood. I started to vomit, but he pushed the filthy stuff into my mouth. When a Cossack stops beating his wife, it means he doesn't love her any more. He doesn't beat her in private, but outside in front of everyone, and while he's doing it, he talks to the neighbors. All the men have beards just like the Jews.

"Where was I? Oh, yes, he takes me to the *stanitza* and I can't speak a word of their language. I already had hair on my head, but not as much as the Cossack women. Everyone came to watch him untie me from the horse. An old woman, dressed in pants and as ugly as a witch, began to mumble and spit. It was his mother. She ran at him and began to hit him with her fists and he drove her away with his whip. Then a young woman—it was his wife—came rushing up, screaming and cursing. I stood there like a clay image, ragged, half-naked, barefoot, as emaciated as the dead. I didn't know what to do but they all kept pointing at me as if asking, 'What do you need such a carcass for?' They looked me over as if I were a freak. He had already defiled me but I started to make my confession. What does a woman remember? 'Hear, O Israel.' 'I put my spirit into thy hands.' And a few benedictions. I spoke to God in Yiddish, knowing He understands all languages. 'Father in heaven, take me to you. Death is better than such a life.' But when one wants to go, one doesn't. They brought me into the house and put me to tending geese. They tried the Cossack for bringing home a foreign woman. The young men wanted to behead him, but the old men sided with him.

"What? No, I have no children. That's all I would have needed. He had children by the other one, and they loved me more than their own mother. She'd fly into rages when he wasn't around and beat me until I bled. But then she'd get sorry and bring me a bowl of soup. At first I wouldn't eat unkosher food but finally I had to. I threw up more than I swallowed. They know nothing about Jews. They live like savages. Do you know how they take a bath? They go outside and the husband pours a bucket over his wife and then she pours one over him. All the while the neighbors chat. When they kill a pig, it's a great event. Instead of cutting off its head, they all stab it with spears—men, women, and children. The old crones run up with a pot and catch the blood.

"They got to like me. Even the old bitch. I learned some Cossack, and they picked up some Yiddish. The old woman was always fighting with her daughter-in-law and she began to make up to me. I understood about one word in ten, but she kept on raving and chattering until I had water on the ear. You know they hardly fed her. She slept on a pile of straw and was half eaten by vermin. She didn't have a tooth in her head. Her son didn't know she existed. I gave her whatever I could. When she was dying, she left me her bracelets. I hid them carefully. The daughter-in-law would have devoured me if she had known.

"I thought about only one thing, running away. But where can you run to on the steppes? There are wild animals everywhere. It's so hot in summer that the earth burns your feet. In the winter the snow is piled as high as your head. I didn't have clothes or money. But even if you have money there's not much to do with it. One thing I did not forget: I was a daughter of Israel. When I opened my eyes in the morning, I said, 'I thank Thee.' He'd ask me, 'What's that you're mumbling?' and I'd answer, 'None of your business.' If I'd known their language I could have converted them. They said to me openly, 'We want to become Jews.' If I'd been a man something would have come of that. But what use is a woman? I myself can't tell up from down. They know a little about the Christian holidays, but it's all topsy-turvy. Their priest has a wife. If his wife dies, he has to take another right away. Until he does, they won't listen to him bleating. During Lent they don't eat milk, butter, cheese, or eggs. Only cabbage and vodka. They have everything there but salt and wine which are as expensive as gold. The country's fine except for the flies and locusts which descend like the plagues of Egypt. And they give you elflocks...."

"How did you manage to get away?"

"What's the difference? I'm here. My mother came to me in a dream and told me to leave. When a Tartar passed through, I gave him the old woman's bracelets. He sold me what he had on him—a *bashmet* and a pair of their shoes—they're called *tshuviakis*. I started off trusting in God and good angels to lead me. A small flame ran before me and showed me the road. If I'm lying, may I not see another Yom Kippur. Animals chased me. A huge bird swooped down and tried to carry me off. I screamed and it flew away. But, dear friends, if I told you everything, we would be here for three days and nights. I got help. Yes, help was sent to me. But to whom or what was I running? I didn't even find a grave. I am all by myself in God's world, shamed and despised. When I remember all I went through, I spit on myself."

"So why have you come to be blessed?" Zeinvel Bear asked.

"I keep wandering. So as not to stay in one place. Perhaps there is some comfort for me somewhere in the world. When that blessed woman put her hands on me, a stone dropped from my heart."

Zeinvel Bear pointed with his finger, "See, a falling star!"

VI

The door of Lady Pilitzky's bedroom opened. The

194

moon shone through the curtains. Lady Pilitzky opened her eyes. "Is that you, Adam?" she asked in a soft, intimate voice.

"Yes, Theresa. Did I wake you?"

"No, I was just napping."

"I can't sleep. What should I do about that Jew? About all the Jews? I let in a few and suddenly there's a city. Savitzky is boiling. He's already consigned me to hell. Our dear neighbors are also conspiring. Each of them has his own little Jew, but when it comes to me, they're all pious Christians. This business with that mute is a farce. Even the Jews are laughing at me. It's just another of those damned Jewish tricks."

"Why are you standing? Sit down or come into bed."

"All right, I'll sit. I'm hot. Why has it turned so warm in the middle of the night? Maybe the world's coming to an end or something of the sort. I don't want those Jews around any longer. Gershon's a crook, and that Jacob's a trickster. Why should a woman pretend to be dumb? I just don't understand it."

"Perhaps she's not pretending. She may really be a mute."

"You said yourself that he admitted she wasn't."

"I said nothing of the kind. All I said was that he remained silent and didn't protest. Who knows what goes on among these people? They're a special tribe. It's best to ignore them."

"How can I ignore them? They have a finger in everthing."

"Your Catholic administrators aren't any better."

"What is any good? The whole of Poland's collapsing. Mark my word, we'll be completely eradicated. What the Jewish lice don't eat, the Prussians or Muscovites will. You won't find our nobility crying. No, they consider every Polish defeat their personal victory. Things like this only happen in Poland. Every other country's anxious to prosper; we strangle ourselves."

"I don't know, Adam. I don't know anything any more!"

"Why did you start with that Jew? It was like spitting in my face."

Theresa hesitated.

"But that's what you enjoy."

"Not when it's a Jew. You shouldn't have done it. I used to sleep at night. Now I don't. I wake every few minutes. I'm beginning to think I'm possessed. Theresa, I want to bring this matter to an end."

"What matter? What kind of an end?"

"I'll take some men and we'll march down to Pilitz and cut off a few Jewish heads. The rest of them will just pack up and run."

"Adam, you're mad. Whose heads? We have enemies all around us. Do something like that and you'll find youself standing trial."

"Because of some Jews?"

"You know your enemies are just looking for something. All right, they hate the Jews, but if they find it useful, they'll take their side."

"I must do something."

"Do nothing, Adam. Go to sleep. Lie perfectly still with your eyes closed, and sleep will come. We must bide our time. Adam, dear, we must wait. What else is there to life? You wait and the days pass, and death comes and everything is over."

"I can't just lie waiting for death. Those spinster cousins are too much for me. They walk around glaring at me as if I were their worst enemy; and they're always whispering. This castle is filled with whisperers. You'd think I was keeping them imprisoned. If they're so unhappy, let them go elsewhere. I can't support all my distant relatives. It's not my fault that my uncles and aunts produced only spinsters."

"I've been saying just that for years."

"Yes, it was you who poisoned me against them. That's the tragedy. But now that your venom's worked, suddenly you're their protector and good angel."

"I knew it. Sooner or later everything ends up being my fault."

"Well, it's so. You're the cause of all my troubles. I've quarreled with everyone on account of you. You've isolated me. But I want to be finished with all this." Pilitzky's voice rose to a scream.

"Why must you shout? You'll wake everyone. You know that they eavesdrop."

"Here no one needs to eavesdrop. They all know everything. I can see it in their faces and hear it in their laughs. Theresa, this time you've gone too far."

"I? No, it was you who pushed me, Adam. If I were at the point of death, I would say it over again. You did it. When I testify before God, I will not change my story. No one but you was responsible. I came to you as an innocent girl and you—"

"I know, I know. That story's already grown a beard. You were pure as snow, as innocent as a white rose, and so on. What do you want me to do? Return your hymen?"

"No, all I want from you is a little peace."

"I can't go on living like this. What makes you think Jacob won't talk? I don't want those dirty Jews pointing their fingers at me."

"He won't say anything. He'll keep still. He has his own troubles. His wife's a puzzle—I don't know the answer, but there is one. He's as frightened as he is large and awkward. Maybe he ran away from jail. God knows what. Sooner or later the truth will out."

"Yes, and my shame also."

"You wanted it that way, Adam. For years you urged me to indulge you in your fantasies. God

197

alone knows how I struggled against you and what I endured."

"Don't mention God."

"Who else? I have no one but Him. You drove our children to their deaths. It was as if you killed them with your own hands. Me you made—I dare not say the word; it would disgrace the souls of our parents in heaven. What you have done can not be undone."

Both husband and wife lapsed into silence and then Pilitzky said, "I ordered Antonia to kill the hog tomorrow afternoon."

"No, Adam, I am no longer interested. I don't want it to happen. Let the beast live."

"I have already told Antonia."

"I was not serious when I said it. I don't want to watch. It doesn't help anyway. Holy Mother, what has become of me? God in heaven strike me dead this instant. I want no tomorrow."

Theresa moaned, half in pain and half in disgust. Her body contorted on the bed as if she had been seized by a spasm.

"Take me, death."

10

The Jews of Pilitz were preparing for the High Holidays. The beadle blew his horn daily to scare off Satan, the Seducer, who led men into sin and then testified against them in heaven. Sarah, having moved back to Pilitz from the manor, in addition to holiday preparations, made ready for childbirth. Jacob had placed *The Book of Creation* and a knife under her pillow to discourage those she-devils who hover around women in labor and injure the newborn—Lilith, for example, or Shibta who broke the necks of children being delivered. Jacob had also acquired a talisman from a scribe which had the power to keep off Ygereth, the queen of the demons, Machlath, her attendant, as well as the Lillies who resembled humans but had bat wings, ate fire, and lived in shadows of the moon and tree trunks. As for Sarah, she secretly practiced the magic native to her village. Though now a daughter of Israel, who had learned the prayers said on the High Holidays, still she wore on her throat a piece of a meteorite; and she took the shell of a newly hatched chick, mixed it with dry horse manure and frogs' ashes and drank the concoction in milk. Another charm required her to sit naked on a pot in which mustard seed was burning, allowing the smoke to enter her. The prediction of the women of Pilitz was that she would give birth to a boy since her stomach was not round but pointed upward. Jacob had already bought a gold embroidered skull cap from a traveling pedlar as well as a bracelet that protected from the evil eye.

On Rosh Hashana it was Jacob who arose to begin the prayer, an honor which Gershon had bitterly opposed. On the previous Sabbath he had delayed the reading of the Torah while he railed against the community for allowing a stranger to stand at the lectern as its representative, but the elders had outvoted him. Jacob stood in his prayer shawl and robe singing "the King" and Sarah could not keep back her tears. She could remember him when he had been a barefooted slave who slept in her father's barn. Now he looked like a venerable sage. She, too, had changed, wore a gold colored dress, earrings which Jacob had ordered from a goldsmith and on which money was still owed, and a string of imitation pearls. She held a prayer book in her hands and its brass covers reflected her image—the image of a lady. Her lips moved in silent prayer. Jacob had been so scrupulous in his teaching that she knew more than most of the women around her. How strange it all was: her love for Jacob at first sight, his leaving her and returning to get her, their years of wandering together. Those had been years of constant danger and her life had almost been forfeited many times. God alone knew how many miracles had been required to rescue Jacob and her.

Next to her in the women's gallery stood Beile Pesche, Gershon's wife, dressed in silk and velvet and with a string of real pearls around her neck. But Sarah didn't envy her her finery, felt herself to be superior. Beile Pesche was old, couldn't read, had to listen to a woman reader, and was married to an ignoramus who was not allowed to represent the community at prayer. But Sarah was young, could read and understand a little Hebrew, and was married to a scholar. If the town only knew what a scholar Jacob really was! More than that, Jacob was Pilitzky's administrator, and was received at the castle. Those years that separated Sarah from her peasant past stretched behind her like an eternity. What had occurred before must have happened to someone else. It was as if she had read about it in a story. She had once been Wanda, the wife of Stach, a drunken peasant. Whenever that thought came to her, she shivered, but often she went days without remembering it. She had become a Jewess. What Jacob had said was true: she had been born with a Jewish soul and he had merely brought her back to her point of origin.

Jacob's voice rang loud and clear as he sang and intoned. Her eyes misted. What had she done to deserve these blessings? She bore his child in her womb. Why had she been chosen from all the other Polish women? Her only special merit had been the suffering which had set her apart from childhood; sorrow and longing had always been part of her. She had had strange thoughts even before she could talk. Often she had cried for no reason. Asleep or awake she had odd dreams whose meanings she had not understood until now. She had always been afraid to talk to Jacob about them, fearing he would think her mad. When her grandfather had died—her father's father—she had seen the dead man standing among the mourners, and he had walked with the peasants as his body was carried for burial. She had wanted to scream out to him, but he had raised a finger and put it to his nose as a sign for her to be silent. Only when the cortege had reached the graveyard had the image dissolved slowly like a pocket of mist when the sun starts shining.

The next night her grandfather had come and left flowers on her bed.

She had had other visions as well, had foreseen Jacob's arrival and for this reason had refused other men. The truth was that since childhood she had been expecting and longing for him.

Around her now, the women motioned and made signs to her, assuming that she heard neither her husband intoning the prayers nor the ram's horn being blown. When they spoke to each other, they did so disregarding her presence. Only Beile Pesche loudly warned that she was no mute at all but a fraud. So great was this woman's hatred that when Sarah nodded a silent Good New Year to her after prayers, Beile Pesche turned her back. At home the holiday dinner Sarah had prepared was waiting, the head of a fish, carrots, all the customary dishes that are eaten on Rosh Hashana. Jacob said the benediction over the wine and passed the goblet to her so that she might drink, and cut her a slice of chalah with honey. As she ate, she imagined she saw God in the pale, blue sky, seated on a fiery throne with the book of life and death open before Him, while angels trembled and fluttered their wings and the hand of each man inscribed his fate for the year. A secret fear gnawed at her. Perhaps her death had already been decreed. If so, at least Jacob and the baby must be allowed to live.

When the meal was over, Jacob went to the study house to recite Psalms. Sarah lay down on the bed. She could feel the child moving in her

202

womb. It would soon be Yom Kippur when those who have lost their parents say the memorial prayer. But whom should she pray for? Jan Bzik, her father? She had asked Jacob, who had concluded after some hesitation that she should omit that part of the prayer where the names of the dead are mentioned. For she, Sarah, had not been orphaned through the death of Jan Bzik. Her real father was the patriarch Abraham.

II

In the middle of the night Jacob felt himself being shaken. He opened his eyes. Sarah stood by his bed.

"Jacob, it's begun."

"What, the spasms?"

"Yes."

Though he was still exhausted and longed for sleep, he rose quickly, yawning. Then he remembered and was afraid. In the half light Sarah's bloated body seemed a barrel taut with suffering.

"I'll go for the midwife."

"Wait. Perhaps there's still time."

She spoke in a whisper. No matter what happened, she continued to insist, she would not utter a word, not even in labor. But who could be certain how flesh and blood would behave at such a time? Jacob was surrounded by danger. He went and opened the shutters. The half moon that shines during the ten days of repentance had set, but stars glittered. Should he bring her something to eat, he wondered. That summer she had made gooseberry, currant, and blackberry jam, and some cherry wine. He glanced at the water barrel, saw it was half empty, and decided to go to the well for more water. He would not have left a woman about to go into labor alone if there had not been charms and inscriptions on the wall to protect her.

But even so he kept the door open and he directed
her to recite the incantation a scribe had written
out for her:

The mountain is high; the sky is my skin.
The earth is my shoe; the sky is my dress.
Save me, Lord God.

Let no sword cut me,
No horn gore me,
No tooth bite me,
No waters flow over me.
Under the black sea lies a white stone.
In the throat of the hawk a hard bone is stuck.
YUHAH will guard me!
SHADDAI will save me!
TAFTIFIAH will be a wall for me.

During the period between Rosh Hashana and
Yom Kippur the townspeople attended night
prayers at the study house. Jacob had not gone
this year because Sarah was approaching labor.
But he had seen Gershon walking with the others.
Only a few days before this wilful man who
dictated to everyone had been threatening violence if Jacob was allowed to become reader; he
had even implied he would denounce Jacob to the
nobles. Everyone knew how Gershon had acquired
his wealth; during the massacres monies and other
valuables had been entrusted to him for safekeep-
ing by someone he knew. The man had perished
and when his heirs had asked for their father's
fortune, Gershon had denied ever receiving it,
perjuring himself. Yet now he went with his wife,
his daughters, and his sons-in-law to night
prayers. Did he believe he could fool the Almighty?
Despite the thirty-odd years he had lived in the
world, Jacob was continually astonished at how
many Jews obeyed only one half of the Torah. The

very same people, who strictly observed the minor rituals and customs which were not even rooted in Talmud, broke without thinking twice the most sacred laws, even the Ten Commandments. They wanted to be kind to God and not to man; but what did God need of man and his favors? What does a father want from his children but that they should not do injustice to each other? Jacob, leaning over the well, sighed. This was the cry of the prophets. Perhaps it was the reason the Messiah did not come. He pulled up a pail of water and hurried back to Sarah. She stood at the threshold bent double with pain.

"Get the midwife."

Leaving the pail of water standing, Jacob ran for the midwife, but when he knocked at her shutters, nobody answered. Jacob hurried to the study house and entered the woman's section, although it was not the correct thing to do. But childbirth is dangerous. He looked around and saw she wasn't there.

"My wife's in labor," he said aloud. "Where's the midwife?"

Several of the women scowled and slapped their prayer books, angry at the interruption. Others whispered words of advice and informed him that the midwife was delivering another child. One woman, however, closed her prayer book and rose.

"Life is more important than anything," she said. "I'll go to your wife."

Still in search of the midwife, Jacob found himself traveling down a street filled with bumps and holes and small hillocks. The house of the woman in labor had been described to him and he knew it was one of those he was passing but couldn't decide which, not hearing any screams. The only sound disturbing the silence was the chant rising from the study house. "Adonai! Adonai! Gracious and Merciful God." How strange the prayer sounded echoing in the dark with that peculiar intonation characteristic of night prayers. Despite all their catastrophes, the Jews still spoke of God as merciful and gracious. Jacob stared vacantly about him, uncertain whether to continue his search or hurry home. Sweat ran from his face, wetting his shirt. "Father in Heaven, preserve her," he said aloud, looking up at the sky crowded with stars. When his first wife, peace be with her, had given birth, he had been scarcely more than a boy. What went on among women had been a mystery to him, protected as he had been by his mother, sisters, aunts, and cousins. He had been reading when the women had come in to tell him that he was a father and wish him mazeltov. It had been that way with the second and third child also. But now all of this was so distant it seemed to have taken place in another life. Raising his voice, he called out the name of the midwife, and his cry echoed as though he were in a forest. Then, turning, he ran back home to find a fire already burning in the oven and a pot of water boiling. The woman who had come from the study house had also laid out linen and towels and had lit a wick in a shard of oil. Her sleeves were rolled up and her face wore the expression of one who is an expert in female matters. If she hadn't been there, Jacob would have asked Sarah how she felt. Sarah lay silent on the bed, her face contorted.

"Did you get the midwife?" the woman asked.

"No, I couldn't find her."

"Well, don't get upset. Nothing's happening yet. It doesn't go that easily." And she thrust another piece of wood into the oven.

Behind the anguish in Sarah's eyes was the trace of a smile which seemed to say, "Don't worry so." Jacob looked at her with both love and astonishment. This was Wanda, Jan Bzik's daughter, who every afternoon had brought food to him on the mountain. On her head was the kerchief worn by daughters of Israel, and around her throat a talisman. The walls of the room were hung with charms and verses from the Psalms, and under the pillow lay *The Book of Creation*. He had wrenched this woman from generations of gentiles, robbed her of mother, sister, sister-in-law, all her family. He had even deprived her of her speech. And what had he given in return? Only himself. He had wed her to dangers from which only a miracle could rescue her. For the first time he realized the ordeal to which she had been subjected, and came close to her and stroked her head. Responding like a peasant, she caught his hands in hers and kissed them. If the other woman had seen, the people of Pilitz would have had more to gossip about and ridicule.

III

Can a mute cry? Can she scream in pain? Sarah wept and screamed but said nothing. From the first, signs had indicated a difficult labor. The afternoon following the night of her first spasms she still had not given birth. Her body was wet with perspiration and her eyes protruded. The midwife hurried in and out; there was an assistant, an old crone who delivered the peasants' babies and who had left her turnip patch to run to the bedside; she also bustled about, her unwashed hands black with loam. Neighbors entered, having heard it was a difficult labor, and offered contradictory advice and suggestions. Some of the women stayed outside talking to Jacob, others approached the bed to signal to the mute. Various magical attempts were made to ease the delivery. A young nursing mother squeezed milk from her nipples and gave it to Sarah to drink. A piece of matzoth left over from Passover was placed between the suffering woman's teeth and she was directed to hold it there. A pious matron, noted for her acts of charity, placed her hand on Sarah's stomach and recited a spell. The man who had read the Torah on Rosh Hashana was sent for and he intoned the following passage, resting one hand on the mezuzah: "The captive exile hasteneth that he may be loosed and that he should not die in the pit." He also repeated the verse beginning, "And the Lord visited Sarah," three times, continuing to the words, "at the set time of which God had spoken to him." It was known that Beile Pesche had a bowl inscribed with sacred letters which if placed on the navel of a woman in labor pulled the child out—sometimes the woman's intestines as well if it were left on the body too long. But when Beile Pesche was asked to lend it, she said it had been broken.

When darkness fell and Sarah continued to scream, the women started to bicker. Should she be given the milk of a bitch mixed with honey? Or pigeon droppings in wine? A tip of the lemon used at Succoth was offered and a coin blessed by the pious Rabbi Michael of Zlotchev. Nothing worked. There was only one hope left—the most powerful of all remdies. A long string was brought and attached to Sarah's wrist, its other end carried to the study house and tied to the door of the ark. Sarah tugged with her wrist as commanded, but instead of the door opening as it should have, the string snapped. This was a bad omen. The midwife said: "I'm afraid there'll be no bread from this oven."

"We must at least try to save the child."

The women spoke loudly, believing there was no need to watch their words.

"What would the widower do with a newborn baby?"

"Oh, he'll find a woman to help."

"Imagine, God already decreed this misfortune on Rosh Hashana," the pious woman remarked.

"No, you're wrong, the fates don't become final until Yom Kippur."

The words Sarah had been trying to hold back tore themselves from her throat:

"Don't bury me yet, I'm not dead." She spoke in Yiddish.

The women drew back.

"Oh, my God, she's speaking."

"It's a second miracle."

"Miracle nothing. She's not a mute."

"Gershon was right."

One of the women called out that her head was spinning and fainted.

Jacob, who had run to the beadle's to fetch more Passover matzoth since the piece in use had fallen from Sarah's lips and was spattered with blood, was not present. Everyone in the room began to yell at once and there was such a tumult it was heard on the street. From all sides people came running to Jacob's, among them the burial society women who supposed Sarah had died and were ready to lay the corpse on the floor and light the candles. Soon there was such a crush in the room that the bed on which Sarah lay was almost broken. Terrified, she started to shout in her native Polish:

"What do you want from me? Get out of here. You play at being good, but you're all rotten. You want to bury me and marry off Jacob to one of your own, but I'm still living. I'm alive and my baby's alive too. You're rejoicing too quickly, neighbors. If God had wanted me to die, He wouldn't have made me go through what I have."

Sarah's Polish was not that of a Jewess but that of a gentile and the women turned pale.

"That's a dybbuk speaking."

209

"There's a dybbuk in Sarah," a voice called out into the night.

Many strange events had occurred recently, but the Jews of Pilitz had never heard of a dybbuk entering a woman in labor, and of all things during the days of repentance. Now everyone came, screaming and running. Mothers warned their daughters not to go see the dybbuk unless they wore two aprons, one in the front and one in the rear. Even school children tried to shove into the room where Sarah lay uncovered, but the women turned them back at the door. The stool on which the wick stood was jostled and the light went out; the oil spilled when someone attempted to light it from the oven. Those on the inside sought to get out and those on the outside tried to squeeze in. People blocked the door and quarrels started. Madness, it seemed, had become universal in Pilitz. Bonnets and kerchiefs fell to the floor, dresses were torn; a string of beads was ripped from a woman's neck. Rising above all this came Sarah's periodic screams. The darkness in the room frightened her and she spoke in a mixture of Polish and Yiddish.

"Why is the room so dark? I'm still living. I'm not in the grave. Where's Jacob? Jacob. Has he run off? Has he forgotten his Wanda?"

"Who's Wanda?" someone asked.

"Let me have light. I'm dying," the woman in labor moaned.

A piece of kindling was found and lit and fiery shadows danced on the walls. In the semidarkness all the faces seemed distorted. The midwife who had been out of the room pushed her way through the crowd.

"What's come over you? Who's Wanda? Push down hard. Push, daughter."

"He's too big, too big. He takes after Jacob,"

Sarah cried in Polish. "He's tearing out my insides."

"Who are you? How did you enter Sarah?" a woman inquired of the dybbuk.

Realizing what she had done, Sarah did not reply. The spasms subsided momentarily and she lay exhausted, her hair damp, her body bathed in sweat, her lips and nose swollen. Her legs felt as heavy as logs, her fingers as if they had been stretched. She knew what a dybbuk was, having heard the women speak about them frequently.

"Who are you? How did you enter Sarah?" the women demanded again.

"I entered and here I am," Sarah said. "What do you care? Get out of here. All of you. I don't need you. You're my enemies."

She was speaking in Polish.

"Who is Wanda?"

"She is who she is. Get out of here. Out of here. Let me die in peace. Grant me this. Have pity on me."

The spasms returned and she let out a terrifying wail.

IV

Jacob had been told that a dybbuk had entered Sarah and his arrival started the crowd milling again. Somehow he managed to squeeze his way through.

"What's going on here?" he asked, annoyed and fearful.

"There's a dybbuk inside of her," a woman answered. "It talks Polish. It calls itself Wanda."

Jacob shrugged. "Where's the midwife?"

Sarah's mouth twisted into an expression of mockery.

"No midwife can help me," she said in Polish.

211

"Your son is too large for my hips. Both of us are on our way there," and she pointed toward the cemetery.

Jacob stood, knowing all was lost, speechless with sorrow and shame.

"Save her," he begged those around him. "Please save her."

"No one can save me, Jacob," Sarah said. "The witch predicted I wouldn't live long. Now I see she was right. Forgive me, Jacob."

"Who are you? Where do you come from?" a woman asked.

"Bring the rabbi," another woman cried. "Let him exorcise the dybbuk."

"It's too late for that," Sarah said. "What's he going to drive out? When you bury me, I won't be here any more and you won't have to trouble yourself gossiping about me. Don't think I didn't hear your nasty talk." Sarah's tone changed. "I heard every word. But I had to play the fool. Now I'm dying, I want you to know the truth. You call yourself Jews but you don't obey the Torah. You pray and bow your heads but you speak evil of everyone and begrudge each other a crust of bread. Gershon, the man who rules you, is a swindler. He robbed a Jew whom the Cossacks killed and because of that his son-in-law's a rabbi and—"

Jacob turned white. "What are you talking about, Sarah?"

"Be quiet, Jacob. My sorrow speaks, not I. I can no longer be silent. I kept still for two years, but now that I'm dying, I must talk. I'll burst if I don't. Thank you, Jacob, for everything. You are the cause of my death but I don't hold it against you. How is it your fault? You're a man. You'll find another woman. They're already talking of matches. The town won't let you remain single long. Pray for me, Jacob, because I have forsaken the God of my parents. And I don't know if your God will

212

allow me into heaven. If you ever meet my sister Basha or my brother Antek, tell them how their sister died."

"What is she saying? What is she saying?" voices asked from all sides.

"It's a dybbuk, a dybbuk."

"Yes, a dybbuk. What are you going to do about it? I'll be in my grave along with my child before you can harm me."

Sarah suddenly started to howl. The spasms had begun again. Jacob was pushed from the room and rebuked for being there. He found himself among the men, women, and girls who had not been able to get in. Questions came at him from all sides but he did not answer.

"Why don't they bring the rabbi?"

"They went to get him."

"First they must remove the child and then the dybbuk," one man said.

"Why didn't Gershon's wife lend her bowl?"

"Because she's so noble."

"What's the sex of this dybbuk, male or female?"

"Female."

"I never heard of one female entering another."

There was silence and everyone listened to Sarah's groans. Men bowed their heads; women covered their faces as if ashamed of Eve's curse. The midwife stuck her head out the door.

"Run and bring the bowl. She's sinking fast."

Jacob lunged. "Let me in."

"No, not now."

The rabbi had entered the street, accompanied by his father-in-law, Gershon, and his brother-in-law, the ritual slaughterer. The latter was carrying a utensil, which was at first thought to be Beile Pesche's bowl, but turned out to be a pan filled with burning coals. A ram's horn was stuck in the rabbi's pocket. At Gershon's command the crowd parted and the dignitaries walked through. Trailing behind, carrying a white robe and a prayer shawl, was Joel, the beadle and town grave digger. Gershon, as befitted his position, began to talk loudly.

"Women, make way for the rabbi. We are going to exorcise the dybbuk."

"No men can come in now," a woman called from inside.

"We can't just stand here and wait."

"It's not a dybbuk," Jacob said. "There's no dybbuk."

"What is it, then?" Gershon asked, even though Jacob and he were not on speaking terms.

"Leave her in peace."

"Men, in that room is a demon residing in the body of a woman. Dare we permit her to defile this whole community?" Gershon said, haranguing the crowd. Then, pointing at Jacob, he continued, "He came to us a mere teacher but now he's become a big man. He has a wife with a devil inside her. Because of such people plagues are sent down."

"First the child must be removed," a woman said sagely.

"Perhaps there isn't any child in her womb," another woman suggested. "It may be the dybbuk."

"I have seen the child's head."

"Demons have heads too."

"Demons have hair."

"No."

"If she dies with the child in her womb, the whole community will be imperiled," the rabbi warned.

"Shouldn't we blow the ram's horn out here?" the beadle asked.

"No, first we must implore the dybbuk to leave her," the rabbi announced.

Again there was silence. Roosters began to crow, answering each other. These fowl would be

214

sacrificed on the day before Yom Kippur; there was something both solemn and awesome in their recitative as if they already knew what lay in store for them. The dogs, hanging around the butcher shops, started barking. A warm breeze blew from the fields and swamps; the night had turned hot and humid. Jacob covered his face with his hands.

"Father in heaven, save her."

V

I will say nothing, Jacob decided. Now that she is speaking I must be still. He stood, lips tightly sealed, determined to endure his tribulations to the end, knowing that now he could not escape unharmed. Sarah mortally ill, probably delirious, had divulged their closely guarded secret. Prayer alone was left to him but his lips refused to open even to prayer. Sarah's fate had been decided by heaven which had determined also that he and probably the child too must die with her. I must recite my confession, he thought, and he murmured inwardly: We have trespassed, we have been faithless, we have robbed, we have spoken basely.... He heard people talking to him but the words made no sense. Sarah wept continually, and then finally became silent. But she could not have died, because again they were speaking about driving out the dybbuk. The men were arguing unsuccessfully with the women who were now in charge, about entering the room. A compromise was reached: the men would stand in the doorway. Admonishing the dybbuk, the rabbi pleaded with it to desert the woman's body, but no voice issued from Sarah. At the rabbi's command, the beadle blew the ram's horn; first a long blast, then three staccato ones, then nine swift grace notes in succession. A few minutes later, Pilitzky's carriages drove up to the house accompanied by retainers bearing torches. The entourage resembled an invading army or demons parading in Gehenna. Pilitzky dismounted, inquiring:

"What's going on here, Jews? Has the devil taken over?"

"My lord," someone answered, "a dybbuk has entered Jacob's wife. It's been screaming from her throat."

"I don't hear any screams. Where is she?"

"She's in labor. It was screaming before. Here's Jacob."

Pilitzky glanced at Jacob.

"What's going on with your wife? Is she talking again?"

"I know nothing, my lord. I have ceased knowing anything."

"Well, it's clear enough to me. She's as dumb as I'm blind. I want to speak to her."

"My lord, no men are allowed," the women called from inside.

"Nevertheless, I'm going in."

"Cover her. Cover her."

Pilitzky entered and addressed Sarah, but she did not answer. The women listened in silence. The younger matrons had already gone home to nurse their babies, and many of the older women had hastened off to the study house. The rabbi had left too. Gershon lounged against a tree outside, appearing asleep on his feet. He had removed his hat on Pilitzky's arrival and had been about to run and kiss his master's hand, but the lord of Pilitz had turned his back on him. This was Jacob's second sleepless night, and he stood numb from fatigue but with his eyes still open. He had wrestled with God as had the Patriarch Jacob, but his defeat had brought more than a dislocated thigh. He, Jacob, the son of Eliezer, had been utterly destroyed by heaven. No longer did he fear anything, not even Gehenna. He deserved no better, having cohabited with the daughter of Jan Bzik and then illicitly converted her. What did he expect? In these days justice ruled untempered by mercy. Jacob heard Sarah groaning.

"Gracious lord, let me die in peace."

"So you are not dumb. You never have been. This was a little comedy that you and your husband played."

"It's the dybbuk, my lord, the dybbuk," someone interrupted.

"Silence. You don't have to tell me. I know what a dybbuk is," Pilitzky said, raising his voice. "When the devil enters a woman, he speaks with his own voice. She uses *her* own. That's the same voice I heard when she thought I meant to harm her husband. Isn't that true? What's your name? Sarah?"

"Let me die, worthy lord, let me die."

"You'll die, you'll die. And when your soul leaves your body, I won't stop it. But for the moment you're living. Tell me, why did you pretend to be mute?"

"I can tell you nothing."

"If you won't, your husband will. We'll pour hot oil on his head, then he'll talk."

"My lord, what do you wish from me? Have you no pity for the dying?"

"Tell the truth before you die. Don't go to the grave still lying."

"The truth is that I loved him and still love him. I regret nothing, my lord. No, nothing."

"Who are you? You speak like a mountaineer, not like a Jewess."

"I am a daughter of Israel, my lord. Jacob's God is my God. Where is the rabbi? I want to make my confession. Where is Jacob? Jacob, where are you?"

Jacob pushed his way through the crowd.

"Here is my husband. Why don't you eat

217

something? Women, give him something to eat. Don't be so pale, Jacob, and frightened. I'll sit with the angels and look down on you. I'll see that no harm befalls you. I'll sing with the choiring angels and pray to God for you."

Sarah intoned all this in Polish and the women stood open-mouthed. Neither Sarah's way of speaking nor her manner was that of a daughter of Israel. Suddenly they remembered she didn't look Jewish, that she had a snub nose, high cheekbones, teeth which were strangely white, strong, and sharp, unlike those found among the Jews. Pilitzky asked:

"Where are you from? The mountains?"

"I have nobody, my lord, neither father, nor mother, nor sister, nor brother. I have erased them from my mind. My father was a good man, and I'll meet him if he's in heaven. Remember, all of you, don't hurt Jacob. You can find him a wife when I'm dead, but don't torture him with your talk. I'll defend him. I'll kneel before God's throne and pray for his safety."

"You were born a Christian, weren't you?"

"I was born when Jacob found me."

"Well, everything's clear."

"What's clear, my lord? It's clear that I'm dying and will take my child with me to the grave. And I had hoped that God would grant me a son, and that I would still have a few good years with my husband..."

Suddenly Sarah started to sing in a half yodel, half sob. The song was one Jacob had often heard on the mountain, the ballad of an orphaned girl who fell into the hands of a forest spirit and was carried to a Smok's cave. The Smok made her his concubine and, forced to endure his demonic love, she longed for the mountains, the Gazdas, and her lover at home. Now it seemed as if Sarah no longer knew where she was. She lay, her cheeks swollen, her eyes half shut, her head uncovered, and chanted in a hoarse voice. Pilitzky crossed himself. The women wrung their hands. Suddenly Sarah was silent, her thoughts turned inward. Then, again, she started chanting; Jacob's eyes clouded and he viewed everything as if through water. He remembered a passage from the Book of Aboth: "Whosoever profanes the Name of Heaven in secret will suffer the penalty of it in public." He wanted to go and comfort Sarah, wipe the sweat from her brow, but his feet were like wood. Pilitzky took him by the arm and led him outside.

"Look, you'd better leave town," he said conspiratorially. "The priests will burn you. And they'll be right to do it."

"How can I run away at such a time?"

"She'll be dead shortly. I pity you, Jew. That's why I'm warning you."

Pilitzky stepped into his carriage and drove off.

11

The baby, a boy, born the next day, arrived crying too loudly for a newborn child. Sarah remained in a stupor and the women took care of the infant; a young mother with an abundance of milk nursed him. It was the day before Yom Kippur and the townspeople were busy with the sacrificial fowl and preparations for the holiday. Yet Gershon demanded a meeting of the community elders. What was said in this secret conclave was never told; but the rabbi forbade the cheder boys to read the Shema at Sarah's bedside, and prohibited attendance at the ceremony requesting peace for the male child customarily held on the Sabbath after the birth. The rabbi went further and instructed his brother-in-law, the ritual slaughterer who also performed the circumcisions, that for the time being the child should not be circumcised. Pilitz was in an uproar. The uninstructed misunderstood the rabbi's decision and maintained that it was Gershon who had instigated his son-in-law to humiliate Jacob. But those who knew the Talmud explained the verdict. According to the law, the child is born into its mother's faith. It was clear Sarah was a gentile— even the name substantiated that she was a convert. But what rabbinical court would have upheld the conversion of a gentile when the punishment for such an act was death? How could the community accept her when acceptance meant a criminal indictment? God forbid. Misfortunes and evils could only attend such an act. In the study house, Gershon demanded that Jacob be excommunicated, publicly exhibited in an ox cart and driven out of Pilitz. What a heinous crime, Gershon shouted. Jacob from mere lust had passed off a gentile as a daughter of Israel. Now even those who had sided with Jacob agreed with Gershon. And since Gershon remained out of favor with Pilitzky another envoy was sent to explain the position taken by the Jews.

The next day Sarah still lay helpless. The women refused to visit her knowing that according to Polish law she too had committed a capital crime. Only the old woman came a few times to inquire after her and leave some chicken broth which Sarah couldn't swallow. Yom Kippur would begin at sundown and although eating before the fast day was considered an act of piety, Jacob had no food in the house nor could he have tolerated eating. He sat at the bedside and recited Psalms. The woman who was acting as wet nurse had taken the child to her own home and Jacob could not go to visit his son since he had no one to leave with Sarah. Nor was it certain that the family would have permitted him to enter their house, for though he had not as yet been officially excommunicated he soon would be. The townspeople, he noticed, no longer passed by his house. His acts, in a perverse way, were an offense to the government, the community and to God. He was ashamed to say the verses of the Psalms. How could his lips utter such holy words? How could his prayer be acceptable? Now he was receiving his retribution in all its harshness. Any day he might be burned at the stake.

As he sat with the sick woman, holding the Book of Psalms in his hands, he made a spiritual accounting. His family had been killed; for five years he had been Jan Bzik's slave, sleeping with the cattle in the barn or with the mice in the granary. True, he had lusted for Jan Bzik's daughter and had wanted her as his wife. But had not the author of the Psalms, King David, lusted for Bathsheba? And if the Bible was to be accepted as the literal truth, then David had committed a far worse sin than he had. God had forgiven David. Why not Jacob, who had never sent a man out to be killed in battle?

But Jacob knew that these thoughts themselves were forbidden. The Talmud explained that King David had not been a sinner, that Uriah the Hittite had left a divorce for Bathsheba before he marched out to battle. The Gemara and the Midrash also defended the people of the Bible. But, just the same, those great ancient figures had lusted carnally, and had married outside of their nation. Moses had taken an Ethiopian as a wife, and Miriam had become leprous when she slandered him. Jehudah who had given his name to the Jews had had intercourse with a woman he thought was a harlot. King Solomon, himself, the greatest sage, had married the daughter of Pharaoh, and yet the Song of Songs and the Proverbs were holy. And what of the Jews now? Did they all strictly obey the commands of the Torah? His years of wandering with Sarah had made him aware of many wrongs he had ignored before. Legalisms and rituals proliferated without diminishing the narrow-mindedness of the people; the leaders ruled tyrannically; hatred, envy, and competition never ceased. Before Yom Kippur the Jews made peace with one another, but the night after quarrels broke out all over again. Perhaps that was why God sent men like Chmielnicki, why the exile lasted so long and the Messiah did not come.

Jacob dipped a finger in water to moisten Sarah's lips, bent over her, touched her forehead, and whispered to her. She lay as if already in the beyond, sunk in contemplation, receiving, it seemed to Jacob, the answers to those unanswerable questions that the living ask. Her chin trembled; the veins of her temples throbbed. It was as if she were arguing with the higher powers. Is that how it is? the smile that occasionally came to her lips seemed to say. How could I, Jan Bzik's daughter, ever have known that? I wouldn't have guessed it in a million years.

She is good, he thought, really a saint, a thousand times better than any of the others. Have they been to heaven and learned what God likes? Worry and fear, the isolation in which he found himself, had made him rebellious. He was even ready to struggle with God himself. Of course, God was the only God, awesome and all powerful, but it was only fair that his justice be universal. He should not be a tyrant like Gershon, fawning on the strong and spitting at the weak. Was it Sarah's fault who her parents were? Had she had the freedom to choose her mother's womb? If such as she must burn in Gehenna, then there was even inequity in heaven.

Dusk was beginning to fall, and the Jews were going in slippers or in their stockinged feet to pray. They wore white robes, prayer shawls, and on their heads gold-embroidered miters. The women were adorned with capes, fancy headgear, dresses with trains. Candles burned in the windows. A wailing rose from the houses. Everyone in Pilitz had lost someone in the massacres, and now Jacob's anger turned to pity. A tortured people. A people whom God had chosen for affliction, raining down on them all the tortures in the Book of Punishment.

The door opened and the old woman entered bearing half a chicken, a chalah, and a piece of fish for Jacob to eat before the fast started. No one else would come near him but at her age she had nothing to lose. Her face was yellow as wax, dry as a fig, and the wrinkles on her forehead were like the script on an ancient parchment. For a few moments she stood at the sick woman's bedside, her eyes still young, looking up at Jacob with a motherly understanding. Her hairy chin shook as she made an effort to speak. Finally she said:

"Let your prayer for a good year be answered. Everything can still be all right. God is good."

The old woman raised her voice in a wail.

II

Late that night, Sarah opened her eyes. Her lips moved and Jacob heard her half-choked voice coming to him as if from a distance. He had the feeling that her voice and body were no longer connected. He bent over her, and she muttered in Polish.

"Jacob, is it Yom Kippur yet?"

"Yes, Sarah, Yom Kippur eve."

"Why aren't you in the synagogue?"

"I'll go there again as soon as you are well."

Sarah closed her eyes and meditated on this. Jacob thought she had fallen asleep. When she opened her eyes again, she said:

"I will be dead soon."

"No, you will get better and live many more years."

"Jacob, my feet are dead already."

He tried to feed her some broth, but her teeth locked, and the soup dribbled out. He remained leaning over her, clasping her hands. He had prayed so much in the last days and weeks, but now he had given up and even the wish for prayer had evaporated. Heaven had not listened to his supplications. The gates of mercy had been closed to him. He looked at Sarah, realizing that he was her murderer. If he had not touched her, if she had remained in her village, she would still be healthy and vital. Every sin, no matter how small, ends in murder, Jacob said to himself. He felt a love such as he had never known before, but equally a helplessness. There was a midnight silence in the room. Two candles standing in a box of sand flickered and cast shadows. The kerchief had fallen from Sarah's head and her scalp, covered with short hair like a boy's, was the color of straw and fire. He didn't know what to do. Should he go and get someone? Disturb people on the holiday? No one could help anyway. He sat on a stool by the bed, unable even to think now. Within him there was a great emptiness. Crush me, Father in heaven, crush me! In the Psalmist's words, "And my sorrow is continually before me." Now his only desire was to die with her. He had forgotten the child. He wanted to descend into Sheol from which none return.

Suddenly Sarah opened her eyes and spoke, her voice firm and clear as if she were again well.

"Jacob—see Father."

Jacob looked around.

"What did you say?"

"Don't you see him? There he is." Sarah stared at the door.

"Good evening, Father," she said. "You've come for your Wanda. You haven't forgotten. I'll come with you soon, Father. But wait, wait another few minutes. How well you look, Father, all in light."

Jacob turned to the door and saw nothing. Sarah was silent. Her eyes began to shrink in their sockets, the pupils contracting into opaqueness. Jacob spoke to her but she did not answer, nor give any sign that she heard. Then she said:

"See Grandmother too. How beautiful you look. I was was your favorite granddaughter. You've come for me too. Oh, how I loved you. You and Father. Now we'll always be together."

"Sarah," Jacob said. "You'll get better. You are the mother of a child. You have a son."

"Yes."

"You must live—for him and for me."

"No, Jacob."

He continued to call to her but she did not answer. Her eyes stayed shut. She lay absorbed in meditations that could not be interrupted. Something was happening within her. Jacob could see that the journey to where she was going was not easy. She seemed to be engaged in a dispute with some power external to her, arguing with it, struggling. Whatever power was forcing her from life also would not accept her in death. An accusation was being made and her glazed eyes seemed to be imploring: No more. No more. I'm tired. Leave me in peace. Jacob sought to have her make her confession, wanted her to die with the words, Hear O Israel, on her lips, but it was too late for that. How strange that these gentile spirits had found their way here on of all nights Yom Kippur eve. But who knew the secrets of heaven and earth? Again and again, Jacob turned to look at the door. Perhaps he too would see the ghost of Jan Bzik.

His head slumped forward and he fell into the sweet forgetfulness of sleep. He awoke, glanced at Sarah, and knew that she was dead. Her jaw had sagged, one of her eyes was open, one closed. The face was no longer recognizable. Now the struggle

226

had ended, her chapped lips seemed to say, I've passed through everything. All is well now. The face was peaceful and acquiescent; this was no longer the sick, the tormented, the martyred Sarah who had estranged herself from both Jews and gentiles, and lost her home and her language. The corpse, at last beyond the reach of finite good and evil, forgave. Sarah's body was here, but her spirit had already climbed to heights unreachable for flesh. Jacob's sight became as if visionary, and he saw her entering a heavenly mansion. He did not cry but his cheeks became damp. His love for her had begun with lust; now nine years later he watched over the body of a saint. But the burial society, Jacob knew, would refuse to inter her in a Jewish Cemetery. Moreover, the gentiles threatened him direly. Nothing that was related to this earth was of any importance to him now. In the presence of this peace, all anxiety left him. He bent down and kissed her forehead.

"Holy soul."

The door opened and a few men and women from the burial society entered. A tall man in a fur hat and white robe cried out:

"What are you doing? That's forbidden."

"He's out of his head," another said.

A woman put a feather to Sarah's nostrils. The feather did not move.

III

Gershon breached custom once more and called a meeting of the elders and the burial society immediately Yom Kippur ended. After the debate had gone on for an hour, Jacob was sent for. He was sitting watch over the corpse, but the beadle now took his place. Offered cake and wine by the rabbi's wife, Jacob refused.

"A second Yom Kippur has begun for me," he said.

"You should eat. One fast day is sufficient," the rabbi answered.

At the insistence of those present, Jacob took a spoonful of rice and a cup of water. The meeting wanted information from Jacob, nothing less than the complete truth.

"What you have done bears on the welfare of the whole community," the rabbi pointed out. "We imperil the town if we break the law. You know well enough what we have suffered. So tell us the truth. If you have sinned, don't be ashamed. This is the night after Yom Kippur and all Jews have been purified."

The speech was unnecessary since Jacob had already decided to tell the truth. As soon as he started to talk everyone became quiet. He told them who he was, who his father and grandfather had been, how Polish robbers had captured him and sold him to Jan Bzik, and how he had lain illicitly with Bzik's daughter, how the Jews of Josefov had ransomed him, how, longing for Wanda, he had later returned to the village, and how, since she could not speak Yiddish correctly, she had pretended to be mute. So quiet was it in the study house that the buzzing of a fly could have been heard. Every once in a while a listener sighed. This was not the first strange story those assembled had listened to. Ever since the massacres all sorts of peculiar things had been heard of: Jews turned Christian or Mohammedan; daughters of Israel married to Cossacks, sold into harems; women who remarried only to find their husbands returning. Stories to tell for generations to come! Yet, that a young scholar from a fine family should fall in love with a peasant girl, convert her in defiance of both the Jewish and gentile law—this was something new. Gershon's yellow eyes bulged, his mustache quivered like a tomcat's, and he clenched his fist on the table. The others glanced at one another and shook their heads. The moment Jacob stopped talking, Gershon said:

"You have betrayed Israel. You're a monster!"

"Men, this is no time to preach morality," a white-bearded elder interrupted.

"You know the law," the rabbi said hesitantly to Jacob. "Your son is not a Jew. The mother was not converted with the consent of the community."

"She went to the ritual bath. She observed the laws."

"That is immaterial. She was not accepted. Moreover, the laws of this country apply to us, too."

"These are unusual times. Is it the child's fault?"

"He was born and conceived in sin."

"Must he remain uncircumcised?"

"Take your bastard and go elsewhere," Gershon shouted. "We're not going to pay with our heads for your lechery."

"What about the body?" the white-bearded elder asked.

"Interment in the cemetery is out of the question."

They were still arguing when Jacob rose and left. He walked slowly through the streets with bowed head. Now he knew what he was: a branch torn from its trunk. Excommunication was certain. He wanted to see the child but decided it was more important to watch over the corpse. While he had been sitting night and day at the sick bed, he had been meditating. What happened was no accident. Everything was preordained. True, the will was free, but heaven also made its ordinances. He had been driven, he knew, by powers stronger than himself. How else could he have found his way back from Josefov to the mountain village? It had been his feet that had led him. And Sarah had hinted, even before she became pregnant, that she would die giving birth. The night before, her words had returned to him, and he knew she must have been granted some prophetic power. But whom could he tell such things? Who would believe him?

But now he at least understood his religion: its essence was the relation between man and his fellows. Man's obligations toward God was easy to perform. Didn't Gershon have two kitchens, one for milk, and one for meat? Men like Gershon cheated, but they ate matzoth prepared according to the strictest requirements. They slandered their fellow men, but demanded meat doubly kosher. They envied, fought, hated their fellow Jews, yet still put on a second pair of phylacteries. Rather than troubling himself to induce a Jew to eat pork or kindle a fire on the Sabbath, Satan did easier and more important work, advocating those sins deeply rooted in human nature.

But what could he, Jacob, do? Become a prophet and castigate the people? He who had himself broken the Torah?

He arrived home and relieved the beadle, sat down to watch over the body. The corpse lay on the floor now, covered by his overcoat, the feet towards the door. Behind the head, the stumps of yesterday's candles still burned. The previous night, it had seemed to him several times that the corpse had moved, and he had uncovered Sarah's face, and tried to wake her, suspecting catalepsy. But hour by hour, she had grown stiffer. The body was altering, and one could see that she was moving further and further from this earth. Jacob raised the eyelids, but the pupils were blank. Even the expression of acquiescence had vanished. Clearly, she was no longer there. Unable to gaze at her longer, Jacob covered her again. He took out the Psalter from his bookcase and began to recite the

Psalm: "Deliver me out of the mire, and let me not sink.... Reproach hath broken my heart; and I am full of heaviness.... Make haste, O God, to deliver me; make haste to help me, O Lord."

IV

The clatter of horses' hoofs sounded in the night. Jacob knew what that meant. The door slammed open and a dragoon with a plumed helmet and twisted mustache thrust his head in. He saw the corpse lying on the floor and was silent for a moment. Then he spoke:

"If you're Jacob, come with me."

"Who will watch over the body?"

"Let's go. I have my orders."

Jacob bent and for the last time uncovered Sarah's face, which seemed to be smiling. He had closed the mouth but the jaws opened again; the teeth no longer seemed to fit the gums; the tongue was lumpy and blackish. He wanted to say goodbye but he didn't know how. I should take some clothes or a shirt, he thought, but he didn't move. Again he covered the body and said:

"All right, I'm ready."

The moment he was in the street he thought of his prayer shawl and phylacteries and asked the soldier to let him return for them. But the soldier blocked his way. The moon, not yet full, had crossed the sky to the horizon. Everywhere, shutters were closed. Even the grasshoppers and frogs were silent. A mounted dragoon held the first one's horse by the reins. Jacob had the feeling that he had lived through this before or seen it in a dream. He thought of calling out to the people not to leave Sarah's body unattended, but was held back by a youthful embarrassment. He was trembling, not from fear but from the cold. He recalled that the night before a mouse had approached the body and he had had to chase it away. But what difference did it make whether the corpse was eaten by mice or worms? The first dragoon dragged out a long chain, tied one end to Jacob's wrist, and attached the other to his saddle. The second dragoon dismounted to help, the two handling the prisoner like butchers trussing an ox to be led to slaughter. They spoke, but only to each other. Only now did Jacob remember the child. Well, the boy would have neither father nor mother. He had been born under a dark star. Jacob wanted to ask the soldiers to take him to the house where the baby was but realized that his request would be refused. He fixed his eyes on the chinks in the shutter where could be seen the glimmer of the candles burning at the head of the corpse. Does she know what's happening to me? he asked himself. Or is her soul so distant it is no longer connected with this world? The dragoons rode slowly, Jacob following. He realized they were taking him to another town. Pilitz was left behind, and they moved past fields that had already been harvested. He was marching to his death, yet Jacob breathed in deeply, filling his lungs with the cool night air. For days now he had done nothing but sit with the sick woman and then with her corpse. Inactivity and stale air had enervated him. He was no longer accustomed to not using his body. His feet wanted movement, his hands demanded work. Now he walked between the horses, fearful they might step on his feet or crush his ribs, although surely such a death was more honorable than being hanged. He wanted to recite chapters from the Psalms, but the chatter of the soldiers distracted him. The taller of the dragoons, the one who had arrested Jacob, said:

"All right, Czeslaw, how many men do you think Kasia's had already?"

"More than you have hairs on your head."

232

"She only has one bastard."

"You can have her for half a grivnik."

"Still, she has a way with her."

"It's all false. She smiles at you with one eye and at your worst enemy with the other. She'll kiss you all over, but the moment you go she curses you and your mother. Then she's off to the priest to confess how she accidentally stepped on a cross of straw."

"That's a fact. Now all she talks about is getting married."

"Why not? Once she's your wife, she'll tell you to go whistle. You'll rot in camp and she'll do what she wants. You'll come home and she'll have a belly ache. With strangers she'll dance; with you she'll groan. Every year she'll present you with another bastard."

"Well, I've got to marry someone."

"Why?"

"Should I take my horse for a wife?"

"Your horse would be more faithful than Kasia."

Jacob wondered how a man who had just looked on death could speak so. Didn't these men ever contemplate their own fate? They lead me to the gallows and never bother to ask why. As if guessing his thoughts the soldiers became silent. The horses' pace slackened. Jacob, cooled by a breeze, felt a calm such as he had never known before, and raised his eyes to the sky. So, the heavens were still there, created by the same God who had formed both the rider and the horse. He had made the chain strong. Suddenly it occurred to Jacob that sometimes chains could be broken. Nowhere was it written that a man must consent to his own destruction. Instantly his mood changed. He was angry. Powers slumbering within him awoke. He now knew what to do. He wanted to laugh. The moon had set, he noticed. Edging over toward Czeslaw, the smaller of the two dragoons, he struck his horse with an elbow. The animal broke into a gallop, veered off into the underbrush. The tall dragoon shouted, reached for his sword. Jacob yanked the chain and the tall dragoon's saddle came apart. The horse stumbled and nearly fell. Regaining its balance, this mare also bolted. Jacob ran into the fields with a speed and lightness that astounded him. There was no place to hide, but the dragoons would not risk injuring the legs of their mounts pursuing him across the stubble. Soon all was silent and he was surrounded by darkness.

I must reach a forest before sunrise, he warned himself, amazed at what had happened. But which way should he run? He had outwitted the powerful, broken the chain of slavery, but despite his escape, he felt no elation. He kept on going blindly and for how long he did not know. Time had become dreamlike. The chain dragged; he felt its weight on his hand. Bending down, he groped on the ground, not realizing at first what he was looking for. He found a stone and used it to pry the chain from his wrist. Where would he hide it? There was no ditch or stream around; like a dog with a bone, he dug a hole with his fingers and buried the chain. Only half awake, he knew he was in the fields, but at the same time he seemed to be in Josefov. He was surprised to discover that Gershon and the widow of Hrubyeshoyv were married. How could this be? Gershon's wife hadn't died. Had the edict of Rabbi Gershom the Light of the Diaspora come to an end? Shaking his head to clear it, Jacob got up and stumbled on across the stubble. Sky and earth fused in the darkness. He heard someone sighing, and knew that it was neither man nor beast but one of those who hover in the night; something wet and warm, like spittle, fell on Jacob's forehead. Under his feet, the earth seemed to sway. He walked dragging his legs as if they were no longer a part of his body. He saw a red pool shining like blood on the ground before him. Billowing smoke mingled with sparks rose in front of him as if from a burning village. He fell face down on the ground, overcome by sleep.

He awoke and it was day. Coils of mist hovered over the naked fields. A crow flew low and croaked. At the edge of the horizon to his left a forest stretched like a sash of blue, and emerging from it like the head of a newborn child, small and bloody red, came the sun.

V

Jacob lay in the forest and slept. But even in his sleep he clutched a heavy stick. The day was warm and the sunlight filtered through the pines. His was the deep sleep of those who have ceased to hope. Each time he woke, he wondered, Where am I running? Why did I escape?—and then exhaustion overwhelmed him again. He dreamed he was in the barn on the mountain and Wanda brought him food. He stood on the rock and watched her climbing from the valley dressed like a queen in jewels and purple robes, a crown on her head, golden milk pails in her hands. When, he asked himself, did Wanda become a Polish queen? Where was her retinue? Why did she need gold milk pails? It must be a dream. He awoke. The forest echoed with the songs of birds. His stomach ached with hunger. He dozed again. Today is her funeral, he said to himself, waking. They will give her a donkey's burial, outside the fence. His grief was too great to permit him to stay awake. Sleep like an opiate drugged him.

He was with her again, but now she was both Wanda and Sarah; Sarah-Wanda, he called her, amazed at the coupling of these names. How strange: Josefov and the mountain hamlet had also merged. Wanda was his wife, and he sat in his father-in-law's library and she brought him the Sabbath fruit. The massacres and the years of slavery had become the dream. But as he told Sarah-Wanda this, her eyes filled with tears and her face paled.

"No, Jacob, it happened."

He heard her speak and knew she was dead.

"What must I do now?"

"Fear not, Jacob my slave."

"Where shall I go?"

"Go with the child."

"Where?"

"To the other side of the Vistula."

"I want to be with you."

"Not yet."

"Where are you?"

She did not answer. Her smile awoke him and for a few moments her image lingered, white and shining, framed between the tree trunks. He reached out his hands and she disappeared. Again he slept and when he awoke the setting sun shone red in the thickets, while above the crowns of the pines, the sky flamed. Jacob remembered that he had not put on phylacteries since he had fled but this was his first day of mourning and so praying in prayer shawl and phylacteries was forbidden him. He moved into the brush searching for food: the blueberries had withered, but not the blackberries, and he gorged himself. Yet he remained hungry. Evening had fallen but the forest murmurs did not cease. Eerie laughter came from the branches, night birds calling. Another nocturnal bird repeated the same shrill warning over and over again like a prophet. The moon rose and dew fell as if through a heavenly sieve. The moss gave off warm, spicy odors. Jacob's head ached. He stumbled through a tangle of underbrush and trees, knowing he couldn't stay where he was. Here

236

he would starve or fall prey to wolves. But there was no path out. He caught sight of a figure among the trees, ran calling to it, and saw it evaporate. Voices were chattering all around him and he wondered if he were already in the hands of the demons. To protect himself, he recited, "Hear O Israel," and then forced himself to envisage each letter of the word, Jehovah. His foot plunged into mud as he skirted a swamp; pine cones struck him as if thrown by hidden hands. He slid on beds of fallen pine needles. He walked toward the moon. The forest was savage yet he knew that even here Providence tended each fern and grub. He listened and heard the many voices around him, each unique, and, uniting all, the inimitable voice of the forest. Overcome by fatigue, he sat down on a couch of moss near a tree trunk. He felt the approach of death and once more cried out to Wanda.

His strength ebbed from him and the earth he rested on became suddenly near and dear. The grave is a bed, he thought, a most comfortable bed. If men knew this, they would not be so fearful.

VI

Sand dunes stretched out and down like steps and at the bottom Jacob saw the Vistula quiet, deep, half silver, half a greenish black. Walking and dreaming, he had come to the edge of the forest. The landscape was as empty as on the first day of Creation. Jacob walked and the moon walked with him. The pleated sand, here and there as white as chalk, brought to his mind the deserts he had read of in the Pentateuch. The sight of the river made him hasten—he had not tasted water since the day before. The closer he came to it, the wider the river became. At the shore, bending down to drink from his cupped hands, he recalled the story of Gideon

237

in the Book of Judges. He sat down to rest in the cool breeze and saw shadowy nets trembling on the surface of the water as if cast by some unseen fisherman. Stars dropped from the sky into the waves and hovering glowworms flared. Jacob again wanted to sleep but some power warned him not to, and, overcoming his weariness, he rose, climbed a pile of rocks and looked about him. Far off to the right, he saw something which could be a barge, a raft, a mill. He walked along the shore toward it.

Nearing the object, he discovered that it was a ferryboat, moored by thick ropes to piles; not far from the boat were a hut and a dog house. As he approached the landing, a barking dog ran toward him and a moment later a man came out of the hut. He was as black as a gipsy, barefoot, half naked, with long, curly hair, and wore trousers turned up to the knee. Scolding the dog in a rasping voice, he walked up to Jacob and said:

"The ferry doesn't run at night."

"Where does it go?"

"Where? To the other side."

"Is there a town there?"

"A stone's throw away."

"What's its name?"

The stranger informed Jacob. After a moment's silence, he asked:

"You a Jew?"

"Yes, a Jew."

"How come you're not carrying bundles?"

"I don't have any."

"If you're a beggar, where's your sack?"

"This stick is all I own."

"So that's it. Some have too much, others too little. In my lifetime, I've seen everything. What happened? Were you robbed?"

"Robbers don't worry me," Jacob said, amazed at his own statement.

"You're right. What have we got to lose? More

238

than your trousers they can't take. But I do keep a spear, and you've seen the dog. Around here, they'd even run off with the ferryboat if they could. And how far would they get? Once we were crossing and this peasant woman's goose jumped into the Vistula. Two men had to keep her from going in after it. We got the goose back later. I said to her, 'Can you swim?' 'No,' she said, 'not a stroke.' 'How come you tried to jump overboard, then?' You know what she said: 'Well, it's my goose, isn't it?' Where are you from?"

"Josefov."

"Never heard of it. It must be far away."

"It is."

"Well, people come and people go. The kings don't even sit still. Everyone's come this way; the Swedes, the Muscovites, Chmielnicki. Whoever has a sword wants to live by it. But someone's got to do the work or we'd all chew rags. I'm a nobody, but I have two eyes in my head. Time's one thing I have enough of. I do plenty of thinking. You must be hungry."

"I don't have any money."

"You're entitled to a piece of bread. Even jailbirds get bread and water."

The ferryman walked into the hut and returned with a slab of bread and an apple.

"Here, eat."

"Do you have a pitcher in which I can wash my hands?"

"Yes. What do you want to do that for?"

Jacob washed his hands with the water that the ferryman brought him and wiped them on his coat. After saying grace, he bit into the bread.

"I owe you thanks, but first I must thank God."

"You don't owe me a thing, or God either. I have bread so I give it to you. If I didn't have any, I'd go begging. God owns everything but the rich receive it all."

"God is the author of all riches."

"If there is a God. Have you seen Him? I had one passenger, an aristocrat, who said there wasn't."

"What kind of an aristocrat?"

"Crazy! But he talked sense. What does anyone know? In India they worship snakes. The Jews put little black boxes on their heads, and shawls. I know. A lot of them used to use this ferry. But along gallops Chmielnicki; there were so many corpses floating in the Vistula the river stank. That's what their God did for them."

"The evildoers will be punished."

"Where? There was a brute of a count in Parchev who flogged I don't know how many hundreds of peasants to death but he lived to be ninety-eight. His serfs set his castle on fire, and down came the rain and saved it. He died peacefully sipping a glass of wine. I say: the worms get everyone, good and bad."

"Yet, you give me bread."

"So! Don't take it as an insult but I feed hungry animals, too."

VII

The ferryman, whose name was Waclaw, took Jacob into his hut and gave him a pillow stuffed with straw. There was only one bench to sleep on so Jacob lay on the floor. The ferryman talked:

"One thing I've learned in my life: don't get attached to anything. You own a cow or a horse and you're its slave. Marry and you're the slave of your wife, her bastards, and her mother. Look at Pilitzky, all his life scared he'll be robbed, while he's being bled dry. When he married that whore, she only had to look twice at a man and he was sending around his seconds. The worst bitch this side of the Vistula. A hunk of filth. She's had a stallion as her lover, and of course the coachman. Did you know her husband finds her lovers? If that isn't being a slave, what is? When I hear such things, I say to myself, Waclaw, not you. You'll be nobody's slave. I'm not a peasant. I have noble blood. True, I don't know who my father was, but what's the difference? My mother came from a fine house. They wanted to apprentice me to a shoemaker and marry me off to his daughter. A dowry and all the trimmings went with her. So did a mother, grandmother, and sisters. The dust didn't settle under my feet. Here at the ferry I'm as free as a bird. I think what I please. Twice a day the passengers come and I do my job. No one bothers me the rest of the time. I don't even go to church. What does the priest want? To put another rope around my neck."

"No, man cannot be entirely free," Jacob said, after some consideration.

"Why not?"

"Somebody must plow and sow and reap. Children must be raised."

"Well, not by me. Let the others do it."

"A woman bore you and brought you up."

"I didn't ask for it. She wanted to have a man, so she did."

"But if there is a child, it must be fed, clothed, and taught, or it will grow up a wild animal."

"Let them grow as they please."

Waclaw began to snore. Yes, it is true, Jacob meditated, only half asleep himself, man goes in harness; every desire is a strand of the rope that yokes him. Jacob fell asleep, awoke, dozed off again, woke with a start. What should he do? Leave and desert the child? But where would he go? What would he do? Marry again? He had already stepped under the canopy twice, and now his two wives and three children were in the other world. He would be more at home there than here. A cold wind was blowing from the Vistula and he tried to warm himself with the heat from his own

241

body. His brain stayed awake and he could hear himself snoring. He mustn't stay here long; people would soon be coming to the crossing, and the dragoons might be on his trail. But perhaps it was better to be caught and hanged.

Jacob fell into a deep sleep, and when he opened his eyes the sun was shining. Waclaw stood over him.

"You got yourself a little sleep, eh?"

"I was exhausted."

"Go on sleeping. There's nothing better. If someone who doesn't belong here shows up, I'll let you know."

"Why do you do all this?"

"Your head must be worth a couple of grivniks..." And Waclaw winked.

As Waclaw left, closing the door behind him, Jacob heard the sound of approaching wagons and realized there must be a road across the dunes. Soon wagons began to pass, shaking the hut, and through chinks in the walls came smells of horse dung, tar, and sausage. He heard many people talking, though it was still early and the ferry wouldn't leave for hours. There was no water in the hut to wash with before praying. So Jacob recited, "I thank," a prayer one could say without ablutions. Blessed spirit, he murmured, where are you now? Your body must have been buried like carrion. He thought of the child, his and Sarah's, the grandson of Rabbi Eliezer of Zamosc and of Jan Bzik. He could not desert it. Did not the first Jacob rear the grandchildren of Terah and Laban? His own son must grow up instructed in the Torah. For God, whose purpose requires both life and death, there was no such thing as good birth. In God's mills even chaff becomes flour.

Rising, he walked to the front wall and peered through the cracks. It looked like market day outside—everywhere peasants, carts, oxen, pigs, calves. On the ferryboat near a sack stood a strange little man in a prayer shawl and phylacteries, his face turned away from Jacob toward the east. His white gabardine and embroidered prayer shawl were unlike any seen in Poland, and he was wearing sandals and white stockings. He bowed so low praying that the phylactery on his head almost touched the deck; he seemed to be reciting the eighteen benedictions. When he turned, Jacob saw the stranger's white beard that extended to his waist, and knew that this man had been sent to him. Degraded as he was, heaven no longer trusted in his wisdom to choose freely, but was leading him step by step along the road that he must follow. Jacob could no longer remain in the hut, but had to go and present himself to the stranger.

VIII

The man finished his prayers, replaced his phylacteries in their cases and put on an *abaya*, the kind of coat worn by messengers from the Holy Land and by Jews from Egypt, Yemen, Persia. Jacob approached the man and greeted him with a Sholom, expecting to receive a reply in Aramaic or Hebrew, but when the stranger spoke, it was in Yiddish.

"A Jew, eh? This place is crawling with gentiles. But I say my prayers wherever I am."

"You must be an emissary from the Holy Land."

"Yes, an emissary. The need in the land of Israel is great. We had a drought this year and on top of that a plague of locusts. When the Arab's in trouble, what's left for the Jews? Starvation is everywhere. And thirst. Water is bought by the cupful. Well, but the Jews all over the world are merciful. Stretch out a hand to them and they give."

"When do you go back?"

243

"I'm on my way now, though I still must visit a few communities. Then I board ship at Constance."

"How do the Jews maintain themselves in the Holy Land?"

The emissary paused to think this over.

"Which ones? It depends. The majority are paupers and what you don't give, they don't have. But there are a few rich men. All of us were struck dumb when we heard what was going on here in Poland. The news came about Chmielnicki—may his name be blotted out—and we had a second Tischab'ov. We ran to the sacred graves and the Wailing Wall and prayed. But we were no help. The massacres must have been already decreed. How do we know what's going on in heaven? Since the destruction of the temple, the rigor of the law has prevailed. But there are signs, many signs, that the End of Days is near."

"What signs?"

"It would take too long to tell you. The Book of Daniel makes it clear to those who understand that the Redemption will come in the year 5426. Don't think we do nothing. The cabalists are busy and have uncovered all kinds of portents. Of course, everything is in God's hands but much can be done through the power of the holy names. Pure and sacred men dressed in white sit and pore over these mysteries. Are you a man of the Torah?"

"I have studied."

"Have you ever looked into the *Zohar?*"

"Occasionally."

"Well, the sacred names govern everything. As the Gemara says, there is an angel for each blade of grass. And if that is so, the Redemption will only come through the holy combinations. Our cabalists fast, study all night, and at dawn visit the graves of saints. The older generation is gone; we have been deprived of our pious Rabbi Isaac Luria as well as Rabbis Chaim Vital and Shlomo Alkabetz. But the tabernacle of peace in Sefad still exists and Yephtah is the Samuel of this generation. But can a man live without bread? Even Rabbi Chanina, the son of Dusso, had to have his share of St. John's bread each week. Jews all over the world must do their part. What is your name?"

"Jacob."

"Give me a little something, Reb Jacob."

And the emissary pulled out a wooden alms box. Jacob blushed.

"You won't believe me but I don't have even half a groschen."

The alms box quickly disappeared.

"How can you travel without money?"

"I am a mourner, I should be sitting shivah."

"So why aren't you?"

"I'm escaping from the gentiles."

"Then, it's you who should be receiving. Does it matter where a Jew suffers? We all have the same Father. Why are you running away?"

Jacob didn't know whether to laugh or cry. Again his story must be told. The secrets he had kept for years were now being divulged to everyone. So seemingly chance occurrences led to a predetermined end. He said to the emissary:

"Come into the hut. My story is long. I must not be seen."

"But what about the ferryman?"

"He is letting me use it."

Before seating himself on the bench, the emissary ascertained that there was no cloth there woven of both wool and linen. He was so short his legs didn't reach the floor and Jacob placed a log for his feet. Then, leaning against the wall, Jacob told everything, denied nothing, from the day the Cossacks took him captive until the night he escaped from the dragoons. The emissary nodded, grimaced, chewed his beard, rubbed his forehead, and occasionally pulled at one of his sidelocks. The deeper Jacob got into his story the more pained the emissary became. He spread his hands, raised his eyebrows, tugged at his beard. His eyes expressed sadness, compassion, astonishment. From time to time, he sighed deeply. When Jacob finished, the emissary covered his face with his hands, which were small and bony, and his lips, hidden behind his beard, murmured and shook as if he were reciting a prayer or an incantation. After a while he lowered his hands. His face seemed altered, grayer, more drawn, with deeper pockets under the eyes.

"The community is right. Your wife was a gentile and so is your son. The child follows its mother. This is the law. But behind the law, there is mercy. Without mercy, there would be no law."

"Yes, yes."

"How could you have thought of doing such a thing? Well, it's done now."

"I am ready for my punishment."

"What? It's all because of the massacres and the destruction. Don't ask me what I've seen here. Nevertheless you are a learned man."

"It was not within my power to act differently."

"It seems it was not. Free will exists, but so does foreknowledge. 'All is foreseen but the choice is given.' Each soul must accomplish its task, or it would not have been sent here. The sons of Keturah were also the sons of Abraham."

"What shall I do now?"

"You must save yourself and you must save your child. First of all, he must be circumcised. When he grows up, he may have to be converted—I don't remember the law exactly but meanwhile let him be brought up as a Jew. It is written somewhere that before the Messiah will come, all the pious gentiles will have been converted."

"I don't remember the passage."

"It's somewhere in the Talmud or Midrash—what's the difference? I'll give you two guldens and when you have money, God willing, you'll give it back. Not to me personally, but to another emissary. Does it matter? The money goes to the Holy Land. The fact that you found me here is odd: I was to have preached a sermon and I would have collected a nice sum of money. But suddenly I was seized by a desire to travel. That's the way Heaven manages things."

For a while both men were silent. Then the emissary said:

"If she has already been buried, you are obliged to pray today. Take my prayer shawl and phylacteries. I'll wait and then we'll have breakfast."

12

The emissary tried to persuade Jacob that it would
be dangerous to return to Pilitz immediately. A
man's life is too important, he said, and anyway
the infant was too small and weak to be moved.
Besides, the day after tomorrow was Succoth, and
a holiday is a holiday. He suggested that Jacob go
to the city with him and stay there until after
Simchath Torah. But Jacob was unyielding. He
longed to see the child, and he wanted to visit
Sarah's grave. Money was hidden in his room;
perhaps no one had as yet stolen it; he could not
suddenly start begging. In his years of slavery and
wandering, Jacob had grown used to overcoming
obstacles. Distances no longer frightened him, nor
dark forests, beasts, robbers; even his terror of
devils and hobgoblins had vanished. The strength
he had gathered had to be used. His escape from
the dragoons meant that the king was not as
powerful as he had imagined. What would happen
to the might of the wicked if the just were not so

craven? Stories he had heard of how the Jews had behaved during the massacres shamed him. Nobody dared lift a hand against the butchers while they slaughtered entire communities. Though for generations Jewish blacksmiths had forged swords, it had never occurred to the Jews to meet their attackers with weapons. The Jews of Josefov, when Jacob had spoken of this, had shrugged their shoulders. The sword is for Esau, not for Jacob. Nevertheless, must a man agree to his own destruction? Wanda had often asked Jacob: Why did the Jews permit it? The ancient Jews of the Bible stories had been heroic. Jacob never really knew how to answer her.

Breakfasting with the emissary on bread, cheese, and plums, Jacob hesitated, then took the two guldens, promising to return them as soon as he could. The emissary who had to stay a few more weeks in Poland told Jacob his route. Passengers, as well as horses, cows, oxen and sheep were still coming aboard the ferry. Amid the hubbub of the peasants, the neighing, bellowing, baying of the animals, the emissary advised Jacob on his future conduct. The Messiah was coming, so why stay in Poland? It was a great act of piety to settle in the Holy Land. When the Redeemer came, the Jews in the land of Israel would be the first to greet him. Moreover, a Jew could breathe more freely in the country of the Turks, where the Torah was respected. Many rich Jews lived in Istanbul, Smyrna, Damascus, and Cairo. Of course there were sometimes hostile edicts and people were falsely accused, but such catastrophes as those that happened in Poland—never. Further, since he, Jacob, had broken the ecclesiastical laws of the Christians, and the Jews too had good reason to censure his conduct, why not bring his child to the Holy Land and settle in a place where scholars were supported? He could always learn a trade or go into business if he wished. God willing by next summer the child would not be too frail to make the journey. The emissary's words were laden with half-spoken promises. He hinted that the Messiah already existed, and that where he was and when he would reveal himself was known to the most esoteric of the cabalists. He said to Jacob:

"My lips are sealed. A word to the wise is sufficient."

The emissary was about to say more, but suddenly the ferry began to move and Jacob jumped ashore. The emissary called out:

"Comfort and aid are coming. We'll live to see it—in our own lifetimes."

II

At dusk Jacob started for Pilitz and reached it by late evening. All the shutters were closed. Pilitz slept. A three-quarter moon shone in the sky. The Succoth booths, covered with green branches, had already been set up, though a few were yet unfinished. Walking abreast of his shadow, Jacob carried an oak stick and in his breast pocket a knife Waclaw had lent him. Jacob now heeded the advice of the Book of Aboth: "If one comes upon thee, to kill thee, rise first and kill him." Passing the market place quickly, he came to the house in which Sarah had died. There was no light, a sign that the corpse had already been removed. Standing momentarily at the door, overcome by terror, he sensed the presence of the corpse, not the body, not even the soul, but something shapeless and horrible. He pushed in the door. The moonlit room resembled a ruin, the bare floor littered with straw and rags; the body must have been cleansed on the spot. Everything had been removed, all the clothing and linen, even the pots from the oven. There was something uncanny, hostile in the fetid air. The room had a wintry dankness though it was still late summer. What's wrong with me? Why should I fear her? Jacob said to himself in reproach. Wasn't she more a part of me than my own body? But he left the door open; his heart pounded, and he breathed heavily. He searched through the straw mattress but realized immediately that the money he had hidden there was gone. Thieves! And Yom Kippur had hardly passed. The men of the burial society might even have stolen it. Despite his anxiety, Jacob was overcome with anger. They had devastated his house. The robbed had become robbers. It was a world of grabbers; whoever could, stole, and now they were going to sit in the tabernacle and invite the Holy Guests to join them. Jacob's few books were missing too. "Naked came I out of my mother's womb, and naked shall I return thither."

After kissing the mezuzah, Jacob left. Be a witness, he said. He strode toward the cemetery. Even at a distance, the new grave was visible, a fresh mound of earth far removed from the others. When he reached the mound, Jacob saw a marker, and on it the words: "Here lies Sarah, the daughter of the Patriarch Abraham." Jacob's eyes grew moist. Here lay Wanda, Sarah, the woman he loved. Although he tried to recite Kaddish, he choked on the words. Darkness enveloped him. Had the moon been extinguished? Throwing himself to the earth, he pressed his face against the grave: I am here, Sarah.

He listened as if expecting her voice to issue from the grave. A ghoulish idea came to him: to exhume her body, or at least to thrust his hand into the earth and touch her. He wanted to kiss her once more. It's forbidden, it's crazy, a sacrilege, he warned himself. Even though it was a sin, he prayed for his own death: I have wandered too long in this world. Everyone I love is there. Lying

251

prostrate, waiting for death, he had forgotten the child. For a while his strength seemed to ebb. His legs became numb and wooden, his brain like stone. He slept as though dead, then awoke. His prayer had not been answered. Rising, he began to mumble Kaddish. The marker had fallen to one side; he straightened it.

Brushing the earth from his face, Jacob stepped back a few paces. He looked for a large rock, wanting like the Patriarch Jacob to lay a stone on the grave of his beloved wife, but there was none. Jacob returned to Pilitz. Passing the study house where a single candle burned, he opened the door. An old man sat at a stand, looking into a book. Jacob recognized Reb Tobias, of whose eight children only one daughter, the wife of Naphtali the leather merchant, remained. In the glimmering light Reb Tobias' face with its matted and dirty beard seemed dark as earth. His gabardine was bloated like the garment of a pregnant woman; since he was ruptured, every few weeks his intestines had to be pushed back in place by a woman, the only person in Pilitz who knew how, and the fact that he had to allow a woman to touch his private parts caused him more grief than the physical pain. Now at midnight he sat studying the Torah. He's not a thief, God forbid, Jacob defended him, but a victim of other people's sins. The thieves are a minority.

Jacob stood watching but the old man did not stir. Deaf and half-blind, he held the book so close his eyelids almost touched the letters and at the same time hummed with a kind of moaning singsong. Because of such men as this, God had preserved the Jews. Suddenly, as Jacob stood there, he knew exactly what he must become: an ascetic who eats no meat, drinks no wine, does not sleep in a bed. He must atone for his sins. In winter

252

he would immerse himself in cold baths, in summer lie on thorns and thistles; the sun would burn him, the flies and mosquitoes bite him. For the rest of his life and until his last breath, he must repent and ask forgiveness of God and of Sarah's sacred soul. Perhaps then he would not have to linger too long in this most imperfect of worlds.

But what if in that other world Zelda Leah claimed him? She was there with her children. But would she want him after what he had done following her death? They had never belonged together spiritually, had never truly mated; most likely she had ascended to realms of purity that he, a man of earthly passions, could never enter. And as for the children, their holy souls were undoubtedly at the very Throne of Glory.

III

Jacob knew where the young woman lived to whom he had given his child, but in the night, with all the shutters closed, her house was indistinguishable from the others. It seemed to Jacob that during even his brief absence changes had occurred in Pilitz. Lurking outside, he listened for a baby's cry. But he could not remain here forever, so, after hesitating, he decided to try one house. He raised the latch to knock, the door opened, and by the light of the moon he saw two beds and two cradles. A man grunted, a woman woke, and a child began to cry. The man asked harshly:

"Who's there, huh?"

"I'm sorry. It's me, Jacob, the baby's father."

In the uneasy silence even the child stopped crying.

"Woe is me," the woman groaned.

"Did they let you out of prison?" the man asked.

"I escaped. I've come for my baby."

Once more there was silence. Then the woman said:

"Woe is me! Where will you take an infant like this one in the middle of the night? He's too small to be moved. The least wind and, God forbid..."

"I have no choice. The soldiers are after me."

"Make a light. Make a light," the woman told her husband. "They'll arrest us. I've heard the count wants the baby. Woe, Woe. What messes people get into."

"I won't give up the child without the consent of the community," the husband said firmly. "They gave it to me, let them take it back. I don't have to suffer for other people's bastards."

"I'll pay you for your trouble."

"It's not a question of money."

The woman, after covering herself with a shawl, stood at the oven and blew into the embers. Then she lit a wick and set it in a shard of oil. Its dim light illumined the unplastered walls, the smoke-stained ceiling, the two benches—one for dairy dishes, one for meat—on which stood pots, bowls, and in a wooden trough covered with rags a loaf of dough. Diapers, swaddling clothes, and straw whisks littered the room. Garbage floated in a pan of slops. A chamber pot stood next to one bed. In one cradle lay the child who had been crying. In the other, beneath a dirty quilt lay Jacob's son: tiny, red, bald, with a large head and pale eyelids. The baby's face looked old and grief-worn. A smile reminiscent of death touched its tiny lips and unformed forehead. Jacob stared. Only now did he realize that he had a son. The woman stood on the other side of the cradle.

"Where will you take such a little baby?"

"It's murder," her husband said, from his bed where he was propped up. His fringed garment was stained; pillow feathers stuck to his skull cap, and his beard and sidelocks were stippled with wisps of down. In his black eyes there was the look of a man trapped by domesticity. Jacob knew they were right, but he realized that if he did not take the baby now he would never see it again. Recalling the dream and Sarah's words, he girded himself stubbornly.

"I'll take care of him. The night is warm."

"It's not so warm. At dawn it gets cold."

"I don't want Pilitzky to get my son."

No one spoke; this was an unanswerable argument. Jacob took out a gulden.

"This is for what you have done. I'd pay more, but they stole everything, even the dishes."

"I know. I know everything. The burial society really outdid itself. They thought that you, God forbid, would never return."

"They all grabbed except us," the husband said. "They stripped the house."

"They took my money out of the straw mattress. And right after Yom Kippur!"

"Don't fast and don't steal, my mother, peace be with her, always said," the woman commented. "She'll intercede for us in Paradise. Other people's property is sacred, she always maintained."

"That's the reason we live as we do," her husband said.

"Where will you take the baby? Well, I'd better not ask."

The woman began to move about the room. She found a basket, padded it with rags and diapers, laid the baby inside and covered it with a quilt. The infant whimpered once. The woman looked at Jacob:

"He has to be nursed every few hours."

"I'll get somebody."

"When? How? Oh Mother."

And the woman began to cry.

Suddenly she said:

"Wait. I'll draw some milk from my breast. Where's the bottle?"

Her husband left his bed. Below the torn shirt, his legs were thin, crooked, hairy. He found the bottle for his wife. The noise in the room had waked the animals. The cat stretched, chickens clucked, worms crawled, a mouse poked its head out of a hole in the floor. The woman turned to the wall and squeezed milk from her breast. After a while she gave Jacob the bottle, its neck stoppered with a bit of cloth, and showed him how to pour single drops into the baby's mouth so that it would not choke. Jacob knew he was risking the child's life as well as his own; carrying the infant, he would be unable to defend himself if attacked. But he could not leave his own child, and Sarah's, among strangers and enemies. If he was destined to live, he would live. Jacob thanked the couple repeatedly, speaking of a debt which only the Almighty could pay. Then he walked out into the night, moving in the direction of the forest, the Vistula, and the ferry. He lifted his gaze to the stars: "Father, what do you want?"

A passage from Psalms came to his lips: "O spare me, that I may recover strength, before I go hence, and be no more."

IV

The moon had set and it was dark in the forest. Slowly Jacob felt his way along a path, pausing occasionally to listen to the child's breathing or to ascertain by a kiss whether it was warm enough. He had endured many tribulations in his life, but never a more anxious night than this one. Praying so hard his lips swelled, he put himself completely into the hands of Providence, knowing he was acting improperly in relying on miracles. But

256

thrusting his burden on God was now his only recourse. He had nothing left but his faith.

Jacob's footsteps aroused the sleeping forest. Twigs snapped under his feet; birds rose from the thickets; animals scurried for cover. He kept one hand raised over the basket to ward off branches. Every conceivable disaster occurred to him. Bears and wild boars inhabited the forest. Several times he thought he heard a wolf howling and reached for the stick thrust through his belt. Let there be day, let the sun rise, he commanded imploringly, realizing that his ambiguous words meant also: Let the Redemption come, and there be an end to this dark exile. It was safer to keep quiet, but instead he recited aloud passages of the Psalms, the Prophets, the Book of Prayer, and cried out to God: I have reached the end of the road. The waters are swirling around me. I lack the strength to endure these afflictions. Suddenly he had a desire to sing and he chanted a Yom Kippur melody which turned midway into one of the mountain songs. Each note reminded him of Sarah. As he sang, he wept.

All at once, a strange light flooded the forest, and for a second Jacob thought Heaven had heard him. All the birds began to scream and sing at once: the trunks of the pine trees seemed aflame. Far off in a clearing between the trees he saw a conflagration. A moment later, he realized it was the sun. Jacob gazed at the child, sat down, and offered it the cloth moistened with milk. At first it seemed to rebel at not receiving the breast, but finally it started to suck. For the first time in weeks, Jacob was joyful. No, not everything was lost; he still had his son. Let him, Jacob, reach the Vistula, he would cross it on the ferry, and find somebody to nurse his son!

At that instant, the name he must give the boy came to Jacob: Benjamin. Like the first Benjamin, this child was a Ben-oni, a child born of sorrow.

Before long he sighted the dunes that bordered the Vistula and knew he had not gone astray. Coming out of the forest, he looked around for the ferry, and walked in the direction where he was sure the crossing lay. The Vistula flowed, red mingling with black; a large bird skimming the surface dipped so low at times that its wings ruffled the waters. The river's calmness, purity, and radiance refuted the darkness of the night. Set against this luminosity even death seemed only a bad dream. Neither the sky, nor the river, nor the dunes were dead. Everything was alive, the earth, the sun, each stone. Not death, but suffering was the real enigma. What place did it have in God's Creation? Jacob stopped again to look at the baby. Did it already suffer? Yes, there were signs of suffering. But such sorrow did not come from anything it had yet endured. Its wide brow seemed furrowed in thought, and its lips moved as if it were saying something. He is only partly here, Jacob thought, no, not yet here; he is still meditating on his past before birth.

Jacob remembered the words his namesake had spoken on his deathbed: "And as for me, when I came from Padan, Rachel died by me in the land of Canaan in the way, when yet there was a little way to come into Ephrath; and I buried her there...."

His name was Jacob also; he too had lost a beloved wife, the daughter of an idolater, among strangers; Sarah too was buried by the way and had left him a son. Like the Biblical Jacob, he was crossing the river, bearing only a staff, pursued by another Esau. Everything remained the same: the ancient love, the ancient grief. Perhaps four thousand years would again pass; somewhere, at another river, another Jacob would walk mourning another Rachel. Or who knew, perhaps it was always the same Jacob and the same Rachel. Well, but the Redemption has to come. All of this can't last forever.

Jacob lifted his gaze: Lead, God, lead. It is thy world.

PART THREE

The Return

13

Almost twenty years had passed and Pilitz, grown
into a city, belonged now to the son of one of
Pilitzky's creditors, who had taken possession
after a protracted lawsuit. Both the lord of Pilitz
and his wife Theresa were dead, he having finally
carried out his threat to hang himself. The widow
had immediately begun an affair with an impoverished young noble and had been so infatuated
that she gave him the last of what she had. One
day he disappeared. Theresa became melancholic,
locked herself in an attic room in the castle, grew
sick and emaciated, and never reappeared. All of
her cousins and relatives deserted her. When the
new owner moved to dispossess the widow, the
bailiff found her dead surrounded by her cats. The
peasants commented that although Theresa had
been dead for days, her cats, ravenous from lack of
food, had not touched the body—evidence that
animals are grateful to their benefactors.

The castle had been rebuilt, but the young noble

was seldom there, spending most of his time in Warsaw or abroad. The bailiff stole, and Gershon's youngest son-in-law, as dishonest as Gershon himself, now leased the manor fields. The peasants starved; most of the Jews were also poor; yet the city grew. Gentile craftsmen now competed with the Jewish artisans, and the priests sent delegates to the king to revoke the ancient Jewish privileges. But when one trade was taken from a Jew, he found another. Jews sapped the trees for turpentine, sent lumber down the Vistula to Danzig, brewed vodka and beer, made mead from honey, wove cloth, tanned hides, and even traded in minerals. And although the Muscovites sharpened their swords and the Cossacks attacked at every opportunity, nevertheless between invasions they bought Polish goods. Jewish merchants extended credit, conducted business with Russians, Prussians, Bohemians, even with the distant Italians. There were Jewish banks in Danzig, Leipzig, Cracow, Warsaw, Prague, Padua, Venice. The Jewish banker did not waste money on luxuries, kept his capital in a bag tucked into his fringed garment, and sat in the study house praying. But when he gave someone a letter of credit, the recipient could present it in Paris or in Amsterdam and get money.

At the time of Sabbatai Zevi, the false Messiah who later put on the fez and became a Mohammedan, Pilitz was torn by dissension. The community excommunicated his followers, but they retaliated by publicly cursing the rabbi and the town elders. Men not only damned but even attacked each other physically. Some of the members of the sect ripped the roofs from their houses, packed their belongings in barrels and trunks, and prepared to fly to the land of Israel. Some indulged in cabala, tried to tap wine from walls, to create pigeons by the arcane powers of the Book of Creation. Others ceased to follow the Torah, believing the law would be annulled with the coming of the Messiah. Still others ferreted out hints in the Bible that to be utterly evil was the way to redemption, and they indulged in every variety of abomination. There was a teacher in Pilitz whose imagination was so strong that while praying in prayer shawl and phylacteries he could fancy himself copulating and have an ejaculation. The cursed sect considered this so great an achievement that they made him their leader.

After a while, most of the Jews recognized their error, realized Satan had seduced them, and lost faith in the false Messiah. But some still conspired and kept up their pernicious idolatry. They met at fairs in distant cities and made themselves known to each other through various signs. They wrote the initials S-Z on the books, tools and other merchandise sold in their stores, and they exhibited talismans invented by Sabbatai Zevi. They were united not merely by the illusion that Sabbatai Zevi would return and rebuild Jerusalem, but by commerce. They bought and sold from each other, formed combines, worked for each other's profit, and intrigued against their enemies. When one was accused of swindling, the others testified to his honesty and threw the blame on someone else. They soon became wealthy and powerful. At their meetings, they ridiculed the righteous—pointing out how easy it was to deceive them.

The city grew and so did the cemetery, until the graves spread to the spot where Sarah lay. Her grave became an issue. Some of the elders said her bones should be exhumed and buried elsewhere, since according to the law she was not Jewish and it was a sacrilege to let her remain among the corpses of the pious. The opposition maintained that digging up her bones was not only wrong but might have evil consequences. Besides, the marker had rotted away, the mound flattened, and no one was sure where the body lay. The wisest thing was to leave well enough alone. And the cemetery kept on growing. As usual in new cities where there is no book of chronicles and no old men to hand down the traditional stories, Sarah was soon forgotten and even Jacob was seldom remembered. Many of their contemporaries had died; new citizens had moved in; and Pilitz now had a stone synagogue, a study house, a poorhouse, an inn—even a community outhouse for those who were ashamed to use the gutter. In a little hut across from the cemetery lived the gravedigger, Reb Eber.

One day in the month of Ob, a tall, white-bearded man, in a white gabardine and white hat, sandals on his bare feet, a bag on his shoulder, appeared at the cemetery. In his right hand he held a stick. He did not look like a Polish Jew. His waist was circled with a broad sash like those worn by emissaries from the Holy Land. Moving among the graves, he poked, searched, bent down to read the headstones. Observing him from a window, Eber wondered what he was doing in the cemetery. Was he looking for someone? The settlement was not old; there were no saints' graves here. Eber went to find out.

"Who are you looking for? I'm in charge here."

"So? There used to be a convert's grave here. Sarah, the daughter of the Patriarch Abraham. They buried her at a distance, but I see the cemetery has grown."

"A convert, here? Has she a stone?"

"No, a marker."

"When did she die?"

"Some twenty years ago."

"I've only been here six. What was she to you?"

"My wife."

"Who are you? What's your name?"

"Jacob. I lived here once, a little after the massacres."

"Was conversion allowed in Poland?"

"She had a Jewish soul."

"I don't know. The place is overgrown with weeds. They added a piece of ground years ago. The whole city fasted."

II

Jacob continued to search, poking with his stick, and sniffing at the ground; then he stretched out on the wild grass, whispering to the earth. The sun was setting when Jacob walked through the city, looked around, stopped, gaped. It was a different Pilitz with different people. Seeing the study house, he entered. A single anniversary candle flickered in the menorah, and above the tables were shelves of books. Jacob took one out, looked inside, kissed it, and put it back. Then he took out another and seated himself. He had come from the Land of Israel to disinter Sarah's bones and take them back. Their son, Benjamin Eliezer, was now a lecturer in a yeshiva in Jerusalem. Jacob had never told him of his mother's origins. There are truths which must remain hidden. Why divide his spirit? Benjamin Eliezer had grown up a prodigy and at thirteen had already dipped into the cabala. This was in the time of Sabbatai Zevi and both father and son were misled by the false Messiah. The emissary Jacob had met on the ferryboat had been one of his legates and in old age had put on the fez.

Jacob had been through so much in those twenty years. The voyage to Jerusalem had taken many weeks and the vessel he had been traveling on had been attacked by pirates. He had seen half of his fellow passengers murdered before his eyes. The baby had suffered from dysentery and would have died if Sarah had not come to Jacob in a dream and given him a remedy. He too had become critically ill. Scarcely had he recovered when a Turk accused him of stealing and the captain had wanted to hang Jacob. A storm had come up and the ship lay on its side for three days. When Jacob arrived at Jerusalem, he found the city suffering a famine. Moreover, there was scarcely any water to drink. Every few years the city was swept by pestilence. Jacob was present when Sabbatai Zevi had been driven out of Jerusalem; he knew Nathan of Gaza and Samuel Primu. During the days of his error, he had worn the talismans of the accursed sect and had eaten on Tischab'ov and the seventeenth day of Tammuz. He had almost put on the fez like all the others. God alone knew how many miracles had happened to him. All that he had seen and endured could not have been told in seven days and seven nights. It is impossible to convey the torment he had undergone when he realized that he was sinking into the lowest abyss! Even his present trip to Poland had been beset by many pitfalls, proving again that no moment is without its misfortune. Every day he experienced another miracle. But that Benjamin should have become an instructor in a yeshiva at twenty and the son-in-law of a rabbi was an unalloyed gift from Heaven. Heaven had decreed that Jacob should not perish a heretic. It had been willed that Sarah and he were to leave issue.

But the disappearance of Sarah's grave was a blow to Jacob, and it seemed that the trip had been made in vain. Jacob wanted to bury Sarah's bones on the Mount of Olives and to prepare a grave for himself close by. He hoped that since he had not been able to be with her alive, at least his body should rest near her in death.

Well, but everything God did was for the good. The older Jacob grew, the clearer this truth became to him. An eye was watching, a hand guiding, each sin had its significance. Not even Sabbatai Zevi had come in vain. False birth pains sometimes precede the true. Jacob, journeying through the Turkish countries from the Holy Land to Poland, had come to know things he had not understood before. Each generation had its lost tribes. Some portion always longs to return to Egypt. There are always frightened spies, Samsons, Abimelechs, Jethros, Ruths. The leaves drop from the tree, but the branches remain; the trunk still has its roots. Israel's lost children live in every land. Each community has within it those who stay apart. Men blossom and wither like plants. Heaven writes the story and only there is the truth known. In the end each man is responsible only for himself.

When Jacob had still been close to the sect of Sabbatai Zevi, they had tried to persuade him to marry. Women of wealth and fine family were available. He had never been free of carnal desires, but a power stronger than passion had said no. Later too, when he had repented, the rabbi and the cabalists had argued that according to the law and the cabala, he should find a new mate. But even when his lips said yes, an inner voice shouted no. It often seemed to him that Sarah was still with him. She spoke to him, he answered. She accompanied him to the ruins and the holy graves, warned him against all kinds of dangers, and advised him how to bring up Benjamin. If he put a pot on the stove and forgot it, she called him when the food was about to burn...

How could he tell such things? He would be considered insane or possessed by devils, but every heart has secrets it dares not tell.

Jacob nodded over the book open before him. How wonderful there were study houses and books everywhere! Jacob had never forgotten the years on the mountain when he had to dig Torah from his memory. His love for books had grown continually. Sometimes when they tried to marry him off he wanted to answer, the Torah is my wife. No day passed without his going over a few chapters of the Bible, and he had read the Midrash many times. His love for the Torah had not ceased even when he belonged to the Sabbatai Zevi sect. A chapter of the Psalms was like manna which tasted exactly as each man wished it to. Jacob refreshed himself with the moral truths of Proverbs; he satisfied his hunger with sections of the Mishna. Everything he studied he explained to Sarah in Yiddish, sometimes in Polish, as if she were sitting beside him. On the voyage he had drawn her attention to the waves, the islands, the flying fish, the constellations. Look, Sarah, God's wonders! It was perilous for a Jew to walk alone on the roads in the Holy Land, but he had wandered with her among the Arabs, through deserts where caravans of camels passed. Sarah watched that no evil befell him. Arabs with wild eyes and knives at their waists gave him figs, dates, St. John's bread, and provided him with shelter for the night. Many times he came upon venomous snakes—which turned away from him. "Thou shalt tread upon the lion: the adder and the dragon shalt thou trample under feet."

But why had he been sent on this long journey if he could not find Sarah's bones and bring them to the Holy Land? His son had tried to dissuade him from the trip. The cabalists had pleaded with him, saying that every Jew was needed in the Holy Land. The pangs accompanying the birth of the Messiah were almost over, and signs indicated that the battle of Gog and Magog was imminent. Satan was drawing up a list of heavy accusations. The Lord of Edom girt his loins for the bitter struggle. Soon would come that battle when the

269

evil hosts would attempt to overturn the scale of mercy. Then would Asmodeus, Lilith, each demon, every hobgoblin, bark, hiss, spit, foam; led by the primeval snake, packs of dogs, adders, hawks, and hyenas would march to Batsrah where the final conflict would take place. Not a single pious Jew, prayer, benediction, or act of piety, could be spared with the Redemption hanging in the balance. Jacob was needed here, not in some distant country. Sarah, too, argued against his going: Why bring my bones when soon the underground caverns will be filled with skeletons rolling to the Land of Israel? But for the first time in twenty years, Jacob demurred. An irresistible power within him forced him to make the trip.

Jacob's losses had been great, but he still had the holy books to cling to. Resigned long since to the loss of both the joys of this world and of heaven, he served God without hope, prepared each moment for the fires of Gehenna.

III

The men who came to the study house for the evening prayer greeted the stranger and asked where he came from.

"From the Land of Israel," he answered. "But once I lived here in Pilitz."

"What is your name?"

"Jacob. In those days I was known as Jacob the teacher, or as Jacob, Dumb Sarah's husband."

There was an outcry. Though most of the men present had not known Jacob, a few of the older inhabitants remembered him well. The man whose wife had nursed Jacob's baby clutched his head, and ran to tell his wife the news. She came into the study house among the men and began to cry and scream as if she were praying for some one who had fallen ill.

"Dear man, a day hasn't passed without my thinking of you. How's the baby?"

"He lectures in a yeshiva in Jerusalem and is the father of three children."

"That I should have lived to see this! There is a God."

Once more she began to wail.

The cantor had difficulty keeping the people silent until after the Minchah prayer, and immediately upon the completion of the eighteen benedictions the tumult resumed. Though few had known Jacob and his mute wife, many had heard of them. Even in the villages outside of Pilitz, the story was told how Jacob had escaped from the dragoons and come in the middle of the night to claim his son. This story had been particularly popular when the Messianists were dominant in Pilitz. That sect had believed in physical action, had contended that Israel should either seize Esau's sword or intermarry with his seed and that of Ishmael until all the descendants of Abraham had become one nation. They cited Jacob and Sarah as precursors of the Redemption. The new lord of Pilitz had even regarded the sect of Sabbatai Zevi with favor. At that time the mound over Sarah's grave was still visible, the marker still there, and women and girls had gone to the grave and recited prayers.

But when it was heard that Sabbatai Zevi had accepted the Koran, the warden of the burial society in Pilitz ordered his men to level the ground over Sarah's grave. Not long after, the new plot of ground was added to the cemetery and soon no one remembered where Sarah lay. Now, hearing that Jacob had returned from the Land of Israel, the secret followers of Sabbatai Zevi approached him, bid him welcome, and one of them invited him to stay at his house. But, refusing to be anyone's guest, Jacob replied he would sleep in the poorhouse. At the mention of Sabbatai Zevi's name, Jacob spat and cried out loudly, "Let his name and memory be blotted out."

Many questions were put to Jacob about what had happened to him. He spoke of the land of Israel, of the Jews living there, of the yeshivas, the holy graves, the ruins. He explained how the true cabalists were attempting to bring about the End of Days. He described the Wailing Wall, the Double Cave, Rachel's grave, and exhibited a few Turkish coins. A young man asked him if on his sea voyage he had seen any of those creatures, half man, half fish, who sing so sweetly that a man must stop up his ears or he will expire with delight. Jacob said that he himself had not seen any. Long after the evening prayer was over, the men continued to talk and converse. Why had Jacob come? someone asked. When he replied that it was to disinter Sarah's bones and transport them to the Holy Land, there was a long silence. Then the warden of the burial society remarked:

"Might as well look for a needle in a haystack."

"It seems that it was not fated," Jacob said.

The people began to turn their backs on him. Everyone had heard of the bones of saints of important people being carried to the Land of Israel—but that a man should return after twenty years to hunt for the bones of some female who had been given a donkey's burial? That was peculiar. Some murmured that the guest must be out of his mind; others suspected him of belonging to the excommunicated sect; still others concluded that he was a liar and had not come from the Land of Israel. The followers of Sabbatai Zevi walked over to him, but everything they said, he disputed. Finally all the older men left, and without Jacob. Soon the woman who had nursed Jacob's child entered, bringing kasha and beef broth for him, but he told her he never ate flesh; neither meat nor fish nor anything else from a living creature, not even cheese or eggs. The woman asked:

"What do you live on? Burning coals?"

"Bread and olives."

"We have no olives."

"Also I take radish, onion, or garlic with my bread."

"How do you keep your strength that way?"

"God gives strength."

"Well, eat the bread."

Jacob washed his hands at the water barrel and sat down to eat the dry bread. A few boys whose turn it was to study at this time of the night began to ridicule the stranger.

"Why are you so scared of flesh?"

"We are flesh ourselves."

"What do you take on the Sabbath?"

"The same as on weekdays."

"You're not allowed to torment yourself on the Sabbath."

"Nor must one torment others."

"What do you put into the Sabbath pudding?"

"Olive oil."

"If everybody lived as you do, what would the ritual slaughterer live on?"

"One can survive without slaughter."

One boy tried to convince Jacob that he was breaking the law, while the others pinched themselves, giggled, whispered. He knew they were ridiculing him, but Jacob answered seriously, clearly. Jacob, who had his own ways of thinking and acting, who interpreted the Torah in his own manner, was accustomed to suspicion and mockery. Even as a child he had been a misfit. Despite his brief association with the followers of Sabbatai Zevi (and even there he had been on the outer fringe), he had always remained aloof. Even his own son, Benjamin Eliezer, had at times reproached him for his strange conduct. In the Holy

273

Land, the community had wanted to support him out of funds given to aid scholars, but he had refused to accept charity, and had done all kinds of hard labor, such as digging ditches, cleaning outhouses, carrying heavy loads usually transported by donkeys. He was offered steady work, but refused to stay long in one place. One day he would go to Safad, another to Schechem; sometimes he journeyed to Jaffa, other times he wandered through the desert on the way to the Dead Sea. When he was sleepy, he would lie down in the sand, placing a stone under his head. There was even a rumor that Jacob was not a born Jew but a convert. Years passed, yet some of those who knew him never discovered that he was a learned man and considered him an ignoramus.

He had always been the same Jacob, in Zamosc, in Josefov, in the hamlet on the mountain, in Pilitz, in Jerusalem. His thoughts seemed clear to him, but others found them confused. At times, Jacob accused himself of stubbornness and disobedience since the Torah itself said that one should accept the majority and follow the leaders of each generation. But even so, Jacob could not be other than he was. Besides he could not forget the years he had spent in Jan Bzik's barn on the mountain, surrounded by animals and savage shepherds. The years with Sarah had left their mark upon him. He had great patience with the weak but he resisted the strong. For long periods he could remain silent, but when he spoke it was always the truth. He had made long journeys to repay half a piastre. He dared defy armed Arabs or Turks. He took the most difficult tasks upon himself, carried the paralyzed, cleansed the lice-infected sick. Men avoided him, but pious women considered him a saint, one of the thirty-six righteous men who are the pillars of the world.

Now Jacob sat in the study house, reproaching

himself for having come. Of the money he had saved for the trip, there was not enough left for the return journey. He had placed himself in a situation where he would have to ask others for help, and, God forbid, he might become sick in Poland, or on the ship where those who die are buried at sea. I am mad, he said to himself. My mother, peace be with her, when she called me a rattlebrain, was right. As soon as he had finished the passages he had set himself, he walked to the poorhouse. The boys had told him he could sleep in the study house, but this he considered sacrilege. His rule was to prefer the difficult to the easy. Sometimes Jacob was amazed at the burdens he required his body and his soul to carry.

IV

Opening the door of the poorhouse, Jacob entered. In the darkness, he heard sighing and groaning, snoring, and the uneasy coughing of those he had disturbed. A man's voice asked:

"Who's there?"

"A guest. A stranger."

"In the middle of the night?"

"It's not midnight yet."

"The candle is out already."

"I will do without it."

"Can you see in the dark?"

"I'll lie down on the floor."

"There's a bundle of straw somewhere. Wait, I'll get it for you."

"Don't bother."

"Once I'm awakened, I can't close my eyes all night."

Jacob stood there while his eyes grew accustomed to the darkness and his nose to the stench. Even though it was summer, all the windows were

275

tightly shut. The moon wasn't shining, but the sky outside was filled with stars. Jacob could discern the sleeping forms of men and women. He was familiar with all of this, the smells, the moaning; it was the same everywhere, in the Holy Land, in the countries of the Arabs and the Turks, in Poland. In whatever town Jacob found himself, he always went to the poorhouse to help the old and the sick, to wash them, rub them with turpentine, bring them fresh straw. Now, bringing a pile of straw and spreading it on the floor, someone was helping him. Jacob had read Shema before coming, so that the holy words need not be defiled by this unclean place; now he only needed to say the last prayer before sleep. He lay down, carefully stretching out his legs to avoid touching anyone. A woman complained:

"All night they drag themselves around, and now they come and wake up sick people. May their legs drop off!"

"Don't curse, woman, don't curse. You'll have time enough to sleep."

"In the grave maybe."

"Who are you? Where are you from?" the man who had brought Jacob the straw asked. He lay on a bench nearby.

"I came from the Holy Land."

"You aren't that Reb Jacob who was in the study house today?" the man said, astonished.

"Yes, I am."

"Didn't anyone offer you a bed? You lived here once. I remember when you first came. You were the teacher. My own son learned the alphabet from you. We were talking about you earlier."

"It couldn't be the same Jacob," a woman said.

"Yes, the same."

"No wonder they call Pilitz Sodom," the man said. "But even in Sodom there was a Lot, and he took in strangers."

"What's your name?" Jacob asked the man

"Mine? Leibush Mayer."

"Reb Leibush Mayer, one should look for the good in people, not the bad. How do you know no one invited me? The truth is, several men did. But it's not my habit to be anyone's guest. What's the matter with the poorhouse?"

"My enemies should rot in poorhouses," said the woman who had cursed Jacob.

"He knows what he's doing," Leibush Mayer defended Jacob. "How many of you here come from Pilitz? The devil knows where you're from. You land in Pilitz and eat up the town. But I came the very first day. There were only three houses here, then. It was right after the massacres. Gershon, may his soul burn in hell, had already grabbed Pilitzky's fields. In those days we didn't even have a quorum. I came with Menasha, my little boy. I'd lost my wife and the other two children. Menasha's gone too, now. I was a carpenter, and there was plenty of work to do. We had one tutor—he left before you came," he said, turning to Jacob. "Another teacher was supposed to come from the other side of the Vistula. Then you showed up. I remember it as if it were yesterday. What do these beggars know about that. You taught my Menasha and he learned a lot. In a few months he could read. Well, and so you took over the fields from Gershon. What didn't happen, then! We've talked about you; we've talked. Just last week I told these paupers here your whole story. Then you show up! But why did you come back from the Holy Land?"

Jacob was silent for a moment.

"To visit my wife's grave."

"Did you find it? The burial society people blotted it out. Don't think, Reb Jacob, there weren't many people on your side." The man's tone changed. "I remember that meeting at the rabbi's the night after Yom Kippur. I went. True, I was only a carpenter, but I was invited. Wasn't I a householder? Didn't I know the small letters? I stood at the door and listened. I wanted to cry out, 'Don't be so harsh. He's punished enough.' But Gershon, his bones should turn in his grave, shook his fist at me. And who gave the verdict? The rabbi, Gershon's son-in-law. We know who was the real rabbi. It was Gershon too who denounced you to the priests. I'll testify to that before God Himself. Gershon almost turned to steam when he heard you'd taken the baby. He almost ruined the man for letting you have it. Did the child live?"

"He has three children of his own now."

"Where is he?"

"In Jerusalem."

"How did you get there with such a small baby?"

"It's a long story."

"They wanted me to be a member of the burial society, but I wasn't going to lick Gershon's boots. They didn't even cleanse your wife's body properly, just threw her into a ditch in her clothes. I was there. I saw it. The beadle was about to recite Kaddish, but Gershon said no. They stole everything you had. The corpse was still lying on the floor, and they were stripping the room. They even took the broom. And they turned the place upside down looking for money."

"I forgave them a long time ago."

"All right, you forgave. But has God? In Heaven everything's written down—from the biggest sin to the smallest. Gershon took to his bed before the year was out. His belly was always big but it swelled up and he looked like a barrel. There wasn't a feather bed large enough to cover him and the town rang with his hiccups. Your wife, Sarah, may she dwell in Paradise, was not at peace in her grave. Maybe I shouldn't tell you, but she came to women in dreams and complained: I am naked and

278

without shrouds. She was also seen walking in the room where she died. Even in summer that room stayed icy. Everyone knew why she walked. The house was finally bought by a gentile."

"It's gone now," Jacob said.

"It burned down. Suddenly one night it blazed up like straw. The women swore they saw her image in the flames."

"Whose?"

"Your wife's."

V

Jacob awoke before dawn. Something heavy lay on his heart; his stomach was swollen; his limbs were weak. Am I getting sick? What's happening to me? he asked himself. His tongue was coated; his head lolled. Never before had he been so ill. He found he didn't have the strength to sit up. He lay amazed, watching the sun through the window, a red ball rising in the east. Dawn was like dusk; the birds twittered feebly. Were the window panes so dusty? Were his eyes misted? Somehow he raised himself and looked around. Men and women lay all about him on straw pallets amid garbage and rags: the old, the sick, the paralyzed, some with distorted faces. They muttered, snored, grunted, whined through their noses. Jacob sank back again closing his eyes.

He was not asleep, yet he saw Sarah standing near him dressed in luminous drapes and surrounded by light. The joy of the sunrise emanated from her. Smiling at him like a mother, like a wife, with a love greater than he had ever known, she said:

"Mazeltov, Jacob. We have been separated long enough."

Jacob opened his eyes. He knew the truth: his time had come. Well, is this what I came for, to die?

Here, and not in the Holy Land? This seemed to him a harsh decree: his son and grandchildren were there; Benjamin Eliezer would not know of his death, would not know he should say Kaddish. But Jacob warned himself not to question the Lord of the Universe. If this was Heaven's decree, so be it. "All that God does is for the good." Jacob glanced at his sack in which he carried his prayer shawl, his phylacteries, and a few books, a Pentateuch, a volume of the Mishnah, a prayer book. How can I recite holy words in this filthy place? he asked himself. He wanted to pray, but his lips would not move. Finally, he began to murmur a chapter of the Psalms, omitting to pronounce the names of God. "None of them can by any means redeem his brother, nor give to God a ransom for him.... That he should still live for ever, and not see corruption."

Jacob dozed off, woke, fell asleep, and woke once more. Even as he closed his eyes, his dreams rushed in on him. Phantoms walked, ran, screamed, behaved in indescribable ways. And when he opened his eyes, they remained for a time etched against the glare of the daylight, speaking a tongue that Jacob understood without hearing. He lay there seeming to sleep. A man with a gray disheveled beard and a wrinkled earthy face put his feet down from his bench and nudged Jacob.

"Reb Jacob, it's morning."

Jacob stirred.

"You don't want to be late with your Shema."

"I have no water to wash my hands."

"Wash your hands in the barrel. They don't bring you pitchers around here."

"I'm afraid I'm not well," Jacob said.

"What? You do look a little yellow."

The man stretched out his hand, touched Jacob's forehead, and frowned.

"I'll go for the healer."

"No, don't trouble."

"Caring for the sick is a sacred obligation."

The man put on his gabardine and his shoes and left. Soon the women and the children began to wake; they yawned, coughed, sneezed. One old crone sat up cursing. Everyone deloused himself. Despite his stuffed nose, Jacob was aware of the stench. Worms crawled on the floor and walls. Rabbis had many times denounced the lodging of men and women in the same room in the poorhouse but the practice persisted, the justification being that Satan had no power over the sick and the old. Modesty did not exist here. One woman bared breasts which hung down like empty sacks. Jacob averted his eyes. His wish had always been to die in the shadow of the holy ruins, near the graves of saints, surrounded by cabalists and ascetics, and to be buried on the Mount of Olives. He had imagined himself bringing Sarah's bones to the Mount and had intended to raise one stone for both of them. He had always pictured his son Benjamin Eliezer standing at his grave reciting Kaddish. Yet it was fortunate that he had had the foresight to carry with him a small bag of earth from the Holy Land. He lay silent while half-naked children crawled over him. A woman rebuked him.

"As if it wasn't crowded enough. The devil had to drag in another."

It was some time before Jacob realized that she was referring to him and he wanted to apologize but he lacked both the words and the strength with which to talk. Jacob listened to what was going on within him. How had it all happened so quickly? He had gone to sleep a strong man and had awakened moribund. His stomach had stopped digesting, his intestines were frozen; his teeth felt loose in his gums. Usually in the morning he had to urinate, but today there was no need even for that. He watched from under his eyelids the

281

women and children eating, and the sight seemed foreign to him. But finally he summoned up enough strength to rise. He washed his hands at the barrel, and walked outside on unsteady legs to cleanse himself of urine before prayers. Standing at the wall, he forced out single drops. The heat was already oppressive. The sun blazed. Next to the poorhouse, in garbage and excrement, grew grass and wildflowers—white blooms, yellow blooms, feathery seed puffs, hairlike green fringes. Butterflies fluttered, and blue-gold flies buzzed on a heap of goat turds as if holding a meeting. A dog limped down the street sniffing the ground. For a moment the wind brought the clean scent of the fields, but then shifting bore only the smell of the outhouses. Feathers whirled in the air as in slaughter houses. Roosters crowed; chickens clucked; geese honked. On a patch of grass and weeds a crow picked at the guts from a chicken. Jacob stood openmouthed. This was the world he must soon leave. He returned to the poorhouse and tried to lift his sack. He could not stay there; the room, as the woman had pointed out, was too crowded. It was one thing to go among the poor to aid them, and another to infringe on the space that they needed. Only yesterday the sack had felt light; now he could barely raise it. At last, having pulled it over his shoulder, he said to everyone:

"Goodbye. Forgive me."

"The poor man is sick. Don't let him leave," screamed the same woman who had reproached him for being there.

"Where will you go, Reb Jacob?" voices called to him.

"To the study house."

"Oh, it's terrible. He can hardly walk," another woman screamed.

"Get him some water."

"Thank you. There s no need. Don t be offended."

Jacob kissed the mezuzah and walked to the study house, which was just across the street, taking small steps and stopping frequently to rest. He heard the voices of the men praying and the boys studying. Lingering in the antechamber, Jacob quickly thought over his life and tried to make an accounting, but his brain was as sluggish as his guts were. Nothing but exhaustion remained. Nevertheless, he marshaled his strength, and before saying the words which are customarily spoken before entering a holy place, he dipped his fingers into the copper font. He remembered having read in a book of ethics that even the man who dies in bed is a martyr. The very act of dying is a sacrificial offering.

VI

Jacob became faint during his prayers and fell sprawling in his prayer shawl and phylacteries. There was consternation in the study house. He was lifted to his feet and a man who had no children took him home and gave him a room; the man's wife assisted Jacob.

Chanina the healer was sent for, and all kinds of remedies were applied—bleeding, leeches, herbs— but to no avail. Jacob grew weaker from hour to hour. His voice became so low one could barely hear him. The next morning he asked for his prayer shawl and phylacteries but lacked the strength to put on the shawl or bind the thongs to his arms. The men of Pilitz came to visit him and the rabbi came also. Jacob asked the rabbi to recite the confession. "And for the sin," Jacob said, as it is said on Yom Kippur; with hands that now lacked the strength to close he fruitlessly attempted to beat his breast. He remembered he had once been powerful. He couldn't even turn on his other side. Merely to open his mouth and swallow a spoonful of warm water was too difficult.

Jacob wanted only to doze. He lay there with his eyelids closed, absorbed in an activity unknown to the healthy. He did not think but something in him approached the higher truths. From nowhere, images came to him: his father, peace be with him, his mother, peace be with her, his sisters, Zelda Leah, the children, Sarah. Even Jan Bzik visited him, no longer a peasant, but a saint from Paradise. They were debating something among themselves but without hostility, and Jacob too was being consulted. Both sides were in their own way right, and even though Jacob was not sure what the question was or what it meant, he was amazed. If only men could apprehend these things while they were still strong, he said to himself, they would serve the Lord differently. No one would lack confidence. No one would become sad. But how could these truths be conveyed to the vigorous? No, it was impossible. Already there was an impenetrable wall between Jacob and those who came to visit him. They wished him a speedy recovery, murmured the customary words of comfort and hope, gave him all kinds of advice, but though he heard them their words seemed empty, unrelated to anything he cared for. He did not want to recover; he no longer needed his body, and his devotion to it had passed.

Already, several times, he, Jacob had found himself outside his body looking down on it as if it were discarded clothing. The body lay, wrapped in linen, huddled in bed, sick, yellow, crumpled. You have already served your time—Jacob said to it—you are torn and stained with sins and must be cleansed. In one night the healthy Jacob had torn free from the moribund; he had traveled over fields, mountains, seas to the house of Benjamin Eliezer in Jerusalem. He had entered the room where his son sat studying by the light of an oil lamp, had spoken to him, given him a sign, but Benjamin Eliezer, engrossed in his book, had not responded. Before long some power had whisked Jacob back to Pilitz and he had again become imprisoned in his body and its suffering.

Jacob's death agony had begun. He breathed hoarsely, his chest heaved, single words of Yiddish and Polish bubbled from his throat. Those present thought he was dead, but when a member of the burial society laid a feather to his nostrils, it still moved. His body in its own way resisted the sentence of death. It tried to hold on, to function again, to digest, eliminate, belch, sweat, but its efforts were like the twitching of a slaughtered animal. The heart fluttered like a half-torn wing; the blood moved sluggishly; the eyes did not see the burning candle. The flame of life was guttering, and those on the other side, who waited for Jacob like relatives waiting on the shore for the ship to anchor, called to him and stretched out their hands. Jacob saw Sarah near Zelda Leah, and even though his thoughts were no longer earthly, he wondered. Well, but up there things happened differently....

Jacob's body died, but he was already so busy greeting those who had come to meet him that he did not look back. His dark cabin with its rags and refuse was left behind on the ship. The voyagers would clean it out, those who must still continue to journey on the stormy seas. He, Jacob, had arrived.

The men of the burial society lifted the corpse, opened the window, and recited the justification of God's decree. They placed Jacob with his feet toward the door and set two candles at his head.

Pious men gathered to recite the Psalms. The news that Jacob had died spread swiftly through the district. Even though he had lived in obscurity for twenty years in the land of Israel, how he had conducted himself was not unknown, and he was thought of as a righteous man. The original cemetery plot was long since fully occupied, so Jacob was given ground in the new part. The body was cleansed and taken to the study house where the rabbi spoke the eulogy. The whole town attended Jacob's funeral. When the gravedigger broke ground for Jacob's grave, his spade struck bones. He began to dig more carefully, and soon a body was seen that had not yet completely decomposed, perhaps because the earth there was so sandy and dry. From the skeleton and from pieces of clothing, the burial society women saw that it was a female. Strands of blond hair still entwined the skull, and it soon became clear that this was the grave of Sarah, who had been buried unshrouded in her own dress. The community had buried Sarah outside but the dead had gathered to take her in. The cemetery itself had ordained it; Sara was a Jewish daughter and a sanctified corpse.

Pilitz was in an uproar. Women cried; the pious fasted. Many came, even young girls and children, for a look at the body that had lain twenty years in the earth and was still recognizable. The cemetery was as crowded as in the month of Elul when everyone visits the graves. All saw the hand of Providence in this event. It was like one of the ancient miracles, a sign that there is an Eye which sees and a scale wherein even the acts of the stranger are weighed. The elders called a meeting and decided to bury Jacob near Sarah.

Thus judgment was rendered. Jacob, enveloped in a prayer shawl, with shards on his eyes, and a stem of myrtle between his fingers, was buried near Sarah. And the community undertook to erect a common tombstone as recompense to Sarah for the injustice done her by Gershon and his men. After the thirty days of mourning, the engraver began to chisel their stone. At the crest were two doves facing each other, their beaks joined in a kiss. But only the outlines were formed in keeping with the Mosaic interdiction against images. Deeply incised were the names of the deceased: Jacob the son of Eliezer; Sarah the daughter of the Patriarch Abraham. Jacob was honored with the words, "Our teacher, the saint"; and inscribed near Sarah's name was the line from Proverbs, "Who can find a virtuous woman?"

The epitaph was completed by a passage from the Bible encircling their names: "Lovely and pleasant in their lives, and in their death they were not divided."